Everything You Have Is Mine

Everything You Have Is Mine

Sandra Scoppettone

LITTLE, BROWN AND COMPANY
Boston   Toronto   London

I wish to give special thanks to
Alana Verber-Fein.
Without her help this book would not exist.

First Edition

The characters and events in this book are fictitious.
Any similarity to real persons, living or dead,
is coincidental and not intended by the author.

Library of Congress Cataloging-in-Publication Data

Scoppettone, Sandra.
    Everything you have is mine / Sandra Scoppettone. — 1st ed.
        p.   cm.
    ISBN 0-316-77646-7
    I. Title.
PS3569.C586E9   1991
813'.54 — dc20   90-48889

10   9   8   7   6   5   4   3   2   1

MV-NY

Published simultaneously in Canada
by Little, Brown & Company (Canada) Limited

Printed in the United States of America

For all of us everywhere, in and out

Everything in life that we really accept undergoes a change.
So suffering must become love. That is the mystery.

— *Katherine Mansfield*

Everything You Have Is Mine

Chapter

One

THE SLASHER came in the night again. He must have. I know that when I went to bed there were only three lines branching out from my right eye. Now there are four.

Looking in the mirror this morning, at home, I didn't notice. But here, in my office, there's a cruel, unforgiving light above my looking glass. I never expected these trenches at the age of forty-two. I thought I'd have at least a decade before I had to accept growing old.

Not that I think I'm old; it's just that I'm closer to the end than I am to the beginning, and sometimes that knowledge is scary. Still, aging is better than the alternative.

And, hell, I have a terrific life: my own business, a happy, long-term relationship (eleven years) with Kip Adams, and a brownstone she and I own in Greenwich Village in New York City. So stop complaining about a new furrow, Lauren. Besides, sometimes I pass for thirty-five, though there are fewer and fewer people fainting when they hear my true age. According to Kip, I'm still attractive. I wear my straight brown, gray-streaked hair to my shoulders, parted on the left, the way I've worn it half my life. My eyes are brown, with dark, long lashes, and I'm told I have a classic nose. Best of all, I don't have to worry about weight. Even so, there's one problem.

I'm short. Five two. I know I shouldn't care, but I do. This is partly vanity and partly because I'm a licensed private detective. Sometimes I face dangerous situations, so I *do* carry a gun — and not one of your wimpy Lady Smith's .38s, either. I tote a Smith &

Wesson Chief's Special with a four-inch barrel. In hot weather, I wear my .25 automatic in an ankle holster. This is particularly handy because it's out of sight. I own, but seldom carry, a Magnum .44.

I've never killed anyone — well, not since I've been a private eye. Before . . . before that . . . ah, hell.

I open my cardboard container and unwrap my croissant. I love drinking coffee out of a paper cup: it makes me feel like I'm in a movie, one of those film noir numbers. If I could I'd wear a trilby. Not really.

I'm a conservative dresser, and today I wear a lavender turtleneck under a pink sweater, and jeans. My matching socks are pink, my Reeboks white.

My jewelry is modest, too. I wear my grandmother's gold bracelet, my wedding ring, and a wristwatch with a black leather band.

I walk to the window, and while I take a bite of the croissant, I look down on Seventh Avenue. It's a quiet morning.

Then the phone rings.

"Lauren Laurano, private investigator," I say.

It's Jill, a good friend and one of the owners of the best independent bookstore in New York.

"Something's happened," she says, ominously.

"What do you mean, 'happened'?"

"I don't want to talk about it on the phone."

If there's one thing I've learned as a P.I., it's that no one ever wants to talk about *it* on the phone.

"Is Jenny all right?" I ask. Jenny is Jill's lover and partner in the business.

"She's fine. Can you come over to the store?"

My watch tells me it's a little after nine, almost an hour before they usually open. "Sure. I'll be there right away."

I finish off my coffee and leave the remainder of my chomped croissant on my desk, wonder when I last ate a complete breakfast, and take my gray wool jacket from the chair where I threw it.

Gordon Peace is washing down the entryway of my building. He's a tall man with orderly blond hair, and today he's sporting a new, somewhat ragged mustache. Gordon is sleek, like a Doberman. He wears tight black jeans and a black T-shirt that shows off his pecs. I assume he's gay, though I've never seen him with anyone of either sex. I know little about him except that he's twenty-eight, wants to be a writer, and, like everyone else in New York, is working on a novel. The only personal dealing I have with him is lending him books. I don't lend books to just anyone, but he takes good care of them and is scrupulous about returning them quickly.

We say good morning.

"How's your novel going?" I ask.

"*Mezzo-mezzo*," he answers, turning a large hand from side to side.

Gordon isn't Italian, as I am, but he often affects phrases in foreign languages.

He snaps his fingers. "Damn. I finished the Jane Smiley book, and I meant to bring it this morning."

"That's okay. Bring it next time, though, because someone else wants to read it."

"Yeah, I'm really sorry, Lauren."

"Don't worry. Next time will be fine."

"I hate to hang your friend up like that. Look, I could go get it. I don't live far from here."

"Gordon, please, it's okay."

"You sure?"

"Positive."

"How's the shamus business?" he asks. His chin rests on his hands, capping the mop handle.

"*Comme ci, comme ça*," I answer, but Gordon doesn't get it. I move around him, open the front door.

"*Ciao*," he says.

Outside, January feels like April. The weather's crazy, and everyone's talking about the greenhouse effect. Mark Twain comes to mind because nobody is doing a damn thing about it.

It takes only a few minutes to walk from my office to the bookstore, but I'm stopped at Seventh Avenue and Tenth Street by a man wearing a sign fastened to his shabby shirt. It says:

> *The rent on my apartment*
> *has been raised to*
> *$250,000 a month.*
> *Please help me so*
> *I won't lose my home.*

It makes me smile. I reach into my pocket and give him one of the small change-filled cellophane bags that I always carry.

A battered bowler sits on his head like a pot. He tips it. "Ah, lass, you're a wonder. This wee bag of change will go toward the terrible rent me landlord's asking for. Thank you from the bottom of me heart."

We both know exactly where the wee bag of change is going, but it doesn't matter. He's presumably homeless, like so many others who strew the streets like litter.

Near the middle of the block I see Joe Carter: Joe of all trades. In his forties, he's tall and slight, his salt-and-pepper hair thin like spider's webs. He wears his usual blue sweatshirt, with gold letters that spell WOLVERINES, and a pair of paint-stained khaki pants. On either side of his prominent nose, his brown eyes are red-rimmed, as though he's been crying, but I know this isn't so because he always looks this way.

Carter is the neighborhood handyman, and though he can find and fix a leak, build bookshelves, rewire a lamp, or replace a pane of glass in record time, there's something about him that I don't like. I've never known what it is or why it bothers me. Instinct, I guess.

"Morning," he says pleasantly.

"Hi, Joe."

"Feels like spring."

"It does," I say, and continue walking. "See you."

"Have a good one."

I grind my teeth at this epidemic phrase, but like a sheep, I answer in kind.

Three Lives Bookstore is on the corner of Waverly Place and Tenth. It's everything a bookstore should be. Warm and inviting, with pine shelves and counter lovingly constructed by Jenny and a friend. Green-shaded lights hang from the ceiling, casting a comfortable glow. There are rugs on the floor, and the room, though small, houses two tables. The larger one displays art and photography books, which are boosted more often than anything else. Novels are seldom stolen. What the hell can you do with a novel besides read it, after all?

I tap on one of the small glass panes. Seconds later Jill opens the door. She's an attractive woman, with dark-red hair that frames her lightly freckled face. Recently she turned forty and has taken on a more serious demeanor. She's wearing jeans and a green sweater, heightening the color of her eyes.

"Want some coffee?" she asks.

"Had some. What's up?"

She locks the front door after me and motions for me to follow her. We go behind the counter, where there are two chairs. No one else is in the store, though there may be an employee in the basement.

As if reading my mind, Jill says, "We're alone, so don't worry."

"*I'm* not worried, *you* are," I remind her.

"Right." Jill sips tea from a mug. "You're the only person I can think to turn to, Lauren."

"Theft?" I ask. A few years ago one of their employees was systematically stealing from them, and they engaged me to discover who the perp was. I did.

"I almost wish it were. It has nothing to do with the store. Well, it does in a way, because she's a good customer," she says in her usual rapid-fire style. Long ago I decided Jill's mind works so quickly her mouth has to fight to keep up with it.

"Who's a good customer?"

"The sister of the woman I want you to talk to."

"What woman?"

"Lake."

"Lake?" I ask skeptically. "This is a person's name?"

Jill nods. "Wait until you hear the rest," she says apologetically.

"What is it, Lake Michigan?" I ask, laughing. That Jill remains unsmiling gives me pause.

"Close but no cigar," she says. "It's Huron."

"Come on."

"It is. What do you expect? She was born in 'sixty-nine."

The date startles me. I often have this absurd reaction, as though I can't believe that anyone could be born after the forties. In 1969 I was a grown woman, out of school and working. And . . . my friends were naming their children Pond, Celery, Sky, etc., so why am I surprised by Lake Huron?

Jill continues, "I've been trying to get her to talk to you for about a week, and she finally agreed this morning. So much time has passed I'm afraid you won't have a lot to go on, but something has to be done."

"Why don't you tell me what happened, Jill?"

"There's no money in it," she says sheepishly.

I can feel a feminist cause in the air.

"All I want is for you to talk with her."

"I don't need money for that." It's true, time is money, but I've never been able to assess that properly.

"That's what I thought. If you can't convince her, then —"

"Jill? What are you talking about?"

"Rape."

Funny how even now that word gets me in the gut. *Rape.* Like a blast from a 12-gauge double-barreled shotgun. I think of Warren and then of the two perps. Warren would have been forty-six now, probably married, with several kids.

"Feeling the way you do, I mean, I thought you'd be . . ."

"Are the police involved?" I ask.

"No. That's the whole trouble. She won't talk to the police. Will you see her, Lauren? Convince her to go to the cops?"

"I'll try," I say.

"Jenny said I shouldn't involve you, that it might be upsetting, but I knew you'd help."

Jenny was right. It *is* upsetting, but that doesn't preclude my lending any help I can.

Jill says, "I'll phone, and you can arrange a place to meet."

"If she lives around here, see if she'll come to Arthur's. How will I know who she is?"

"She'll know *you.*"

Arthur's is on the corner of Charles Street and Greenwich Avenue. The restaurant occupies one good-sized room, and if you sit near the window you can watch the passing parade. These days a lot of that parade is heartbreaking. So many men walking by have AIDS. The look is haunted, unmistakable.

Arthur's is, to say the least, unpretentious. In other words, it's not about food. The place is a good spot to meet people because no one hassles you if you sit for a few hours with one cup of coffee.

Across the street, above a natural-foods restaurant, is the Caffe Degli Artisti. That's where I usually meet paying clients, unless they want to go to a bar. The building next door houses one of the six video clubs Kip and I belong to. I admit it: we're movie freaks. While wondering if I should rent something for tonight, I feel a presence at my table.

The woman who stands above me was not born in 1969. She looks as if she were in her thirties. What's going on?

"Are you Miss Laurano?" she asks in a pleasant voice.

"Sit down," I suggest.

She's tall — well, to me everyone looks tall. Still, this one is about five ten. Her hair's light-red, almost orange, and it's been permed so that the strands frizz around her face, brush her shoulders. She has large blue eyes, like robin's eggs. Her face is heart-shaped, the nose slightly out of line above a generous mouth. All the parts are good, but as a whole they come out ordinary, pedestrian.

She's wearing one of those black and white Arafat scarves, and when she takes off her tweed coat and folds it neatly on a chair, she reveals a tasteful blue button-down shirt and a pleated gray skirt. There's no way this woman could have been born in '69. 'Fifty-nine I might buy.

"Would you like something to eat or drink?" I ask.

"Just coffee, thanks."

I look around, but as usual there isn't a waitress or waiter in sight. Where do they go? I wonder. And who is Arthur? I tell the woman someone will come in a moment, which is true. Then I break the ice. "Well, Lake, I —"

"Ursula."

"Ursula?"

"I'm Lake's half-sister."

"Different mothers or fathers?"

"Different . . . mothers," she says hesitantly. "I wanted to meet you before you saw Lake."

I feel irritated. "To see if I'm suitable?"

"Something like that. My sister is very . . . very shy, and especially so now."

"You want something?" our waiter interrupts in a bored tone.

"Coffee."

He moves away silently, as if he were ice-skating.

"Jill recommended you highly, so it's not that I don't trust you. I just wanted to see if you were the type of person my sister could confide in. I don't want her to have to repeat the story any more than necessary."

"*Am* I the type of person your sister can confide in?" I say churlishly.

"I don't know yet."

At least she's direct. I like this because I'm always direct. I don't understand the need for artifice when you know what you want.

Gracelessly, the waiter plunks the cup and saucer on the table, causing coffee to spill over the rim.

Arthur's is not about service, either.

"What exactly do you want from me?" I ask, trying to sound affable.

"I want you to find the man who raped her."

"And?"

"Turn him over to the police."

I'm glad she doesn't expect me to be judge and jury.

"Lake's very ... well ... fragile, and it's important that she's handled right."

"Is it her fragility that's keeping her from telling the police?"

"In a way. Mind if I smoke?" Not waiting for my response, she takes out a lustrous gold case, snaps the catch, and withdraws a brown cigarette. I can't remember the last time I saw anyone using a cigarette case.

I gave up smoking four years, two weeks, and five days ago. But who misses it?

Ursula says, "Lake's avoiding the police is due more to the circumstance of the rape than to her personality."

"And what *was* the circumstance?" I ask.

"The rapist was her date."

Chapter

TWO

AFTER I TELL URSULA my story, she decides I'm suitable and that I may be a fair detective, too. I try to appear flattered, though what I am is depressed. It invariably brings me down to remember.

We walk along the narrow Village streets in silence, and I admire the architecture. I always spot something new: a brass knocker, a carved wooden door, cement lions, like sentries, guarding a stoop.

When we reach a brownstone on West Thirteenth Street, Ursula stops.

"This is it."

Because of the location, I assume that a student can't afford to live here, but I ask anyway. "Your place or hers?"

"Mine."

I nod, and we start up the front stairs. Ursula takes out a key, slips it neatly into the lock, gives it a half-turn, and the door opens. We're in a hall that leads to the back of the building. There's a set of stairs on the left, but we stop at a door on the right. She uses a key again. Inside is a lovely living room decorated in shades of blue and lavender.

"Sit down, make yourself comfortable. I'll be right back."

She opens a set of lace-curtained glass doors, and before she disappears I glimpse part of an office.

The furniture in the living room is Victorian, as are the fabric coverings, the pictures on the walls, and the collection of knick-knacks on all the surfaces. There's a marble fireplace with wood and paper laid out in readiness. Large windows face the street. A strong scent of a potpourri is present.

I pick up a black-and-white photograph in a standing gold rococo frame. A man and woman pose against a forties car. The man's handsome, with closely cropped hair, wearing slacks and a sport shirt. The woman's in a blouse and skirt. This being Ursula's house, I assume she's Ursula's mother. And that would mean that Lake's father could've been in his fifties when she was born.

While I look at the woman for a resemblance to Ursula, the French doors open and the two women enter.

I replace the picture and stare at Lake. One seldom sees beauty like hers off the big or little screen. I can see a vague likeness to the man in the photo.

Lake is about five seven and looks like a perfect size six. Long blond hair outlines a creamy oval face. Her eyes are indigo spheres, the brows arching thickly above them. The nose is straight and small, the mouth the color of pomegranate juice. She's wearing jeans, Frye boots, and a chambray shirt, her only jewelry a silver and jade ring. When we're introduced, she gives my hand a solid squeeze. I like that. So many young people don't know how to shake hands.

We all sit down, I in a comfortable chair and the two women on the couch facing me.

"Tell her what you told me," Ursula prompts me.

For a moment I don't know what she means. When it becomes clear, I wonder why Ursula doesn't understand why telling my story over and over might be hard for me, even though it happened twenty-four years ago. But I can see that unless I repeat it, Lake's not prepared to trust me.

So I tell again about when I was eighteen, parked one cloudy night at the Lookout with Warren Cooper, a boy I was dating even though I knew then — had always known — the truth about myself.

We were making out when both front doors of his jaunty Ford were ripped open and two men hauled us from the car and dragged us into the woods. Warren was forced to watch while the men raped me in turn. Then one of the men put a gun to Warren's temple and blew off the top of his head. I thought I'd be next, but instead they raped me again, beat me mercilessly until they believed I was dead, and then left me there to rot. With my multiple skull fractures and loss of blood, it took me three excruciatingly painful hours to crawl out of the woods and down the winding road to where I was eventually rescued.

Although the results of that night were incredible, I stop my story here because the rest can hold no interest for Lake or Ursula. The silence in the warm room clings to us like tropical vines.

Lake finally speaks. "You've never gotten over it, have you?"

"It only disturbs me when I have to talk about it. I've been through counseling, so I don't have nightmares anymore. It's something you should do as soon as possible."

"Yes," she replies vaguely.

"Can you tell me what happened?" I ask.

Her pale cheeks flush.

"I know the rapist was a date," I add.

She nods, humiliated.

I discern the expression easily, having worn it myself. "How long have you known him?"

She shakes her head and abruptly begins to cry. Her hands cover her face. There's no sound, only the slight lifting and lowering of shoulders. I look at Ursula. Concerned, she comforts Lake, a hand on her arm.

Uncovering her face, Lake apologizes.

"I understand," I say. I wait a moment, then repeat my question.

"It was a second date," she says haltingly.

"Where did you meet him?"

"You mean, that night?"

"Originally."

She shakes her head but says nothing.

"Go on, Lake," Ursula urges gently. "It's all right."

Lake looks from her to me, then back to Ursula again. "There's something I didn't tell you," she says softly.

"Oh, really?"

I detect a pejorative tone in Ursula's *Oh, really?* Maybe the Victorian decor reflects her spirit.

"What didn't you tell me?" Ursula continues.

"Please don't be mad at me, okay?"

"Mad at you? Why would I be mad at you, Lake?" Ursula seems genuinely puzzled.

"Because you . . . you warned me."

"It doesn't matter. Nothing matters except that you tell Ms. Laurano the truth about everything."

Lake looks at her feet. "He . . . he was a blind date."

"*How could you?*" Ursula exclaims, then, chagrined, claps a hand over her mouth.

"I knew it," Lake cries.

"No. No, I'm sorry, darling. Please, it doesn't matter. Go on."

"Who fixed you up?" I ask.

She doesn't answer.

Ursula says, "Did you hear Ms. Laurano's question?"

Startling us both, Lake jumps to her feet and yells. "Oh, why did I ever tell you? Why did I let you talk me into this? I can't . . . I just can't." Sobbing, she runs from the room.

Ursula says, "I'm so sorry, Ms. Laurano."

"It's not your fault. And I wish you'd call me Lauren."

"All right." Flustered, Ursula paces. "I don't know what to do now. You must think I —"

"I don't think anything, except that your sister's upset and there's something she doesn't want to tell us."

"I'll try to bring her back."

"No," I say. "Leave her alone for a bit. I'll call you later. Maybe she'll feel more like talking then."

◆

I know my croissant will be stale by now, so I stop on the corner of Eighth Street and Sixth Avenue at Gray's Papaya and buy one of their terrific sixty-cent hot dogs. I will also manage to choke down a glass of papaya juice.

While I eat, I stand at the window and think about Lake. Going on a blind date isn't as innocuous as it once was, but I can see why she would do it. It's hard to meet men in New York, so having a friend set up something could seem the prudent way to go. Apparently this is something she and her sister discussed, Ursula warning her about the inherent dangers.

Why is Lake protecting her attacker? Maybe if she'd been dating him awhile I'd understand it better. But why shield a stranger? After hearing my story, Lake must've known I would believe her, be simpatico.

Something is off here . . . something doesn't add up. I pop the last piece of hot dog into my mouth, wash it down with sweet sips of papaya and toss my garbage in the pail. I need to speak with Ursula.

The first pay phone I find has no receiver, and the second doesn't have a dial tone. The third, which is blocks away, has a receiver and a dial tone. I know because someone is using it. The fourth phone is healthy and mine.

After a lengthy skirmish inside my handbag, I locate the scrap of paper on which I've written Ursula's number. Paper is tricky for me. I've thrown away more important letters and documents than I care to think about. Kip says it's because I want to remain unencumbered. Perhaps.

Ursula answers on the first ring.

"Oh my God, I'm so glad you called. I've been trying to get you."

"What's wrong?"

"It's Lake. She's gone."

As Lake doesn't live with Ursula, I ask her what she means.

"She left without telling me — just went out the back through the garden — and I haven't been able to reach her by phone. I'm worried . . . she's so depressed."

"Are you suggesting she might commit suicide?" I ask.

There's a slight intake of breath, as if I've shocked her. "It's occurred to me."

"Has she ever threatened —"

"No, but since the rape . . ."

I ask for Lake's address and assure Ursula that I'll find her sister. When I leave the phone box and walk toward the East Village, I realize that I haven't discussed my fee with Ursula. So what else is new?

Lake lives on Seventh Street between First and Second avenues. The area is having a robust renaissance, with new restaurants, clubs, and boutiques springing up like dandelions. A few years back it was in competition with SoHo for gallery space, but that didn't last. The art scene is no longer here.

Apartments that once rented for $200 a month tops now command as much as $1,000. There are still some stabilized places, though, and I assume that Lake lives in one of those.

I don't like spending time in this area. As much as it's been gentrified, an atmosphere of drug dealing lingers on. Although the real drug scene is farther east, many druggies promenade here like hellish apparitions. Crack and crank remain the twins of death.

Two young men on skateboards zip past me. I cross the street, and a woman on a bicycle blows a whistle as she almost knocks me down. I hate cyclists. They think they're above the law and never obey the lights. This is one of my pet peeves, and I can go on about it at length.

Lake's building is a tenement, as I anticipated. Nevertheless, a sign advertises co-ops for sale. In the vestibule I read the names on the roster. The apartment's on the fifth floor: 5C. I ring, doubting that I'll get a response even if she's home.

Convinced I'm not going to gain entry this way, I ring all the bells, and inevitably someone buzzes me in. Is it faith or foolishness that prompts a person to answer an anonymous caller?

Once inside, I dig into my purse, this time taking out my wallet, which holds my license. Whoever answered my ring will be waiting for me.

I find her on the fourth floor. She can't be more than sixteen, her hair blue on one side, pink on the other. She wears black high-heeled shoes and a black dress that ends midthigh.

"Yeah?" she asks in a granular voice.

I flip open my wallet to my license, hold it up. "Private investigator," I say. It's meaningless but always works.

Fear floods her eyes. "I didn't do nothin', lady."

Lady. It always jars me. Somewhere inside I think I'm no older than this girl. But she calls me *lady*, and I'm forced to see that she could easily be my child.

"It isn't you I want," I say.

"Jackie's not home."

It's amazing what people will tell you. "Really?"

"Cross my heart," she says, and illustrates this by dragging her index finger across her chest twice.

"What's your name?" I ask, because I would if this were real.

"My name? It's Bambi, why?"

"Bambi what?"

"Listen, my ma knows where I am."

"I told you, it's not you I want."

"So what d'ya need my last name for?"

"The record."

"Oh. Well, it's Bloom."

Bambi Bloom. I wonder what Mrs. Bloom thinks of her daughter's hair, and if somewhere, in one of the boroughs, she blames herself for the way her Bambi has turned out.

"When will Jackie be back?"

"He's split. Won't be back."

"Do you know where he's gone?"

"Who, me?" she asks, as though she has no idea who or what we've been talking about.

"Yeah, you."

"Hey, look, lady, I don't know nothin' about Jackie. I mean, he's history far as I'm concerned, you get my meaning."

I say I do, pretend I'm frustrated by this, thank her, and start downstairs.

"Have a nice day," she inexplicably calls after me.

As I continue descending, I hear her door close. I make it to the first floor and hide myself under the stairs. I look at my watch. Forty-two seconds later I hear the faint sound of a door opening and closing, the roll of tumblers in the lock, and then the click-clack of high heels as Bambi Bloom hurries down the steps.

When she's gone I come out of hiding and, on Reeboked feet, make my way to the fifth floor.

There are four apartments to a floor. The ones on the left are A and B. I go to the other end of the hallway. Number 5D is on my left; 5C, Lake's apartment, is across from it . . . the door wide open.

Chapter

Three

═══════════════════════
═══════════════════════

ENTERING someone else's apartment is a tricky business. When the door's shut and locked, aside from the question of who may be inside, there's the feat of getting in; when it's unlocked, there's the knowledge that someone has been there, or is still there, perhaps with a weapon. And if it's wide open, like this one, chances are that nothing good awaits you.

I reach into my purse, take out my gun, and release the safety. My detective's heart is jumping hurdles, and I start to sweat. Carefully, I step into the apartment. My back against the wall, I wait, gun in both hands against my chest, pointed at the ceiling. I'm in the kitchen and I can see part of the living room. The place is a mess, and I assume it's been burglarized or tossed. I listen for sounds as if I have a stethoscope on the core of the flat. All I hear is my breathing. I don't think anyone's here, but there's a possibility I'm wrong. I've been known to be — once or twice!

I edge my way along the wall toward the living room. At the archway I step into the room and adopt the standard combat stance, gun held straight out in front of me, as I sweep the room from side to side. No one's there. Three closed doors lead to other areas. I figure one for a closet, one for a bedroom, and one for a bathroom. Someone could be hiding behind any of them, and this is not "Let's Make a Deal."

There are overturned chairs, broken glass, books swept from their shelves, CDs and tapes scattered everywhere. I move toward the first door. When I reach it I turn the handle slowly, shove it open, then, again in combat stance, move into the doorway. It's the bathroom, a small WC. I do the same at the second door, which turns out to be a closet with only cleaning supplies inside. The third door is to the bedroom.

This room's in the same disarray as the living room. To my great relief, the closet door's open, allowing me to see it's unoccupied. What I assume were its contents are strewn around, along with those of emptied bureau drawers. There's no one in the apartment, dead or alive.

After I put on the safety, I return my gun to my bag, go back to the kitchen, close and lock the front door. I stand there as I recover my composure and confidence.

I know this isn't a burglary because a CD player, television, and VCR are still here. The apartment was tossed: someone's looking for something. Can this be a coincidence? Or is the break-in tied to the rape? This doesn't make sense, but neither does happenstance.

A key turns in the lock. I guess it's Lake, but I take no chances. I secure my gun and make myself ready.

As she comes through the door, I say, "Don't be afraid," and lower my gun.

My warning does nothing to curtail her frightened cry, but then she recognizes me and calms down.

"What are you doing here?" She looks around. "What happened?"

"I came to see you. The door was open, and I found the place like this."

For a moment, I think she believes I'm responsible for the toss, but this vanishes quickly. Once again I'm struck by her fragile beauty.

"Who would do this?" she asks guilelessly.

"I thought *you* might know."

"Why would *I* know?"

"It *is* your apartment, Lake."

"So what? Since when does the victim know who the burglar is?"

"I don't think you've been burgled. Take a look around, see if anything's missing."

I follow her through the rooms as she touches certain items, kicks at the remnants of her life with a toe, and idly picks up things as though this is someone else's rubble. We return to the kitchen. At a small wooden table we sit in two ladder-back chairs. I wait for her inventory, but she says nothing.

"Has anything been stolen?" I ask.

"Doesn't seem to be."

Would Kinsey Millhone believe her? I don't either.

"What's the point of this?" she says plaintively.

"I think we can conclude that someone was trying to find something. Have any idea what that might be?"

"No. Honestly."

Experience has taught me that when a person says *honestly*, or *to tell the truth*, 75 percent of the time he or she is lying.

"Do you think this has anything to do with the rape?" I ask bluntly.

Her cheeks flush like ripe peaches. "I can't see how it could."

"Can we please talk about it, Lake?"

"Why do you care? Has Ursula hired you or something?"

"There hasn't been any discussion of money. But yes, I guess you could say that. She's very worried about you."

"She think I'm going to kill myself or something dumb?"

"Yes."

Lake looks at me as if I'm an alien she's never seen before. "God, that's so typical."

"Of what?"

"Old people."

I try not to identify. "Meaning?"

"They always think the worst. At least Ursula and my mother do."

"Then you wouldn't do anything like that?"

"Kill myself? You kidding? I'd like to kill *him*. Why should I kill *myself*?" She goes to the refrigerator, gets a can of soda, starts to close the door, then asks me if I want one. It's a Diet Orange Slice, my favorite. I say yes.

When she sits opposite me again I say, "So a friend fixed you up?" as if our earlier conversation had never been interrupted.

Lake examines her long, clear, manicured nails, like an anthropologist looking for cracks that will offer clues. As they're in perfect repair, she abandons this diversion.

"No," she says softly.

"Then how did you get the date?" I ask.

After six or seven hours she murmurs, "The paper."

"A matchmaker ad?"

"No."

"A personal ad?"

"Yes," she admits.

I feel like Ursula, wanting to ask how she could do such a thing, but before I can, she showers me with a deluge of words.

"I know you don't understand, but you don't know what it's like out there. You're married." With a thrust of her chin she indicates my wedding band.

"I have some idea." I think of my single friends and their similar complaints.

"I thought it would be a good way to meet a man who liked the same things I do. Hell, I thought it would be a good way to meet a *man*. You can't just pick people up, you know."

I say nothing, remembering that I once urged a friend to place an ad. I'm unnerved to think of what might have happened, though Lorraine was trying to find a woman, not a man. Still . . .

"I was lonely," she submits, as if seeking a pardon.

"What's his name?"

She looks humiliated. "Joe Smith."

I pass quickly over the answer so she won't feel foolish. "Did you answer an ad or put one in?"

"Answered."

I'm glad. It'll make it easier. "Which paper?"

She hesitates. "The *Village Record.*"

"What did the ad say?"

"I . . . I don't remember."

I find this odd. "How about the date of the ad, do you remember that?"

"Yes," she replies almost truculently. "December sixth."

"You didn't keep it?"

"No, but I have his letters," she breaks through my suspicions. "I'll get them."

I feel a quiver of excitement: letters will help.

When she returns, she's holding a blue velvet candy-sized box, the lid embossed with flowers.

"The letters are gone," she says, perplexed.

She hands me the empty box. "I guess we know now who and why," I say.

"Pardon?"

"The toss." I sweep my arm from side to side.

"You think *he* did this?" She's frightened.

"Who else would want those letters?"

"You're right."

"How many letters were there?"

"Four or five. Five."

"Handwritten or typed?"

"Typed. Well, on a printer. Near letter quality."

"You mean you think he used a computer?"

"Right." She frowns, as if *computer* is a dirty word.

Something bothers me. "Where did you keep this box?"

"On a shelf in the back of my closet, behind some blankets."

"You live alone, don't you?"

"Yes."

"Then why did you hide the letters? Who from?"

"I just . . . it's habit."

"Habit?"

"My stepfather used to go through my things, looking for evidence."

"Evidence of what?"

She shrugs. "This and that, you know."

"I don't."

"Well . . . drugs, mostly, I guess."

"Did he have reason?"

"No," she answers absolutely.

"You said drugs *mostly*. Did he look for other things as well?"

"Yeah."

"What?"

"Stuff that had to do with boys."

Lake's embarrassed, as if she'd been the intruder, instead of her stepfather. I wonder if incest has played a part in her life. Lately it seems as though every other person I meet has had an incestuous experience.

This isn't a good time to ask her.

"Does anyone else have keys to this apartment?"

"Why?"

"I suppose I find it odd that you hid the letters from no one."

"I told you —"

"I know. Habit." I'm not buying. "How long have you lived away from home?"

"Since I started school. Two years."

"Do you hide other things?"

"Like what?"

"I don't know. That's why I'm asking you." I can see that she's becoming annoyed and impatient with me, so I quickly ask another question. "Can you tell me what was in the letters?"

"Oh, you know," she says wistfully, probably remembering her expectations. "We traded information about ourselves. And ... sometimes he included lines of poetry."

"His own?"

"No. Quotes."

"Do you know who he quoted?"

"Mostly Browning, sometimes Millay."

"What else?"

"Nothing."

"Think carefully. There might be something that could lead us to him. Why else would he steal the letters?"

"I ... I can't remember anything."

I decide to let it go for now. "So when did you meet him?"

She looks down at her hands, then picks at a scab on a knuckle.

"Lake, why are you protecting him?"

"It's not that."

"Then what is it?"

"I'm afraid. Especially after this," she says, meaning the toss.

"Did he threaten you?"

"He said if I told anyone ... he said he'd kill me."

"And that's why you wouldn't go to the police?"

"That and the circumstances. After all, it was a date, wasn't it?"

"Date rape is becoming more common all the time."

"Even so ... answering the ad and everything. It doesn't make me look good."

I can't argue with her there. In the past few years the police have changed their attitude toward rape victims, but there's still skepticism from certain cops.

"When did you meet him?" I ask again.

"Three weeks ago."

"And the rape occurred on your second date?"

"Yes."

"What does he look like?" I click on the silver Tiffany pen Kip gave me for Christmas and open to a clean page in my notebook.

"He's tall, maybe six four. Thin. I don't know."

"How old is he?"

"Thirtysomething."

"Eyes?"

"Blue. A funny blue. I can't explain what I mean."

"His hair?"

"Brown."

"How does he wear it?"

"Regular."

"Sideburns?"

"You mean long or short? Short."

"Any facial hair?"

"No."

"Distinguishing features? Big nose, pockmarks, details like that?"

"That was the thing about him. He was so regular-looking. Handsome, but not unusual. Do you know what I mean?"

"I think so. Where did you go on your first date?"

"Uptown. We went to a restaurant called My Pierre, on Seventy-eighth, off Broadway. See, we'd agreed in the . . . the letters that we adored French food. In fact, we're both Francophiles."

There is something about the way she refers to the letters that puzzles me, but I don't know what it is, so I continue. "Was it a big or small place?"

"Medium."

Too bad. The smaller, the more chance I'd have of someone remembering them.

"Oh, God," she says.

"What?"

"I'm talking about him like he's someone I care about, like we have a relationship. God." Her face folds like a lawn chair and she begins to cry.

I wait, not touching her or saying anything to interrupt the flood of tears she needs to shed. When it's over I hand her a tissue.

She dabs at her eyes, nose, and cheeks. "It seems so ludicrous. I'm telling you all this intimate stuff about this guy, and the god-damned creep raped me." She gives a small, fluty laugh. "It's not funny, but it is, you know?"

"Yes. Can you go on?"

"Sure."

"Where did you go after dinner?"

"The movies. A Lelouch double bill."

Naturally. "And then?"

"For coffee."

"Let me guess. A French café?"

She smiles wanly at my feeble attempt at humor. "Yes. One I'd never been to. I can't remember what street it's on or the name, but it's near the theater, which is on Seventy-fourth."

"On a cross street?"

"Yes. He had an espresso and I had a café au lait. We shared a dacquoise. Then he brought me home."

"Did he want to come in?"

"No. He didn't even try to kiss me goodnight. He said he'd call. I remember feeling fabulous while I got ready for bed. The phone rang. It was him."

"What time was it?"

"About midnight."

"Late for a call."

"Not this call. He wanted to say what a perfect evening it was and that he missed me already. He said it in French."

Spare me. "Did he ask you for another date?"

"Not then. He phoned the next day. Our schedules made it impossible to get together for almost a week. The first time I'd met him at the restaurant, but this time I invited him here."

"You didn't think that was risky?"

"No," she says defensively. "And you wouldn't have either."

I don't comment.

"I mean, God, he was so polite, so charming."

"He came here and what happened?"

"The second he was inside and closed the door, he grabbed me with both hands, turned me around, and pushed me toward the bedroom. I started to scream and he put a hand over my mouth, still forcing me ahead of him. I couldn't believe it was happening. You can't imagine." She met my eyes. "Oh. You can. Sorry."

"It's okay. Go on."

"Do you need to know the details?"

"Not unless there was something different about it, like a signature."

"Signature?"

"Something kinky or unusual."

"There wasn't."

"After it was over, what then?"

"That's when he threatened me. Then he let himself out. That's it." She closes her eyes as if trying to black out the images. "I lay there for hours. I felt paralyzed. Finally, about two in the morning, I was able to move, and I ran a bath."

"When did you tell Ursula?"

"A few days later. I couldn't tell her before. I couldn't go to classes or speak to anyone."

"Why did you keep the letters?"

Bewildered, she says, "I don't know. I forgot about them. I don't think I thought of them once until you asked about the ad. Funny, isn't it? If I had I would've torn them to shreds."

I ask her for a recent photograph, and she gives me one of her sitting against a tree. I offer to help her clean up the place, but she says I won't know where anything goes, which is true.

"I think you'd better call Ursula," I suggest.

"What for?"

"To ease her ancient mind," I say, smiling.

Lake grins. "Okay."

After advising that she call a locksmith, I urge her again to see a therapist or rape counselor. I take down her phone number and say I'll be in touch.

When I hit the street, it's nearly 1:00. I'm starving. I have two choices: I can eat in a restaurant alone or join Kip at home.

I choose Kip.

Chapter

Four

FOR THE LAST THREE YEARS Kip and I have owned a brown-stone on Perry Street. We occupy the first two floors and rent the third to our friends Rick and William. The fourth floor is a problem. The fourth is Mr. and Mrs. PITA. That's what we call them. It's an acronym for Pain In The Ass. Their real names are Alice and Josh Whitfield, and they're leftover hippies. They've lived in the apartment for fifteen years and pay $250 a month. With new tenants we could get more than $1,000. But our desire to evict them isn't only monetary.

What we hate is that they smoke. Both pot and cigarettes. The smell permeates the halls and sometimes slithers under our door. We also fear they might nod out and set fire to our house. Their lease doesn't expire for another year, and then we'll have to take them to court. Terrific. It'll be a long, messy battle, and I don't even like thinking about it.

Sometimes, as I approach our building, I can't believe that I own a part of the Apple. As a child growing up in New Jersey, I dreamed of living in Greenwich Village and owning one of the little houses that line its streets, but I never thought it would be possible.

I go down the four steps to the front door. Inside, I walk to the back of the hall and use what was probably once the servants' entrance.

The door leads to the kitchen, which we've completely redone with pine counters and cabinets. The square wood New Haven clock on the wall tells me it'll be about two minutes until Kip finishes. I open the fridge and stare in as though I'm looking at television.

This is how Kip finds me.

"Is it detective work you're doing, or are you on a treasure hunt?" she asks.

I come out of my trance, and when I see her, her head cocked to one side, a small smile frolicking at the corners of her lovely lips, I feel it, almost as if I'm seeing her for the first time. This doesn't always happen. I mean, come on, eleven years is a long time to keep that response alive on a daily basis. Still, every once in a while that fluttery feeling gets me.

Kip is a looker. Life has left its impression on her, so she doesn't have Lake's ethereal beauty, but to me she's captivating . . . dazzling . . . sublime. Others find her attractive, though perhaps don't use my superlatives to describe her.

She has a patrician nose, brown eyes like liquid chocolate, wavy brown hair going gracefully gray, and a slender body (not as thin as it was when she was in her thirties, but who notices?) that's curvaceous and exciting.

She wears a silk blue blouse with the sleeves rolled back twice at the cuffs, pleated navy slacks, no belt, and gray boots. I love the way she dresses: she's one of those people who look great in clothes, and she can carry off almost any style or color, except for shades of yellow, brown, and black. Black is better on me.

"I think," she says to an imaginary crowd, "this one needs the type of help I'm not equipped to give."

I laugh, close the fridge door, and put my arms around her. "Have I ever told you that you make my pulse race?"

"Not in those words," she answers, and bends her head to kiss me.

I'm continually astonished by how much she can still arouse me after all these years. We both have work to return to, so we draw back from what could turn into something more than a sexy kiss.

"What are you doing?" she asks.

"Kissing you."

Smiling, she says seductively, "I know that. I know that very well. What I mean is, what are you doing *here?*"

"I live here."

"Very funny. You have a lunch date with Susan."

"Oh, Christ," I say, slapping my forehead. "I forgot." I grab the phone.

Susan answers on the first ring. "So you got a better offer, do I care?"

"I'm sorry, Susie."

"Don't tell me, let me guess. Michelle Pfeiffer hired you and insists on lunch or no deal."

"I knew you'd understand."

"Hey, call me crazy, but I know lunches with movie stars are more important than twenty-year friendships."

"Are you mad?"

There's a beat of silence, and then she hangs up. I laugh. We've been doing this for years when one of us asks a dumb question or says something ridiculous. I call her back.

"What?" she answers.

"Tomorrow?"

"Same time?"

"Yes."

"Try not to forget, okay?" she says, laughing.

"I'll try."

Kip's heating up leftover vegetable soup. "Want some of this?"

"Sure."

"You must have a case."

"How can you tell?"

"Lauren, don't you think I know you by now? Staring into the fridge, forgetting your lunch date . . . the absentminded detective. So, what and who?"

We share our work with each other, though we never identify the people. Kip's a therapist, hypnosis her specialty, and we often talk about her patients (to me they're "patients"; to the rest of the world they're the more acceptable "clients") but always use code names. I tell her about Lake and wish I could use her name because Kip would love it. Lake Huron indeed. Instead, Lake becomes Youthful Beauty, Ursula becomes Big Sis, etc.

When I finish my tale, Kip reaches across the table and puts her hand over mine. "God, honey, does it bring everything back?"

"In Technicolor," I say. She understands how one memory can lead to another and why I may be brooding about Lois. She'd crossed my mind, but I'd relegated thoughts of her to the "don't think about this now" department.

Lois was my first lover. The road that led to her began when I was in the hospital after the rape and beating. A man named Jeff Crawford started the whole thing.

I awoke one afternoon to find a handsome man sitting at my bedside. I thought he was Paul Newman until he introduced himself, leaving out the most important part of his identity. I assumed he was a cop.

I hadn't been in love with Warren — I knew I preferred women, though I'd had no experience — but I'd liked him and I cared deeply about his murder. Later, in therapy, I learned that I unconsciously felt responsible for his death. Something like, *If I'd been unafraid of what people thought of me and hadn't pretended to be heterosexual, we wouldn't have been there that night, and Warren wouldn't be dead.* My doctor pointed out to me that Warren probably would've been there with another girl, and I knew that was true. Still . . .

Jeff came to see me every day, and it never occurred to me to question why he was being so attentive to a stranger. I thought it was what all cops did on a case. When my mind and body had healed some, he told me he was FBI and brought me books of mug shots to see if I could identify my rapists (I always think of them as *my* rapists). For four days I pored over pages of photos, until I found the first one: Charlie West. West had so many priors that his sheet was six pages long. From West to Tom Bailey took only a day.

Aside from what they'd done to Warren and me, they were wanted on a kidnapping charge. But the FBI couldn't prove anything and hoped to get West and Bailey through me. It worked. Of course, Charlie and Tom were back on the street in less than ten years. Even now I sometimes look over my shoulder to see if my rapists are there. My luck continues to hold.

It was after the trial that Crawford approached me.

"You have guts," he said. "We need someone like you. The way you look, no one would ever suspect you."

I'd been planning to go to college and told him so.

"Go. With our blessing. We'll use you only occasionally until you graduate. Think of it as a way to make up for Warren's death."

He pushed the old guilt button, and before I knew it I'd capitulated. The summer before I went to Smith, the FBI trained me with pay. I told my parents I had an office job. I hated lying to them, but there was nothing else I could do. No one was to know.

While in school, I avoided affairs with women because I knew the Bureau was watching me. There wasn't a doubt in my mind as to how J. Edgar would feel about having a lesbian working for him, and I desperately wanted to avenge Warren's death. So I continued going out with men and even had a sexual relationship with two. I didn't find it repulsive, but I didn't enjoy it. It wasn't because of the rape. The rape had its effect on me, but it was not the cause of my sexual preference. Long before, perhaps as a toddler, I was programmed to love women. Simply put, lovemaking with a man leaves me cold.

When I graduated, I became a full-fledged agent. Within six months I met Lois, and we fell in love. She was four years older than I and had been an agent for three years. When it became apparent that she felt about me as I did about her, we consummated the relationship. It was completely clandestine, but we managed to be together a great deal.

Two years after our affair began, Lois and I worked together for the first time. We were busting an underworld kingpin. Everyone on the case was nervous and edgy.

To this day I'm not sure how it happened, and only God knows why. Three minutes into the operation, holding my gun in front of me as I'd been trained, I turned a corner of the perp's building. Dark though it was, I saw a glint of light bounce off a gun I believed was pointed at me. I fired, and I killed Lois.

There was an investigation, and though I was exonerated, our affair was revealed, and I left the Bureau. Even if it hadn't surfaced that Lois and I had been lovers, I would've resigned. I had no heart for the job anymore. I had no heart at all.

Devastated, I remained celibate for two years and drifted from job to job. I finally had a few relationships, but they didn't succeed. I kept looking for someone to take Lois's place, and it didn't work.

When I was thirty-one, working for Pan Am as a reservation clerk, Jenny and Jill introduced me to Kip Adams, and everything changed. Kip (her real name is Christine, but her younger brother couldn't say it, and "Kip" stuck) urged me to do more with my life. She helped me see that I enjoyed investigative work: becoming a P.I. was her idea. I had no trouble getting a license and opened my office six months after Kip and I met.

In spite of the past, I consider myself one of the lucky ones. I have what most people want: love and work I enjoy.

"Want some more soup?" Kip asks.

"No thanks. I have things to do."

Using a line from a horror movie (at one point, desperate, having seen everything available on tape, we sunk to things like *The Howling* and *Nightmare on Elm Street* — all five parts), Kip says, "Places to go, people to kill?"

I laugh. "Something along those lines."

We stash our bowls in the dishwasher, and I check my answering machine at the office. Nothing.

"Who do you have this afternoon?" I ask.

"Please, don't remind me."

"Chicken Head," I stated, using a code name for a guy who can't eat anything but chicken.

She nods. "And Forever Fran." F.F. has been with her for almost fifteen years, refuses to leave, and threatens to commit suicide if Kip drops her. All of her patients aren't this extreme. Some are just ordinary neurotics.

"God, what a day. Poor lamb."

"Don't," she says.

"Don't what?"

"Don't say the L-word."

"Louie Lamb Chop?" I say, more incredulous at the lineup than sympathetic.

She nods; her eyes close against the appalling afternoon that stretches ahead. Louie Lamb Chop got his name because one day he came to his session beaming, and when Kip asked why, he said, "I'm feeling great because I've got my lamb-chop list done for the month." Don't ask!

"Are they all you have?"

"Ain't they enough?"

"Plenty." I kiss her quickly. "I feel for you, kid."

As I'm leaving, Kip says, "Don't forget, we're having dinner with your parents."

"Forget? Who, me?"

"Go pick a lock!"

Christ, I love her.

Chapter

Five

ON MY WAY to the *Village Record* offices, I spot two new Korean grocery stores. I can't imagine how they make money, as there must be half a dozen of them in every ten-block radius. They seldom fold, so they must know something I don't.

Their biggest draw is the incredible salad bars. They offer hot and cold food and change the menu daily. Often Kip and I fill the plastic containers with fruit or vegetable salads, but sometimes we get ribs, pasta, or chicken. The point is, when you don't want to cook and you don't know what you want to eat, these places are great.

I pass a black man sporting a high-top fade, hair shaved on the sides, the center high, like the top tier of a wedding cake.

Three young girls walk toward me; all wear jeans slit across the knees. This is meant to appear genuine, as if they've been in the same accident, but instead it looks like what it is: a costume, for which they've each paid forty or fifty dollars. Why?

The *Record's* offices are in a new, and incredibly ugly, beige building on Seventh Avenue between Eleventh and Twelfth streets. The five stores at street level have never been occupied at once. There are unrented stores all over the Village. Something is *not* going on.

The *Village Record* began publishing in the fifties but has since undergone many changes. Once considered a bohemian rag, it's emerged as a paper of stature, though slightly to the left.

I ring for the elevator. Six years later it arrives. No one gets out. The doors remain open for four months, then finally close.

Though this is a new elevator, the speed of the ride brings to mind a car trip to the beach on the Fourth of July. I'm convinced there are battalions of men and women whose only job is to slow down elevators as soon as they're installed. When the doors open at the fifth floor I've grown older, wiser.

I enter the *Record* offices. This is my first foray to this location. In the old days the staff occupied two rooms on the first floor of a tenement, and battered manual typewriters sat on old wooden desks. Now there's a high-tech look to the place, halogen lighting, chrome and metal. The walls are painted a stark white, and four black leather chairs make up the waiting room. Clicking computer keys sound like insects on a summer night.

There are many cubicles, but only one person can be seen. She sits behind a waist-high counter and doesn't look up. I view the crown of her head with its black curly hair and watch long, red-nailed fingers sail over the keys.

I wait.

I clear my throat.

I finally say, "Excuse me."

"Sure," she answers.

"I beg your pardon?"

"You asked to be excused, I excused you."

"Is this a gag?"

She looks up. "Is what a gag?"

I decide against *I said, you said.* The woman's in her twenties. Her elaborate eye makeup is turquoise and purple. She has crimson lips and a dark complexion. I can tell she's been visiting a tanning salon.

"I'd like to see someone about placing an ad."

"That would be in the advertisement department."

I smile at her. "You're Ms. . . . ?"

"Rabble," she answers, and howls with laughter.

I stare.

"You don't get it," she says, disappointed.

"Get it?"

"Ms. Rabble."

I must have a blank look on my face because she says angrily, *"Miserable, miserable."*

I get it. "Oh, I see. Well, Ms. Miserable, Miserable, I —"

"You don't get it," she says, disgusted. "What d'ya want?"

"I'd like to talk to someone about placing an ad," I repeat.

"What kind?"

Suddenly I'm embarrassed that Ms. Rabble might think I want to buy a lonely-hearts ad for myself. Why do I worry about what she thinks? They say you care less after fifty. I hope it's true.

I show her my P.I. license and she sits up straight, raises her hands above her head. "Okay, you got me. I confess."

I'm not amused but smile anyway — the big one that displays my dimples. "I'd like to speak to someone in Classifieds."

"Go down the main hall and it's the second door on your right. Talk to Ms. Terious."

"I get it, I get it," I say, walking away from her.

"You don't get it," she mumbles behind me.

The second door on the right is open, and Ms. Terious — who according to the nameplate on her desk is Bobbie Finn — is wearing a pink, long-sleeved rayon blouse with a jabot at the neck. The desk prevents me from seeing the rest of her outfit. Her hair's cut Prince Valiant–style, with uneven bangs. The shade of brown is curious, as though she's tried to match a paint chip. I suspect Ms. Finn is her own beautician. She has bored blue eyes, and an ivory-colored powder lies on her face like waffle batter. I didn't know anyone still used the stuff, except my mother.

I scan the small room. Posters of rock groups plaster the walls. There are two flowerless gardenia plants on the windowsill.

"Can I help you?" she asks.

"I'd like to know something about a classified ad."

"Like what?" From an ashtray that says Hard Rock Cafe, she picks up a lit cigarette, takes a long drag, and exhales a smoky squall.

I resist giving a lecture on the evils of tobacco. "The personals. It's not for myself," I add quickly, a craven pipsqueak.

"It's for a friend," she says wearily.

"No."

"A relative."

"No." I show her my license.

"Is that supposed to make it clear?"

"I'd like to know how to find out the identity of someone who placed an ad."

"Confidential," she says.

"Yes, but —"

"No buts. That's our policy."

"A crime's been committed."

She raises both brunette eyebrows. "What kind of crime?"

"Rape."

"Oh Christ. Look, I know about the animals out there, and my heart goes out to the girl. But the paper's not responsible for what happens when two adults get together. I mean, it's not like they take lie-detector tests before they place the ad. We can't monitor every connection that's made. In fact, we can't monitor *any* of them. So whoever she is, God bless her, she doesn't have a case."

"Ms. Finn," I say calmly, "my client's not interested in suing the *Record.*"

"You say that now, but wait. When push comes to shove, everybody sues everybody. This is a suing state. A suing nation."

"All I'm interested in is the identity of the man who raped my client," I assure her.

"Do you have any idea of the idiotic lawsuits that go to court every day? A woman right in this office is suing another woman because Robert jumped out of her window when the second woman was taking care of him. I ask you, as an impersonal person, was that the second woman's fault? No. Still, the suit goes on. Three years now."

I know I shouldn't engage in this, but I can't help myself. "But if the second woman was supposed to be watching him —"

"Please." She holds up a hand, palm out. "The second woman couldn't keep her eyes on Robert day and night."

"But if Robert was likely to do something like that, the first woman shouldn't have left him in the care of the second woman in the first place." Why am I doing this?

"Aha! Now you're cooking. That's the basis of the second suit, by the second woman."

"Was he depressed?"

"Who?"

"Robert."

"Depressed?"

"What I'm getting at is, if he wasn't depressed, how could the first woman know he'd jump out the window?"

"The first woman knew it was a possibility, but she didn't warn the second woman. Now, of course, the first woman claims that Robert never did anything like that before and that maybe he jumped because the second woman wasn't giving him enough attention."

I feel like there will never be a time when I'm not having this conversation. "Sounds like he *was* depressed. Who jumps out of a window for lack of attention?"

"Robert."

"Did Robert die?"

"Of course not. He landed on his feet, like all cats do."

A cat.

"But he's never been the same since. That's the basis for the first woman's —"

"Ms. Finn," I interrupt. "Can we talk about the problem at hand, please?"

"What problem? Oh, yeah. The suit your client is bringing against the paper."

"No. My client is absolutely not interested in suing the paper," I say firmly. "My client was raped by someone who took out an ad in your Personals section on December sixth of last year, and I want to find him."

"It can't be done," she says. "Not through us. We promise confidentiality, and that's what we provide."

"But you're protecting a criminal."

"Can't be helped. Standards. Don't you know about standards? Ethics? Morality?"

I recognize that this avenue of pursuit's at a dead end. "Can I see the editor?"

"No."

"Why not?"

"The editor has the same standards I do, so it would be a waste of everyone's time. And I'll tell you something. The kind of person who would do such a thing is not going to give us his real address, and he's going to pay cash. In other words, the person is not going to leave clues."

I know she's right. Still. "Maybe if I describe him to you you'll remember something."

"Remember something." She sighs. "Is this person fifteen feet tall? Does he weigh six hundred pounds? Does he have three eyes? Does —"

"I get your point." I decide it may help to read the ad. "Do you sell back issues?" I ask.

"How many you want?"

Sitting upstairs at Exquisites, I sip my coffee and tuck into a wedge of mudcake. I'm sure there's an underground kitchen that, through chutes, sends out the same mudcake to every bakery and restaurant. Some places call it mud*pie*, but theirs is exactly like the rest. I know. There's nary a spot in town I haven't tested. Okay, so I'm a chocoholic. Who cares? There are worse things to be. My mother comes briefly to mind, but I close that door with a thud.

I open the *Record* for December 6 to the personals column. It's been a long time since I've read this paper, let alone looked at the ads. I don't mind saying, even if it makes me seem antiquated, I'm shocked.

The things people want to do to each other are mind-boggling. I can't even picture some of them. Sprinkled sparingly in with the smut are a few innocent-sounding ads. I circle these to show Lake.

After finishing my dessert and coffee, I cross Sixth Avenue to a bank of phones. I call my machine. There are three messages.

The first is from my father, who reminds me about dinner. The second's from Lake, saying she has something to tell me that she should've told me before. So my suspicion that she was holding back information is correct. There's nothing like a little validation to make one smile, even about the worst things. The third message is from Ursula, asking me to call her back.

I return Lake's call first. After two rings a man answers. I'm surprised but ask for her.

"Who's this?" the man says.

"Who's *this?*"

"Who you calling?"

"Ms. Huron," I say.

"She's not available now. You wanna leave your name?"

I'm not sure I do. Then something like static scorches the line, and I can hear a woman's voice but not what she's saying. The mouthpiece is covered, uncovered, and then Ursula is shouting through the wire.

"Who is it? Who is it? Is it Lauren?"

"Yes."

"Oh, God," Ursula sobs. "She's dead. Lake's killed herself."

Chapter

Six

═══════════

LAKE'S PLACE crawls with cops, most of whom I know from other cases. I'm particularly fond of one. His name's Peter Cecchi (pronounced Check-key). We're both third-generation Italians and our fathers are not Mafia, don't come to the dinner table in undershirts, and are educated. We admit that there *is* a Mafia and that movies like *Moonstruck* and *Married to the Mob* accurately portray some Italian-Americans, but there's a whole other group of us who are never seen or heard from.

Another reason I like Cecchi is that he never tries to pin the crime on me. This dumb ploy is used by certain writers, and I find it totally unbelievable. Why would the P.I. want to kill all those people? Worse, why would the cop believe, despite being proven wrong over and over and over again, that the P.I. was guilty?

Cecchi's a tad under six feet and extremely attractive. His abundant black hair's shot full of gray, and his dark eyes look beautifully wounded, as though he's seen more than any person should. A meticulous man, under his open black topcoat he wears a dark-blue suit, a light-blue shirt, and a silver-gray tie.

We say hello and I ask where the body is.

"In the bathroom."

"How?"

"Hung herself."

"You're sure?"

"Want to see?"

I don't but know I must. As we walk through the rooms I note that Lake put everything back in its place. Why tidy up and then kill yourself? I don't understand this, but I know it's not unusual. In the bedroom the bathroom door yawns open like a greedy maw. I step inside and confront ruthless reality.

Around Lake's throat is a brown belt. Looped and tied to a pipe is the other end. A chair, presumably kicked over by her, lies on its side. Horror has replaced beauty, extinction existence, and the delicacy of life leaves its monstrous mark on me again. I turn away.

"Any note?" I ask, recalling Lake's scorn at the idea she might commit suicide.

"No."

"Where's the sister?"

"We sent her home with the brother."

"Brother?" Strange — neither Ursula nor Lake mentioned a brother.

Cecchi flips some pages in his notepad. "Mark Bradshaw, age thirty-six. Stockbroker. Married and divorced twice. No kids. He's a stepbrother."

"How?"

"Lake's mother married twice. Bradshaw's her stepson, no blood relation to Ursula or Lake."

There are a lot of marriages in this family. "Has anyone told the parents?"

"Bradshaw's going to do that as soon as he gets Ursula calmed down. I think the stepfather's dead. One of the fathers is, anyway." He shrugs, perplexed.

We leave the bathroom.

"What's your connection, Lauren?" he asks when we're back in the kitchen.

"Ursula hired me."

"The rape," he says flatly.

I nod.

"I guess the kid couldn't live with it."

"Somebody couldn't," I say.

Cecchi raises a salt-and-pepper eyebrow.

"I don't think she did this." I tell him about Ursula's concern and my conversation with Lake. And as I do, I wonder if Ursula's suggesting suicide was a setup for murder, but I keep this rumination to myself. "Also, I had a call from Lake on my answering machine saying she had something else to tell me. I suspected she wasn't revealing everything when I interviewed her."

"Interesting," he says.

I can see Cecchi believes, as I do, that Lake's call to me doesn't belong in the profile of a suicide. Instead, it advances a "what's wrong with this picture?" angle.

"You get anywhere on the rape?" Cecchi asks.

"I'd barely started. Who found her?"

Cecchi consults his notebook again. "Terrence Ford. A friend. Door was open."

I file the name. Had Lake phoned Ursula, as I'd advised? I should've called her myself. More interested in food (not unusual) and in seeing Kip (also not unusual), I hadn't reported to Ursula. Now I remember that she also left me a message. After Lake's. What had she wanted?

Cecchi and I leave the apartment together. The temperature has dropped, and I think I smell snow in the air. I like snow, but not in the city. I put up the collar of my jacket and stuff my hands in my pockets.

"Where to now?" he asks.

"Back to my office, I suppose."

Cecchi makes an indecipherable sound. I think sometimes he envies my autonomy as a P.I. But he has five children (two biological and three adopted) and needs a steady income.

"All right if I call you tomorrow about the autopsy?"

"Sure. How's Kip?"

"Fine. And Sophia?" I ask about his wife.

We tell each other to say hello to our mates, and we agree that the four of us should get together soon. Peter Cecchi is an unusual man and, specifically, an unusual cop.

After we say good-bye I feel in a quandary. I want to go on with the case because even if Lake's death was a suicide, that doesn't negate the rape. The man may not be a murderer, but he's a rapist, and he's out there.

I need to speak with Ursula, even though it's not the most auspicious of times. Also I'd like to meet this stepbrother. I should call, but if I do I'm less likely to gain admittance. Despising drop-ins, I decide to become one.

A man opens Ursula's door. He's tall and well built, his auburn hair an assembly of wiry ringlets. His face is indistinct, as though someone has tried to erase his features, and his expensive gray suit is more revealing than his dull brown eyes.

"Mr. Bradshaw?" I ask.

He shows surprise. "Yes."

"I'd like to speak with Ms. —" For a moment I don't know what Ursula's last name is, then remember she and Lake have the same father. "— Huron," I say.

"Who are you?"

I tell him my name.

"I'm afraid she can't see anyone now."

"I think she'll want to see *me*." I'm not sure at all, but it's a time-tested line.

"Oh?"

Why do they always say "Oh?" like that? "Please tell her I'm here," I insist.

He gives me the once-over, as though what I look like will decide him. It does.

"Come in."

When I'm inside he leads me to the living room, where earlier today I questioned Lake. Now she's dead. I feel this knowledge like gloomy weather.

"How'd you know my name?" he asks warily.

"Lieutenant Cecchi told me. You *are* Lake's brother, aren't you?"

"Stepbrother. What do you want to talk to Ursula about?"

I ignore the question and sit in a wing chair, though Bradshaw doesn't make the suggestion. "Lake didn't mention that she had a stepbrother."

"I didn't realize you knew her so well," he says. A swift supercilious smile dances across his lips.

"I met her this morning." I want him to see that I'm up-front, truthful.

"Ah," he says.

Ah. I hate *ah* almost as much as *oh*. I wait him out.

Finally he says, "Then it isn't odd she didn't mention me."

"I suppose not. Could you tell Ursula I'm here, please?"

He leaves. I want to look in a drawer, open a cabinet, but there're none in this room. I don't know what I'm looking for, though I've never let that stop me before.

Mark Bradshaw is back. "She'll be with you in a moment."

"Thanks. Were you close to Lake?" I ask.

"Close?" he repeats, as if it's a new word.

"Were you friends?"

"I wasn't living at home when my father married Helena."

"When you were growing up, why didn't you live with *your* mother?"

"I don't think that's any of your business," he says sharply.

Maybe not, but now I definitely want to know the answer. "It was unusual at that time for the father to get custody," I prod.

I watch while he works a muscle in his cheek, silent.

"Lauren," Ursula says, entering. Her eyes are swollen, like puff pastry.

"I'm so sorry," I say.

She sits on the couch and sinks into the cushions. Her hands shake as she reaches for an antique silver cigarette box on the coffee table. Bradshaw is ready with a light.

"I called you," she accuses.

"I know."

"Why didn't you phone me after you saw Lake?"

"Then Lake called you and told you I'd seen her?"

"No. I assumed you had. You said you would," she states, as if whatever a person promised were a fait accompli. "You did see her, didn't you?"

"Yes. Her apartment had been tossed. Somebody was looking for something," I explain.

"I didn't notice anything out of place," she says, her eyes focusing on the ceiling as though a picture of Lake's apartment, as she last saw it, will appear there.

"She obviously put things away."

"What was taken?" Ursula asks.

"According to Lake, only the letters from the rapist were missing."

Suddenly Ursula emits a moan, her head drops into her palms as though she's been hit from behind, and she sobs.

I wait and watch.

Bradshaw jumps to his feet, goes toward Ursula, then backs away, unable to comfort her, unsure of what to do. He whirls around and glares at me accusatorially, as if to say that Ursula's grief is my fault. But before he can voice his thoughts, Ursula speaks.

"I knew it, I knew she was in despair. I told you," she indicts me.

"The idea of suicide was ridiculous to Lake," I say.

"What do you mean?"

Bradshaw sits on the couch, legs cramped behind the coffee table.

I repeat my earlier conversation with Lake about Ursula's fears.

"And you believed her?" Bradshaw asks.

"Yes. There was nothing in her manner that led me to conclude she'd turned against herself. She was angry at her rapist. And there's something else. Something important."

Both Ursula and Mark become still and appear to be holding their breath.

I say nothing, waiting to see which one will ask.

It's Bradshaw. "What is it?"

"She left a message on my machine."

"And?" Bradshaw again, impatient, falling for my ploy.

"I don't know," I answer provocatively.

"What's that mean?" Ursula snaps.

I notice that they don't look at one another, which seems artificial.

Bradshaw says, "What was the message?"

I can't stall any longer. "She said she had more to tell me."

"But not what?" Ursula asks, and I wonder whether it's hope I hear in her tone, or just curiosity.

"Not what," I concur. "Still, if she were going to kill herself, why would she leave me that message?"

Now they look at each other, then, apparently learning nothing, turn back to me.

"I think Lake may've been murdered."

"Murdered?" Ursula echoes.

"Who?" he asks.

I shrug.

"The rapist?" she asks.

I shrug again.

Bradshaw says, "What is it you want, Miss Laurano?"

"I'd like to know that, too," Ursula says.

I'm in a funny position. Supposedly I'm working for Ursula, or at least I *was*, yet I'm acting as an antagonist. Standing up, I say, "I guess you don't want me on the case anymore."

"What case?" she asks genuinely.

"The rape, if not murder."

"She wasn't murdered," Ursula says authoritatively. "And I can't see that there's any point in . . . in going on with it, under the circumstances." She lowers her eyelids on the last three words, as if they are shameful, soiled.

I put the murder theory on the shelf. "But the rapist is still at large," I counter.

"How much do we owe you?" Bradshaw asks.

"*We?*"

He gestures clumsily at Ursula.

"I don't think I understand your relationship to Ursula," I say.

"I don't think you need to," he answers acidly.

Covering, Ursula says, "We're friends."

"So what's your bill come to?"

I ignore him. Did Ursula kill Lake? Bradshaw? Or are they in on this together? Why do they want to get rid of me? "Another woman might get raped if we don't find this guy."

She disregards this. "I want to pay you for the time you've spent. What're your rates? We never —"

"They're three hundred a day plus expenses, but forget it," I say angrily. I don't want her money. I'm furious about her selfish attitude, and I don't like him much, either. All I want now is out. I suppose it's dumb — cutting off my nose, like they say — but I can't take the money.

I slam out of the potpourri-scented apartment, exit the building, and run down the front steps. Filth and all, it smells better outside than in.

Chapter

Seven

RESTAURANTS COME AND GO in New York, like politicians. The restaurant we choose on Bleecker Street, Arlecchino, is not going anywhere; it's too good. I'm distracted, as I can't get the case off my mind. There are too many unanswered questions.

We finally arrive at the dessert course, and Kip, my mother, Katherine, and I have zabaglione, a custard confection made with egg yolks, sugar, and marsala wine. I say *finally* because as good as any restaurant is, let's face it, I'm always ready to cut to the dessert. My father, Silvio, who lacks a sweet tooth, drinks an espresso.

Everyone says I look like him, and I suppose that's true. I don't have a widow's peak or black hair, but our eyes are the same, and our noses both have a Roman bump. My mouth resembles my mother's, which is lucky because my father's lips are thin.

They're in their sixties, in good health — except for my mother's . . . disease. My father still practices law. And God knows what my mother does now.

She made a life out of being wife and mother, though she had dreams and aspirations of her own. I know because she tells me about them as often as she can, tells me how she gave up who she might've been had she not married my father and, presumably, had me. She might have been: a) a writer; b) an actress; c) a historian. There's a d, e, and f, sometimes even a g, but they change from conversation to conversation depending on how much she's had to drink.

It's taken me a long time to admit that my mother's an alcoholic, even though I say the word almost blithely. I suppose I had my own reasons for protecting myself from the truth, but she didn't fit my picture of what an alcoholic looked like.

I never saw her pass out, never came home to find her lying on the kitchen floor, the way some kids did. She never abused me. However, like any unattended disease, it's gotten worse. There are the repetitions, the long, boring stories, the rhythm off by a beat, the uninhabited eyes. And it's then I wonder, was she *ever* there? I don't like to think about that, and this is when my denial digs in its heels. Round and round we go.

At the same time she lives a circumscribed life, continuing to dress well, remaining neat and clean, with only my father to see to, so she "gets away" with it. Still, there's an impression of furious offense that she conceals under irritating little diversions.

My father colludes. Somehow, for some reason, this all suits him. But for the last twenty or so years this has been their business, and I try to detach with love when I can.

They are not without charm and grace, wit and intelligence, and this is what makes it so difficult.

To say that they're horrified by my occupation is too mild. I'm an overprotected only child, and my father's take on life is that death and violation lurk behind every tree. When Warren was murdered and I was raped and beaten, though my father was incredibly supportive and sweet to me, he felt vindicated. We try to stay off the subject of my livelihood, but it always comes up, usually like this:

"What insane case are you working on now?" he asks.

"Arson and mass murder."

He puts his hands over his ears. "I don't want to hear that stuff, Lauren. It makes me sick."

I glance at Kip and my mother, who both shake their heads no, meaning that to point out he asked me would be useless. Instead, I smile benignly.

"Did you ever think of becoming a magician?" he asks.

This is a running joke. Well, almost a joke. What he means is, have I thought of becoming anything other than a P.I.? Even though he knows the answer, I play my part and tell him no, but I'll give it my fullest consideration. For the moment this mollifies him.

Kip, though not blind to their flaws and failings, is fond of my parents. And they of her. There's no deception about our union. They consider her their daughter-in-law. I'm aware that this is an unusual attitude, and makes my relationship with them an easier one than most of my friends have with their parents.

We speak of films we've seen, books we've read. My parents are dedicated readers. I suppose that's why I always have a book in my purse or pocket. I'm grateful to them for this legacy.

The meal's over, and the check comes. We don't fight for it because we understand that picking it up is important to my father. As usual, he overtips. And as usual, he and my mother argue about this. He wins. Surprise.

At the parking lot we wait for the man to bring up their car.

My mother says, "Let's get together again soon." She's never in the moment, always planning the next dinner, the next event.

"Think about being a carpenter, Lauren," my father says. He imagines this is funny, having no idea how many women are carpenters these days.

"I might accidentally cut off a finger," I say.

He winces. "You're right. Forget it."

The car arrives, tires squealing. The attendant, a face like a crumpled newspaper, steps out and looks at my father with a gimlet eye.

Unnecessarily, my father tips him. We three women look at each other: we know, we understand, we have compassion.

"I wish you'd let us drive you home, girls," my father says, as always. We haven't been able to break him of using the G-word.

That we walk the New York streets without them on other nights doesn't matter. We politely refuse the offer, then kiss good-bye. Now they'll drive home to New Jersey, to the town and house where I grew up. I thank God I'm not going with them.

When they're gone, Kip slips her arm through mine and we head for home.

"She held it pretty well," she says.

"Three manhattans — I'd be on my ass."

"One, and I'd be on mine."

"Think she'll ever quit?" I ask, knowing this is an impossible question for Kip to answer.

"Probably not as long as your father protects her."

"Yeah," I say sadly, and squeeze her arm between mine and my body. We didn't have a chance to talk before meeting my parents, so I fill Kip in on the case, using real names now because the status has changed, become public.

"You don't believe it's a suicide, do you?" she asks.

"I don't think you make a phone call saying you've got something else to tell if you're going to punch your ticket ten minutes later."

"I think you're right. Any suspects?"

"Two so far." I tell her about Lake's half-sister and stepbrother.

"Do you think they're lovers?"

"Possibly."

"Motive?" she asks, like a proper detective's mate.

"Don't know yet."

At Third Street and Sixth Avenue we cross to the other side. The Waverly Theater, which has joined the odious Odeon Cineplex (really Cineplex Odeon) stable, has been showing the same films for three months. These two theaters were made from the balcony and orchestra of what was once a single, inexpensive neighborhood movie house. Now it's $7.50 a ticket, $15 for the two of us. This to sit in cramped quarters, the screen in your nostrils. Remember when movies were a dollar, and popcorn was fifty cents? The films have gotten worse, and the popcorn's grown stale.

We walk the Sugar Gauntlet. It's what I call the strip between the theater and West Fourth Street. I've dubbed it this because there in a seductive row are Ben & Jerry's ice cream parlor, a candy store, and Mrs. Field's cookies. At least David's Cookies is no longer there. Sometimes I have to go completely out of my way to avoid this block.

As we pass, Kip puts a protective hand at the side of my face, like a blinder on a horse.

"You're all heart," I say, my nose twitching to the sweet smells wafting from the stores.

"You couldn't eat a cookie after that meal, that dessert, could you?" she asks.

I say nothing.

"You could," she affirms.

I take the Fifth.

The Village is quiet for a Friday night. The usual hordes of boys from other boroughs and New Jersey are absent. But we're not spared the sight of a well-dressed man peeing against a building. It continues to astonish me the way so many men use New York as their personal urinal.

The homeless hold out paper cups, begging for change as the Yuppies pass them by. To be fair, I recognize that one can't respond to every request.

We turn at West Fourth and walk toward Seventh Avenue. I feel the heat from Kip's body against mine, and I get ideas. Fantasies ripple through me. I quicken our pace. This surprises her; usually she complains about my walking speed. I'm always a beat behind her, my legs shorter than hers.

Kip says, "In a hurry?"

Smiling, I look into her eyes. "Yes."

She understands and smiles, too. We say nothing more for the rest of the walk, but as we turn onto Perry we're almost jogging.

Inside, as the door swings shut, we embrace, kiss, and undress each other. Because we're not in a movie, there's nothing graceful about this, but it's urgent and exciting.

Our hands tour each other's bodies. I kiss her breast and feel the nipple grow hard in my mouth. She sighs softly and . . .

The phone rings.

"Don't answer," she whispers.

"I won't."

We lower ourselves to the floor and continue our investigation, as though we've never been here before.

The machine picks up the call, and I hear Kip's voice telling the caller what to do after the beep. This feels surreal, as though there are two Kips in the room.

She slips her hand between my legs.

The caller speaks.

"Lauren, this is Cecchi," he says. "I've got the prelim on Huron."

I look at Kip.

Her eyes beseech mine.

I can't help it.

I crawl across the carpet, pick up the phone, tell him to wait, then turn off the machine. "What?" I ask.

"She was strangled manually."

"Murdered," I say, not surprised.

"Right."

"Have you told her sister yet?" I wonder if Ursula will want me back on the case.

"I'm going to, after I tell the mother."

"Let me know how she takes it."

He agrees, and we hang up. As I make my way back to Kip, I think about Lake, her youth, her ethereal beauty erased by the pressure of thumbs in a matter of seconds. Death is cunning, adroit, expecting us at our earliest convenience. We must be vigilant. Lake was not.

I look at Kip. The street light streams through the half-opened Levolor blinds, creating stripes across her naked body. Her nipples are erect, her mouth slightly open.

Lake is dead, but I'm alive.

Chapter

Eight

THE PHONE drills my ears. I wish I could unplug, but it's my conduit to the world, my line to financial security, such as it is.

Ursula's voice, low, depressed, speaks my name. But how should she sound, her sister dead, murdered?

"I need to see you, Lauren. I'm sorry about what happened, but things have changed now."

"Yes, they have."

"There's something . . . maybe I should tell the police, but I don't know, I think . . . could you come over this afternoon?"

I tell her I will, and we set a time. I remember Lake's last recorded words to me, and I wonder whether what Ursula has to tell me has anything to do with what I never got to hear from Lake.

I finish my coffee, toss the cup at the basket, miss. I look at my watch. I have several hours before my appointment with Ursula. Is she going to rehire me? If she is, there are things I could check out. But what if she isn't, and I investigate on my own time? What would V. I. Warshawski do? I do it, too.

The weather continues to be curious, as though this is San Francisco. Festooning the sidewalks are the street people: drunks, addicts, crazies. They beg for money, talk to themselves, rage against society. I find myself agreeing with some of their diatribes and wonder what this means.

On Sixth Avenue, between Fourth Street and Eighth, illegal vendors sell their wares. Each day they bring their bounty in shopping carts, wagons, even cars, and display it near the curbs. Some sell jewelry, incense, sunglasses, but the majority peddle used books and magazines. I often wonder who buys last year's copies of *The New Republic* or *Time*.

There's one guy who sells "almost new" current books in front of Dalton's. I admire his moxie. He says the books have only been read once, which I've pointed out to him doesn't make them any less used. But he persists in this delicate distinction. Occasionally I pick up something from him at a good price, even though I feel guilty about not buying from Three Lives. Today nine books are featured on a clean beige blanket.

"Hello, Richard," I say.

He nods. Richard's on the short side, with unruly black hair and mouse-colored eyes. Stubby fingers meander through his floppy mustache. He wears an army jacket, fatigues, and a baby-blue bicycle cap, striped down the center, the small visor turned up.

I look over the swag. The new Penelope Lively is ten dollars. I pick it up, turn it over, riffle the pages, as if this will enlighten me.

"Ten is a lot for this," I say.

"Don't buy it," he answers with a shrug. "Wanna buy in Dalton's for full price, I could care less. This book'll be gone by the end of the day. No, my mistake. It'll be gone in a hour. I'll betcha a C-note it's gone in a hour."

Richard tries to make bets with me all the time. It's tempting, but I resist and return the book to the blanket.

He looks both ways as though scouting for enemies, leans toward me, and whispers, "Nine."

"Eight," I say.

"You're killing me. I paid eight."

"You paid eight, Richard, you were robbed."

"I know I was robbed. I get robbed every day of this fucking world. You wanna know why? Because I'm too nice. You know? Too nice. That's me. What the hell, I'll letchu have it for eight-fifty and make fifty cents on the deal, which it won't even buy me a cup of coffee."

"You *are* nice, Richard. I'll take it." Kip loves Lively.

Laconically, he nods his head, as though to prove he's a nice guy, robbed again.

I fork over the money, and Richard looks at it with disgust. "You don't know the overhead I have," he says seriously.

"You're too nice, Richard."

"I am, you're right. I'm too fucking nice."

We say our good-byes, I tuck the book under my arm and walk toward the subway.

My Pierre is on Seventy-eighth, off Broadway, as Lake told me. The decor is tasteful. Simple, spare lines, white walls, peach table-cloths. No fleur-de-lis anywhere.

At this hour, the place is empty of customers. Busboys make last-minute additions to tables. The ring of crystal, the tinkle of silver-ware are the only sounds in the room. Waiters in black tuxes and rose-colored cummerbunds stand around anticipating the lunch crowd. A tall man in a dark suit, who I assume is the maître d', approaches me. He has a bald, freckled head and a florid cast to his skin. I suspect he has the occasional cocktail.

"May I help you, Madame?" he asks, a discreet, experienced glance at my wedding ring. "We are not quite ready for *déjeuner*."

I can't tell if his accent's real. "I'm not interested in lunching," I say, trying not to make it sound like an insult.

It doesn't work. "*Pourquoi?*" he asks sullenly, lower lip extended like a child's.

This ends my knowledge of French. "Because I'm looking for someone." I show him my license.

He takes my wallet from me, scrutinizes the document, touches the thing as if it's in braille.

"You are not the police, then?"

"I'm a private investigator."

"Ahhh."

This is slightly more irritating than *ah*.

"You are looking for someone who is employed here?" he asks hesitantly.

"A customer."

"Which one?"

I reach inside my bag for the photo of Lake. He exchanges my wallet for the picture, nods many times, then sighs. "Beautiful."

"Do you recognize her?"

"No." He extends the photo between two fingers, as though it's obscene.

"You're sure?"

"*Oui.*"

I forgot I knew that one. "Perhaps one of the waiters or busboys will remember her."

He glances at his watch, claps his hands twice, and the men join us. As the picture's passed around, there are many civilized comments on her looks, but no one recollects her. I describe the man she was with.

A waiter with a wasted face and worried brown eyes steps forward. I wonder if he has AIDS.

"I remember," he says. "He left a lousy tip."

So it's money, not beauty, that inspires recall. Is this news?

"Now I remember the girl," the waiter goes on. "She seemed nervous, dropped a fork."

"How did he pay?" I ask. "Cash or credit card?"

"We do not accept cards," the maître d' says, nose twitching, as if the idea is preposterous.

"Cash," I say to no one. "Was there anything unusual about this man?"

"The ring," says the emaciated waiter. "It's not that it was unusual. I only noticed it because my nephew has one."

My detective's heart soars. "Can you describe it?"

"It's silver, with eagles holding a ruby stone. One side has the date, the other the name of the school."

"Which is?" I ask.

"Easton."

I recognize the fancy private boys' school on the Upper East Side.

"And the date?"

"Couldn't see that. My nephew's from the rich part of the family," he adds sourly.

As though it's the first time, I marvel at how readily people reveal themselves.

"My father," the waiter goes on, unable to stop now, "got shafted. My uncle drove him out of the business. It was in the family for years. My father should've had his share."

I nod sympathetically. "Does anyone else have anything he can tell me?"

No one does. I thank them all and leave.

I look at my watch. I've done it again. I find a phone and call Susan.

When she answers she says, "You're going to be late."

"Don't you have any other friends?"

"None as dear to me as you, pea-brain."

"I'm calling from a booth, so don't hang up, okay?"

"And?"

"I'm not going to make it."

"Really?"

"I'm uptown," I say lamely.

"Oh, then of course I understand. How could you possibly get downtown if you're uptown?"

"There's someone I have to see."

"Uptown," she puts in.

"Downtown."

"This better be good, Lauren. Who?"

"I can't tell you."

She hangs up. I laugh. Later I'll go to her place bearing a box of Almond Joy (her favorite) and beg forgiveness.

At least I have a new lead. The Easton School. Since I'm uptown, it seems a shame that I'll have to make another trip up at another time. For me, traveling above the theater district is like taking an ocean voyage.

But it can't be helped. Now I have to see Ursula, find out what she wants, and, to the best of my ability, try to determine whether she's guilty of murder.

Chapter

Nine

BACK DOWNTOWN, on my way to Ursula's, I pass a middle-aged man who's wrapped in a befouled blanket, drinking beer from a can with a straw.

To the world at large he says sincerely, "I did give some thought to running for mayor."

I can't help laughing. He hears me and pirouettes; his dark, demented eyes peer into mine.

"But I decided all I want is a house and a wife," he challenges.

Carefully I move around him and hear him shout at my back. "Is that too much to ask?"

Actually, it isn't, but I have my doubts as to whether this man will ever have a house. A wife — well, who knows?

Ursula answers after one ring. Today she's wearing a brown suede skirt and a green sweater. Even with a hint of makeup her face is pale. She leads me into the lavender-smelling living room, and I take a seat on the flowered couch. She offers me tea. I decline.

"What can I do for you?" I ask, all business.

"You're angry," she states.

"No. Why do you say that?"

She shakes her head, begins to cry.

I crush my instinct to comfort her, and wait it out. I know from experience that I'll get more from her this way. A heartless business. My cold cunning is duly rewarded in moments.

"I'm sorry," Ursula says, taking a tissue from her skirt pocket, dabbing her eyes. "I thought you'd be through with me after . . . after I threw you off the case."

"It's happened before," I say insouciantly, impervious to insult. I wish. "What did you want to tell me?"

She stares at me a moment, weighing her need for absolution against my obvious indifference to rejection. A shift in her eyes tells me she'll forgo forgiveness and get on with it.

"I want you to know that I forgot all about it until this morning, or I would have ... I think I would've brought it up before, especially when Lake was ... was ..." She drifts off.

Alive, I know, is the operative word. Five letters, but so hard to say now.

"I completely forgot that I had it. She gave it to me before she told me about the rape."

"Gave you what?"

"I found it this morning when I was looking for something in my closet. Lake put it there herself, in the back."

I want to scream my simple question again, but try not to be impatient. Instead I count fabric flowers on the couch.

Ursula goes into her office. She returns carrying a large black canvas case and sets it gingerly on the table.

"Maybe it's nothing — I mean, maybe it means nothing, has no bearing. I just thought since she was so strange about it ..." She unzips a pouch on the front of the case and removes a small rectangular-shaped thing. It's tan and odd-looking. I don't know what it is. Ursula sets it down, then unzips the outer part of the case and flips back the cover. From where I sit I can't see inside, so I rise and stand over the table.

Tucked neatly inside the case is a gray object almost square in shape. It's maybe sixteen by eighteen inches and four inches high. On the upper left-hand side it says TOSHIBA. Deduction takes only moments, and my heart and pulse begin to mobilize like frightened dogs snapping at my innards.

It's a computer!

A laptop.

I have steadfastly and proudly refused to enter the technological times we live in. Kip says that I'm a fool, or words to that effect, and that I could simplify my business life if I got a PC and a few programs to keep track of bills and clients, as she's done. I've resisted a calculator and continue to use a manual typewriter. I still employ a fountain pen — the marbleized kind, from the forties. An old-fashioned woman? Perhaps. But even *I* suspect my motives. No, it's much more along the lines of inadequacy. I fear that if I was to try to learn to use a computer, I might . . . fail. And God and Parents know that that's not permissible. My personal F-word.

"It's a computer," Ursula says redundantly.

"Yes." I shiver slightly.

"Are you cold? Should I turn up the heat?"

I affirm that I'm comfortable temperature-wise. "What's this have to do with . . . anything?"

"I'm not sure." Ursula lifts it out of the case, sets it on the table, and pushes something at the front that opens The Beast.

The unlit screen, like a blind eye, meets my sighted ones. Its little keyboard, with its funny F keys at the top, torments me. And what are those arrows? What do CTRL, ALT, INS, DEL, and ESC mean? And what does NUM LOCK have to do with life? I hate the bugger!

"She was so odd about it when she brought it to me. It was as though . . . I don't know how to explain this so you don't think I'm a nut . . . but it was like the thing was alive to her, and she couldn't live with it anymore."

It doesn't sound strange to me at all. I feel I understand perfectly and am ready to agree to its demise. But unable to help itself, my brain shifts into its work gear.

"What did she say about it?" I ask.

"Just that she couldn't have it in her apartment anymore and wanted to store it here. I asked her why but she wouldn't say."

A ripple stirs my detective's blood. "Do you know what she used it for?"

"I suppose she used it for school papers, letters."

I think back. "I don't recall a printer at her place." I'm absurdly proud that I know a printer goes with a computer, and have to check an arrogant smile.

"This is the printer," she says, pointing to the tiny tan thing.

I'm chagrined and then astonished. "This is a printer?" I look at it and see that it says KODAK DICONIX 150 PLUS. There are various labels and buttons on the cover, and a slot where, I assume, paper goes in or out or both. I remember that Lake said her rapist's letters had probably been done on a printer. I remember, too, that she seemed peculiar about it. I can't make a connection.

"What do you think this has to do with her murder?"

Ursula winces at the word, still unaccustomed to its place in her life. "I told you, I don't know. The truth is, I don't know a damn thing about computers. In fact, they frighten me."

"Really?" I say without shame. "Why?" I hope for insight.

"Maybe it has something to do with math. . . . I was never good at it."

I nod, superior but understanding. I don't see any need to tell her that I flunked Geometry three times. I wonder if it's my short suit in the mathematics department that relegates computers to the arcane for me as well.

"I wish I didn't feel that way. After all, I'm a capable woman, and it's like being afraid of mice or something. Such a cliché."

Here we part company. Mice don't bother me. It's Kip who jumps on tables screeching if she sees one. "I don't mind mice," I say, sounding somewhat macho, I think, and feeling slightly disgusted with myself.

"I know it has a hard drive, so there are probably things in there."

Hard drive. It has a *hard drive.* Does this mean it's difficult to operate? Obviously Ursula knows more than I, but I don't want to appear hopeless. I nod. Steve Jobs in person. "I assume you want me to work for you again?"

"Oh, yes. I'm sorry. I should've asked. Will you?"

"Sure. Is there anything else that has to do with the computer?" I pray for any kind of enlightenment.

"Let me think."

I do. I peek at The Brute and try to convince myself I can easily crack this thing, but Ursula interrupts my fantasy with something so puzzling I have to ask her to repeat it.

She says again, "Lake said there was a moped that went with it."

Moped? Even *I* know this can't be right. A moped is something you ride on. But perhaps there's a piece of computer equipment that's also called this.

"Maybe the moped is somewhere in here," Ursula says, unflapping flaps, unsnapping snaps, unzipping zips on the black case. She pulls out various cords with odd ends to them, a black oblong thing that says AC ADAPTOR, some plugs, but no moped. I'm not surprised.

I toy with asking what the moped does. Will Ursula know? I decide not. "I'll look into the moped business," I say, my words of certitude a front for my insecurity.

"Good," she says, and I wonder if she knows.

Ursula closes the computer and returns it, the printer, and everything else to the carrying case. "Well," she says, as people do when they don't know what's expected of them.

I sit back down to show her that we're not through. She mimics me, waits. Now comes the hard part.

"I have to ask you some questions," I tell her. "About the time of the murder."

"You'll be investigating that, too?"

"Yes."

"But won't the police be doing that?"

"Yes. Still, if you want me to continue on the rape case —"

"You think *he* did it?"

"The rapist?"

She nods.

"It's most likely, don't you think?"

Uncomfortable, Ursula shifts in her seat as if to rearrange thoughts. "So why do you have to ask *me* about the time of . . . of the murder?"

"I have to eliminate you," I say truthfully.

"Eliminate *me?*"

"Routine," I explain, not truthfully.

"But I'm hiring you. And Lake was my . . . why would I kill her?" Her face becomes splotchy with anger and matches her hair.

"I don't know why you would. Or wouldn't. Why does it make you so mad?"

"Wouldn't it make *you* mad if you were being accused of murdering . . . someone you loved?"

"Yes," I admit. "Nevertheless, I have to ask. The police will ask you, too."

"What exactly are you asking?"

I take a breath. "Where were you when Lake was murdered? It was sometime between one and three."

"I was here."

"Can you prove that? Was Mark with you?"

"Yes. No."

"Which was it?"

"I . . . I guess he came later . . . afterwards. No, I can't prove it. But I was here."

"Did you get any phone calls during that time?"

"I don't remember. I know *I* kept calling Lake. And you. I called you."

"Did anyone call you?"

"I just can't remember. I was in a state. So worried. And God, I was right." Tears spring to her eyes.

I appear indifferent to her emotional state and continue callously, "Can you think of anyone else, besides the rapist, who might want Lake dead?"

There's a slight change of expression, like a phantom shadow crossing her face. And then it's gone.

"No, no one."

Too late. I've seen the truth before hearing the lie. Who is it? I wonder. Who does Ursula believe might have killed her half-sister? I won't learn this now, but I know she has *someone* in mind, and that's helpful in itself.

As for Ursula, I still don't know. She can't prove where she was at the time of Lake's murder. But she lacks a motive, as far as I can discern now.

"If you think of anything that might help or remember getting a call, some way to establish your alibi —"

"Alibi? Alibi!" She rises and flounces from the chair to the office doors and back again.

I try to soothe her. "It's all routine. Don't let it upset you. You have to be prepared for the questions the cops'll throw at you."

She targets the carpet with her foot, like an angry colt. "All right. I understand."

At the table she lifts the case, stands it on its end. The canvas handles beckon me. I take The Jezebel's hand in mine, lift it from the table, and walk to the door with it banging annoyingly against my leg.

"It has a shoulder strap," she says, and shows me.

This is no light package. I droop to the right as I tell Ursula I'll get back to her as soon as I find out anything. I don't say that this could be at the turn of the century.

◆

It is on my desk.

Next to it is my lunch: a Black Forest ham and Muenster sandwich, with lettuce and mayonnaise on the cheese side of the French bread, mustard on the side next to the ham. Very important that it not be the other way around.

In a bag is a chocolate truffle bar with hazelnuts from Houghtaling Mousse Pie, Ltd., on Mulberry Street. It was well worth the walk. This bar is so dense and delicious that my teeth ache when I think about it. I NEED IT! The afternoon will be dedicated to deciphering the Toshiba from hell!

On my desk, next to my food, is a pile of computer magazines that I purchased at Soft Etc., the basement part of Dalton's. I could've asked the salesman (no women, I noticed) questions, but I wasn't ready for the soft slap of humiliation that I would surely have had to endure. Besides, I'm stubborn.

It would probably be most prudent to at least scan the magazines before I turn The Devil on, but I'm impatient. I take a bite of my sandwich for energy, then push the release bar in front, as Ursula did, and the computer opens.

I fit a cord into the AC ADAPTOR and the other end (a regular three-pronged plug) into a wall outlet. Curling out from the opposite end of the adapter is a thin wire, like a snake, its head a black plastic gizmo with two holes in it.

I look at the back of The Horror and see, under DC IN 15v, the counterpart to the snake's head I hold in my hand. Adeptly, I push it right in. A feeling of accomplishment so overwhelms me that I consider calling it a day. Actually, it's because I don't know what to do next.

I stare at it while I finish half the sandwich. Then logic lurches to the forefront of my brain. Almost anything you plug in needs to be turned on! Maybe I won't be so hopeless after all. I mean, this deduction only took ten minutes, and we're not talking simple solution. Okay, who am I kidding? A three-year-old could've figured that one out.

On the right side a button marked POWER grins, mocking me. Trembling, I reach out and push it. There's a whirring sound, and I roll back my chair, staring as the screen burps and flickers, finally flashing orange letters that tell me the time and the date. How does it know?

Below that message there is this: c:\>. Next to it is a small blinking thing (also orange), and from the vacant lot of my mind I dredge up a word.

CURSOR.

It seems somehow to be a fitting name. I move my chair back to my desk, and while I stare at the keyboard I finish the other half of my sandwich.

There's a rectangular key marked ENTER, which looks suspiciously like the RETURN key I've seen on the electric typewriter Cecchi has at home. But I've nothing to enter, nothing to return. Cecchi! He uses a computer at work. Even as I'm registering this fact, I know I'm not going to call, ask him anything. First, I don't want to share this with him. Second, I don't feel like having a man explain computer stuff to me. As wonderful as Cecchi is, I know in my bones that condescension will creep into his tone and I'll want to kill him. Third, something makes me want to do this on my own. It's probably called stupidity.

Time for my chocolate. Carefully, I remove the wrapping. It's like a four-inch bar of thick, creamy fudge, and I salivate. I pull off a piece, pop it into my mouth. God. It's almost better than sex. Melting, it slides down my throat, and I'm transported by chocolate decadence. But only for a minute, because The Nightmare is still on my desk, taunting me with its blinking cursor.

So what's the worst thing that can happen if I push ENTER? Are the computer police going to suddenly appear? I laugh out loud. A false sound.

What would Helen Keremos do? Timidly, I reach toward the keys and press ENTER. There is flashing and funny sounds, and when it stops, this is what is on the screen:

```
:   Name   3    Name    3   Name       ::Name    3    Name    3   Name       :
:ARC      3NORTON    3autoexec bak ::ARC      3NORTON    3autoexec bak :
:ASKSAM   3NYZIP     3autoexec bat ::ASKSAM   3NYZIP     3autoexec bat :
:CATUTIL  3PCUSA     3command  com ::CATUTIL  3PCUSA     3command  com :
:DB3GEN   3PKZ       3config   exp ::DB3GEN   3PKZ       3config   exp :
:DOS      3PRODEX    3config   pro ::DOS      3PRODEX    3config   pro :
:EGA      3PRODIGY   3config   sys ::EGA      3PRODIGY   3config   sys :
:EZ       3Q&A       3ddm      qw0 ::EZ       3Q&A       3ddm      qw0 :
:FILMS    3QEDIT     3grasprt  exe ::FILMS    3QEDIT     3grasprt  exe :
:GAMES    3SCANV56   3help     bat ::GAMES    3SCANV56   3help     bat :
:GIFS     3SKYGLOBE  3spatter  gl  ::GIFS     3SKYGLOBE  3spatter  gl  :
:GMK4     3TELIX     3telix    cap ::GMK4     3TELIX     3telix    cap :
:GRAPHICS 3UTIL      3telix1   cap ::GRAPHICS 3UTIL      3telix1   cap :
:INFOLOOK 3WP42      3telixb   cap ::INFOLOOK 3WP42      3telixb   cap :
:JORJ     3WP51      3treeinfo ncd ::JORJ     3WP51      3treeinfo ncd :
:LETTERS  3WT        3             ::LETTERS  3WT        3             :
:LINK     3Ibmbio  0com3          ::LINK     3Ibmbio  0com3          :
:MEMMATE  3Ibmdos  0com3          ::MEMMATE  3Ibmdos  0com3          :
:NC       3Novirus 0dat3          ::NC       3Novirus 0dat3          :
```

Now I know what is meant by "It's Greek to me." I hate to admit it, but I'm overwhelmed. I'm clear on one thing: I need to either ask someone or read something about this. As always, I prefer to read. After hitting the POWER button (probably not what one should do) I unplug the thing, close it up, and settle down with *Compute, PC Magazine, Personal Computing,* and *Byte. Byte!* I can hardly wait.

Chapter

Ten

ALTHOUGH I've been no stranger to funerals these past few years, it doesn't get easier. The names tumble round in my mind like laundry in a dryer. Jerry, Stephen, Gloria, Barry, Mitch, Danny, Tom, Larry, Norma, John, Phil, Jane, Gwyda, Dino, and on and on. I'm too young to have so many friends die. But aside from the usual killers, we're in a pandemic, and more funerals lie ahead.

This one is Lake's. Cecchi and I sit near the back. Young men and women fill the first three pews. Ursula and Mark sit together. On the other side of Ursula is an older version of Lake: her mother, I deduce.

The service is over, and male and female pallbearers wheel the ornate casket up the center aisle. Outside, as usual, the New York air is sullied, and when I breathe I feel my lungs tarnish like unattended silver. We watch as the coffin's loaded into the hearse and the door slams shut with a brutal finality. I want to talk to Lake's mother, but this isn't the time. Ursula approaches us.

"Are you coming to the cemetery?" she asks. Her eyes are red from crying.

"No," I say. "Unless you want us to."

She shakes her head. "Later, I guess about noon, people are coming back to Helena's place. If you'd like to come . . ." Her voice trails off as though she can't bear to speak any longer.

"Where?" I ask.

"Here's the address." She hands me a crumpled piece of paper. "Only if you'd *like* to," she stresses.

"I'd like to," I say, and Cecchi agrees.

We watch her walk to a limo and disappear inside like Jonah in the whale. When the procession is gone, Cecchi suggests a cup of coffee at Rocco's on Bleecker Street, his favorite.

There are new pretensions in Rocco's, which has recently been redone. It's a rectangular room with one mirrored wall. Long pink marble-looking tables jut out from this wall, eight black chairs at each, so that you often sit with strangers. The ceiling, though not mirrored, is made of a material that reflects the room. And from that ceiling hang two chandeliers that bring to mind the Trump Castle in Atlantic City. A long counter runs the length of the room, and an abundance of cookies and pastries fills the glass-fronted cases.

A waiter, wearing a baseball cap backward, arrives with our order. Cecchi's espresso, my cappuccino, Cecchi's one vanilla cookie, my chocolate mousse cake. I can't help it. As I entered the café, I heard the cake calling my name. It would've been rude not to answer.

"So what've we got?" he asks.

"You really want to know?"

"No," he says, because he already knows: we don't have a damn thing.

I should tell Cecchi about the computer, but I don't. This is always a tricky business: I'm withholding possible evidence, a crime; still, I'm working for Ursula, and she has a right to my confidentiality.

"Do you think he ever *answers* ads?" I ask.

"Might."

We stare at each other.

Cecchi says, "You can't."

"Why not?"

"It's too dangerous."

"No, it's not," I tell him. "On the second date, when he comes to my house, you're there."

"You might get tons of guys answering the ad. You going to go out with all those dorks?"

"I'm sure I'll be able to narrow it down."

"Even so. I mean, it's no good, Lauren. It'll take too damn long."

He's right about this.

"Now that I think about it," he says, "I bet he *doesn't* answer ads. Too out of control that way."

Probably true. I tuck into my cake. Perfection.

"I'll be damned if I know where to turn next," he complains. "Hell, we got fibers and prints, but what good are they without a suspect?"

"What if you place somebody at the *Record* in the personal-ad department?"

Cecchi sighs. "One, Donato'd never go for it, and two, Donato'd never go for it."

Donato is his boss. "Why not?"

"Because it'd take too long. This sucker's bound to keep a low profile for a while."

"Unless he can't help himself," I suggest.

"You mean like . . . blood lust?"

I shrug. It's hard to talk about this, as it sounds too much like horror-movie mentality. I return to my cake. Although we're both confident that the rapist will make a mistake, it could be twenty-five, one hundred women later. We know we can't let that happen.

◆

The address Ursula gave us is on Washington Place, between Sixth Avenue and Washington Square Park. Years ago the park was un-sullied and innocent. People played guitars and sang; children ca-vorted while adults lay on the grass, sunning themselves. Now the park's a haven for drug dealers and their customers. Everything changes.

The building has two cement columns framing the doorway. I look on the bell-pad for HURON, and only when I see BRADSHAW do I remember that Lake's mother remarried. We are buzzed in, no questions asked. I assume there's television security.

This is a modest building, with a small elevator. I'm glad I don't have claustrophobia, like my father. When we get out on Eight, I observe that the door to my right is ajar. I ring the bell and we enter.

The tastefully decorated room has two white leather couches and a glass-topped steel coffee table. A Mexican-tiled fireplace con-tributes color to the room. At the opposite end there's a dining table and six elegant green-and-yellow rattan chairs. Light streams in through the windows like laser beams, and spectacular views can be seen from all.

There's a steady hum of people talking. Someone laughs, and it rends the atmosphere like a chain saw. Mark Bradshaw ap-proaches us.

"Thank you for coming," he says formally. He wears a dark suit and tie, and he sweats, creating tighter ringlets against his fore-head. In one hand he holds a drink, in the other a cigarette. There's something strange about this man, as though the last piece of the jigsaw's irreparably damaged. I'll have to interview him at another time.

"Want a drink?" he asks. "The bar's in the kitchen."

We take his suggestion.

Joe Carter, in a white jacket, black tie, and black pants, is the bartender. I've never seen my neighborhood handyman attired in anything like this, and I notice for the first time that he's not unattractive.

"Hello, Joe. You get around," I say.

"That's me," he replies, and flashes an inauthentic smile that doesn't dazzle.

Cecchi and I each order a club soda, then we survey the crowd. The majority are young, like Lake was. I spot Lake's mother.

She sits in one of the rattan chairs and talks with a young man whose complexion is studded with acne scars. He leans over, gives her a kiss on the cheek, and moves away.

"I'm going to talk to Mrs. Bradshaw," I say to Cecchi, and cross the room.

Helena Bradshaw looks up at me with distressed, denim-colored eyes. She's astonishingly beautiful, even though the chin definition has begun to blur. Her hair, which was probably blond, is pre-maturely silver and piled on top of her head. Loose strands, like lacework, adorn her cheeks. She wears a blue wool suit and a white silk turtleneck with a string of amber beads. On her right hand is a large diamond ring, on the left a wedding band. Aside from her resemblance to Lake, she reminds me of someone else, but I can't think who. I guess her age at forty-five or -six. After I introduce myself and give my credentials, she invites me to sit down.

"I'm so glad you came, Miss Laurano," she says. "Ursula told me she hired you. I didn't even know about the rape. Ursula said Lake didn't want me to know. I mean, I'm the mother. If anyone should know, it should be me, don't you agree?" She doesn't wait for my response. "Lake and I are like two peas in a pod. She tells me everything. I can't fathom why she went to Ursula instead of me. Don't misunderstand, I think Ursula's a wonderful woman, but she's not a mother. There isn't anything that Lake doesn't tell me."

I note, of course, that she speaks of Lake as though she's alive. This isn't unusual.

"I can't help wondering if there *was* a rape. Why wouldn't she tell me if there was?"

"I don't know that, but I do believe she was raped."

She grimaces, as if my stating this makes it a hideous reality. "You'd know, I suppose," she says.

I assume Ursula's told her my story.

"It's all so peculiar. Telling Ursula and not me."

Helena's concern with being left out of the process seems to bother her more than Lake's death.

"From the time she was a little girl until . . . well, I thought . . . until now, she made me her confidante . . . and I made her mine. She knows everything about my life. *Everything*," she emphasizes, and there is a faint flicker of sex in the room, as though someone's signaling by flashlight.

I think of my mother and how, when I was a child, she inappropriately told me of her life with my father. During my high-school years, my friends went to her with their troubles and she joined us at slumber parties held at my house. Everyone loved her, said how lucky I was to have her for a mother. They didn't understand that by making me her pal, instead of her daughter, she left me motherless.

"I know all about her boyfriends," Helena goes on jauntily, as if we're at a cocktail party exchanging information about our kids. "Several of them are here. I was just talking to one."

The acne-scarred young man.

"Terrence Ford," she says, identifying him. "Terry. He . . . he found her, you know."

"Yes." Another one I have to interview. "Was he her current boyfriend?"

"Well, actually, no. He's still in love with her. It's so obvious — sad, really. Lake broke up with him a few months ago."

"But they remained friends?"

"Definitely."

"Do you know if he was accustomed to dropping in on her?"

"I don't understand."

Lake hadn't mentioned to me that she was seeing Ford later that day, but why would she?

"I was wondering," I say, "if they had an appointment or if he dropped in."

"I don't know. But what I *do* know is, the idea of Lake's answering a lonely-hearts ad is ridiculous. Couldn't be." She reaches for a pack of Benson & Hedges on the table, extracts one, and lights it with a silver Dunhill.

I say, "Lake told me she answered the ad."

"Oh," Helena says with a thud.

"She said it was hard to find eligible men in this city," I explain.

"You see there, there, and there?" She points to three different men. "Any one of them is eligible."

"Maybe Lake didn't find them suitable," I suggest.

"Why not?"

"I don't know."

"Well, then, we'll simply have to ask —"

Finally, Helena Bradshaw acquaints herself with her daughter's death.

"Oh, God," she says, eyes filling. "I can't believe it. As I watched the casket lowered I kept thinking, Who's in there? What am I doing here? I felt like I was in a movie." Suddenly she brightens. "I could've been."

" 'Could've been'?"

"In the movies."

Another thwarted mother? I wonder.

"Whitey was against it."

"Whitey?"

"My husband. Lake's father."

"And Ursula's father," I state.

"Yes," she says, and looks away for a moment, then back at me. "Whitey said movies were just a reflection of decadent capitalism. Or was it Zach who said that?"

"Zach?"

Helena stares at me as though she hasn't heard or it makes no sense.

"Zach," I repeat. "You mentioned someone named Zach."

"Oh, did I? A friend. Anyway, we were all so different back then. It was the sixties . . . we all lived believing things would be . . . there was the war and other important issues. I'm sure you remember. Then by the time I met Harold, well, I was already into my . . . it seemed too late to start an acting career."

"And you had a small child. I believe Lake was two when you married Bradshaw, is that right?"

She nods, exhaling smoke fumes from her nostrils. This woman has come a long way from the sixties. I try to imagine her wearing a caftan, sandals, hair long, parted in the middle, baking bread, marching against Vietnam, smoking pot, and I find it impossible to see her in any of those guises. She seems more likely to have been plucked whole from Westchester, having never done anything but be an upper-class suburban wife and mother.

"What are your plans?" she asks, as though we've been talking about me instead of her.

"What plans are you referring to?"

"About Lake."

For a moment I wonder if I've missed something; it's like we're doing separate plays. And then I realize this is more narcissistic behavior on Helena's part: she expects everyone to know who or what she means, all the time.

"I want to hire you," she says flatly.

"As you know, Ursula has already hired me."

"I want to hire you, too." She runs fingers back and forth over the string of amber beads.

"That's unnecessary. I mean, if you want me to find out who murdered Lake."

She thinks a moment. "I suppose one could look at it that way. It's the same thing, isn't it?"

I calm myself by counting to three. "*What's* the same thing?" I ask placidly.

She looks at me, as if to imply that I haven't been paying attention. "If you find the person who ... who murdered Lake, then you'll find my murderer, too, won't you?"

"*Your* murderer?" I can feel my patience shredding like cheese on a grater.

She stubs out her cigarette, leans toward me, takes my hand in hers, and speaks to me as though I'm seriously retarded. "Miss Laurano, I can't imagine why you're making it so complicated when it's so simple. Whoever killed Lake will try to kill *me* next." She sits back in her chair, looking satisfied with her explanation.

Teeth clenched, I'm forced to ask why.

She frowns. "Are you really a detective?" she asks.

I nod, feeling incredibly stupid.

"The inheritance," she says.

"What inheritance?"

"The one Lake got from my second husband. He made her a millionaire. But if she were to die, then I'd be the millionaire. See?"

"And if you die?"

"Half goes to Mark, and half to Ursula."

"Are you suggesting that one of them killed Lake?"

She shrugs. "Well, it's always money or sex, isn't it? Motive, I mean."

"Usually. Which puts you in a special position."

"I don't follow."

"It means that along with being a potential victim, Mrs. Bradshaw, you're also the number-one suspect."

"Oh, shit," she says, and breaks her amber beads.

Chapter

Eleven

AS I LEAVE Helena's apartment I realize that if the rapist didn't murder Lake, I have at least three suspects: Helena, Ursula, and Mark. Then there's Terrence Ford, who's a fourth possibility.

It's difficult for me to believe a mother would kill her own child, even though I know it happens. Certainly Helena had the best motive, and pointing out that the others stand to inherit if she's killed is an elementary ploy. Still, the discomfiting mother-daughter scenario shifts my attention.

Now I have a motive for Ursula. Money. But why get me in on the rape case if she was planning to kill Lake? Of course, it might be *for* that reason: so I would think what I just thought! Or perhaps it wasn't premeditated. Perhaps a submerged sibling rivalry rose to the top like curdled cream. Helena said that the motives for murder are usually sex and money, but jealousy is another. Ursula remains in the running.

Since I don't know anything about Terrence Ford, Mark Bradshaw is my favorite candidate. Is it because I don't like him much, or is he really a good choice? Again, there are two possible motives: jealousy and money.

But why am I letting the rapist off the hook so easily? This is surely the course to follow first. I decide to visit the Easton School. This will involve taking the subway up to Times Square, the shuttle from west to east, and then, from Grand Central, a third one up-town. It's too awful. As for buses, they're too slow. I take a cab. Well, hell, at least I *thought* about other means.

*   *   *

The streets and sidewalks seem laundered on the Upper East Side, and even though it's a pleasure not to walk around garbage, it reminds me of white bread. No flavor.

The Easton School is in a redbrick building, circa 1930s. Above the imposing oak doors are etched these words: KNOWLEDGE IS POWER.

Inside, it's hushed, as if no one's there. Then I hear typewriter keys in the distance. I move toward the clacking like a homing pigeon.

The typing comes from an office occupied by three people. The typist remains moored to his work, while a woman with her back to me labors at a file cabinet. Seated behind a desk, another woman, hair the color of a ripe cantaloupe, looks up. She wears a tan sweater set. I didn't know they made sweater sets anymore. On the right side of the cardigan, above her breast, is a silver cat pin with green glass eyes. A nameplate on her desk tells me she's Mrs. L. Barnett. She asks if she can help me, and I say I want to speak to the principal.

A hint of derision crosses her wrinkled face. "Dean," she says. "He's called a dean here, not a principal."

"The dean, then," I say amicably.

She asks suspiciously, "Have you an appointment?"

"No."

She looks at me with what I think is pity.

"Dean doesn't see anyone without an appointment."

"This is a matter of life and death." I take out my wallet, open it to my P.I.'s license, and place it on the counter between us. From where she sits she can't see it. With a groan, Mrs. Barnett rises and walks toward me. She has a body like a forties radio.

"What's that?" she asks, as if the wallet might be germ-ridden. I tell her.

"You're kidding," she says.

"No."

"Well, what am I supposed to do about it, huh?"

" 'Do about it'?"

"It doesn't matter what you are. You have to have an appointment to see Dean Barry."

"Why don't you take this"— I point to my license — "in to Dean Barry and see what happens?"

"What could happen?"

"Tell the dean that I want to discuss a murder involving a former student."

Now she's impressed. I know because her eyes widen and the brows rise like slivers of moons.

"Murder," she whispers, and glances over her shoulder at the two behind the counter. The typing and filing have stopped. They're staring at us, unnerved.

Mrs. Barnett says, "Get back to work. What d'ya think this is?"

In my mind I respond: *I think it's a holdup. I think it's a submarine. I think it's bigger than a breadbox.* How can anyone answer that question? Predictably, the man and woman say nothing and return to their work, irritated, as if Mrs. Barnett is having all the fun.

"Who was murdered? Which student?"

"Confidential," I whisper.

My new conspirator nods, understanding. "Lemme see what I can do." Now she's eager to help because my information gives me a certain cachet. *Knowledge Is Power*, I think.

I pick up my wallet and watch as she strides toward a door, her backside like the Acropolis. She knocks once, then enters. As soon as she's gone, the other two stop working and stare at me. I feel somewhat uncomfortable.

"Hi," I say, to be polite.

Neither answers. Because I'm a detective, I know that conversation is at a dead end.

The dean's door opens, and Mrs. Barnett waves me over.

"He'll see you," she says reverently. I wonder which of us, the dean or I, has elicited this tone.

Dean Barry is a redhead and wears round wire-framed glasses. He stands up to shake my hand. The grip is indifferent. He wears a gray pinstripe suit, a light-blue shirt with a white collar and a rep tie. Cufflinks are initials in gold: MB. Michael? Malcolm? Moses?

Barry indicates a chair, and when I'm seated I read his stationery upside down. His name is Mead. He sits behind the walnut desk and tents his hands beneath a pointed chin.

"Mrs. Barnett tells me you have some information regarding a graduate of this school."

He doesn't want to talk about it, can't bring himself to say the word *murder*.

"Actually, no. I mean, I hoped you'd supply that information."

"Why would I know anything about a . . . about this?"

I put him out of his misery. "The man I'm looking for graduated from here sometime in the last fourteen, fifteen years."

"But I thought —"

"I'm looking for a possible killer," I say.

"Mrs. Barnett gave me the impression that it was the *victim* who'd gone to school here."

"No."

Dean Barry averts his eyes, as if he's embarrassed that he might know such a person, and I realize then that for him, it's preferable for the victim to have gone to Easton than the killer.

"How do you know he went to school here?" he asks defensively.

"He wears the school ring."

"I don't think that's conclusive. He could've gotten it in another way."

"Like having an affair with one of the graduates?" I ask.

He gives a snort of contempt. "Hardly."

"You mean, none of the boys from Easton is homosexual?"

"We weed them out early," he answers with pride.

Good show, I want to say sarcastically.

"It seems to me that if this man is a possible killer, he could've stolen the ring," Dean Barry maintains.

"That's true," I admit. "Or he could be a graduate."

The dean adjusts his glasses, fusses with his tie. "I suppose. What do you want from me, Miss Laurano?"

"I'm trying to identify this man." I explain the particulars and recount Lake's description of the rapist.

"That portrait could fit thousands of boys who've been through here."

"I'm only interested in a few years." I give him the dates.

"Still, we're talking about a large number of boys. Hundreds."

"I realize that. What I'd like, Dean Barry, is for you and your staff to think about this, go through those yearbooks, and make a list of any possible suspects."

"I couldn't do that," he sniffs.

"Why not?"

"You can't possibly expect me to implicate one of my boys."

"But I can," I say simply. "This is murder we're talking about, and 'one of your boys' is a rapist and a killer. The scum don't all live in Harlem, you know. I'll be in touch."

◆

"I don't believe my eyes," says Kip, coming into the living room after her last patient of the day.

"Believe them."

"Why are you reading *Byte*?"

"What do you mean, '*why*'?"

"Want me to spell the word?"

"Not in the mood, Kip," I say. I've been reading these computer magazines for hours. They're maddening because they assume you know what they're talking about. And I suppose that most people who read the things do. I don't.

She sits down next to me, reaches out, and lowers the magazine. "Lauren, I don't mean to intrude, but it's just not your kind of reading, and I have . . . well, let's face it, I'm curious as hell."

I debate whether to tell her everything, give in, get her help. Why am I such a pain? Why do I always have to do everything the hard way?

"I don't feel like going into the whole thing," I offer.

"How about part of it?"

"It has something to do with a case."

"Oh, really? I thought you were going to become a programmer!"

"Crossed my mind," I say nonchalantly.

"FORTRAN, COBOL, PASCAL, or something else?"

I stare at her, and I can see that she's trying hard not to smile. "PASCAL."

"Good." She gets up and leaves the room.

She can be so wicked. But it happens that I've run across these words and know they're programming languages. I pray that I don't have to learn anything about them to understand what's in the hard drive, which, I now know, stores the programs.

Kip sticks her head back into the room. "Calling Big Blue," she says.

Ha! I also know that this is a nickname for IBM. I don't turn. "Yes?"

"I admit I have no idea what you're doing, and it's clear that you don't want any help, unlike usual, still, I thought I'd mention that *Byte* is a bit too technical for the novice. But by all means, do what you please."

She's gone, and I think perhaps she's a bit hurt. *Bit, byte* — it's a whole new world. Relieved, I close the magazine and go into the kitchen.

Kip is boiling water for tea and cutting cheese.

"Want help?"

"Nope."

"Mad?"

"Nope."

"Hurt."

"Nope."

"What?"

"What, 'what'?"

"What *are* you?"

She puts down the knife, turns to me, and strikes a pose, one hip jutting out, a hand on the other, her chin raised. "I am woman," she says.

I laugh and put my arms around her waist. "I know."

She nuzzles my ear, kisses my throat. I'm not immune.

"Lauren?" she whispers.

"Yes?"

"I have something to ask you." Her voice is husky, prescient with wild abandonment.

I graze her lips with mine. "What?"

"Why were you reading *Byte*?"

I drop my arms from her waist, step back, and give her one of my most appalled expressions.

"Why won't you tell me?"

"I did. It has to do with a ca—"

"Don't."

"It's a long —"

"Don't."

The moment of truth. Is this a power struggle? Am I being a child? What I want to do is tell her but make it clear that I don't want her help. There has to be a kind, decent, gentle way of conveying this.

"Okay," I say, "but I don't want your help."

"Why are you screaming?"

"I'm not," I whisper.

"I promise not to help you. This is ridiculous, Lauren. I've been trying, to no avail, to get you to enter the twentieth century for years, I find you in our living room, casually reading *Byte*, of all things, and now you tell me you don't want my help. Why not?"

"Because."

"Why didn't you say so in the first place?" She goes back to slicing cheese. There's something about it that brings to mind a guillotine.

"I hope you remember that we're going to the Js' for dinner tonight."

I don't. "Of course I remember. Listen, Kip, it's not that I don't want your input. . . ."

"Yes, it is."

"Yes, it is."

"Right."

"Well, why should that hurt your feelings?"

"It doesn't."

"It does."

"It does."

"Right." So I tell her.

"Fascinating," she says earnestly. "And you don't want me to show you how to use it?"

"This may come as a shock to you, Kip, but I'm a detective."

"You're also a jerk."

"Thanks. That makes me feel wonderful!"

"Well, I can't help it. It's so dumb. I know you're a detective, but why not let me show you the basics and then you can detect your little heart out?"

I think this over. I ask myself the important question: Is she crossing my boundaries? No. She's my lover, my friend, and she knows how to do something I don't know how to do. She can shorten the process. She's right: I *am* a jerk!

◆

Jenny and Jill's apartment is as warm and cozy as their store because it was also designed and constructed by Jenny. She's always anxious to have a project. Lately she's been speaking of buying a house in the country, redoing it, then selling.

In the living room, on opposite sides of a large white square table, we sit on comfortable couches. The room is lined with bookcases filled with first editions and, here and there, pictures of their friends. Kip and I are in a black frame, both in our early thirties. I don't give it more than a glance because I can't believe we ever looked that young. There is not a speck of gray on either of our heads, not to mention . . . not to mention.

Jenny is about my height, with short, blond, curly hair. At least it's blond tonight. She views her hair like one of her projects and is always changing color, growing, cutting. She's an appealing and lovable person, even though at times she can be paranoid, seeing plots and conspiracies around every bend. But it's not a serious flaw, and I suspect she does it more to entertain than for any other reason.

She wears glasses (contacts are too much trouble), a striped, long-sleeved cotton top, and blue shorts. It doesn't matter that it's winter, and it isn't because the temperature is high: she wears shorts whenever possible, and being at home makes it possible.

They've cooked dinner for us — fish and vegetables — and now we're having what Jenny calls gunk. Gunk is cooked fruit and very good. All three of them are on diets. I, of course, would prefer something chocolate, something sinful, but I go along with the others, having sympathy for their weight problems, which I believe to be minor. I miss a sugary confection but say nothing because, as it is, I know they despise me for my metabolism.

"So, Lauren, what're you going to do?" Jenny asks, referring to Helena Bradshaw's wish to hire me.

We've been discussing various aspects of the case for the last hour. I've asked Kip not to mention the computer. I don't like taking up this much time and rarely do. But the others are fascinated by the case and have besieged me with questions.

"Ursula's my client, but I'll keep an eye on Helena. There's nothing new about a perp hiring a detective to throw one off the trail, and that goes for Ursula, too. It's done all the time."

"And you think that's what the Bradshaw woman was doing?" Jill asks.

I say, "Have you noticed that no one says 'the Bradshaw *man*,' or whatever the name is?"

They look at me.

"Is that true?" Kip asks.

"Think about it. On the news, for instance, they always say things like 'the Helmsley woman,' but do they say 'the Helmsley man'? No."

"I think she's right," Jenny says. " 'The Meyerson woman,' 'the Nussbaum woman' ... they never said 'the Capasso man' or 'the Steinberg man.' "

"Why do they do that?" Jill asks, spooning up some gunk.

I say, "It's probably just more of the same." We don't need to define what "the same" is.

Jenny smiles, an impish gleam in her eyes. "The important thing is you're back on the case."

We all love getting the scoop, being in on things. Not that we trivialize the magnitude of what's happened. Still, it's exciting to be in the know, and we can't deny that to each other.

"We should celebrate," Jenny says.

Without a word or a nod we all get up, grab our purses and coats, and head for the door.

In the hall, while Jill locks up, I see in my mind's eye four half-full bowls of abandoned gunk.

As we start down the stairs, Jenny says, "Soup's On has the best white chocolate cake I've ever tasted. And the mousse is great, too."

◆

The teaching session took forty-five minutes. I'm a quick study. I now know (understand?) the rudiments of computing. And some of what overwhelmed me earlier in the day. The list of strange names that came up on the screen was put there by something called the Norton Commander. It's a program that's known as a shell (who knows why?), and it displays my directories. Or rather, Lake's directories. Kip has identified various programs for me, like WP42 and WP51. These are two versions of WordPerfect, for word processing. Writing. And GMK4 is Grammatik4, to check grammar. GAMES I figured out myself. God, there are a lot of them. I'm now playing something called ALLEYCAT. It's this adorable . . . It's two-thirty in the morning. This is disaster. I can't stop playing this game.

Kip went to bed long ago, after she realized I wasn't going to stop playing BIGRIG. Between BIGRIG and ALLEYCAT there was COMICS, DIGDUG, ASTEROIDS, TREK, and HANGMAN. But I like ALLEYCAT the best so far. There are other games in the Games directory, and I know I'll be trying them out. This is what terrifies me. Oh, not the way it did. My phobia about computers is almost gone. What worries me now is that I won't get anything else done. The damn thing is FUN!

There was nothing of Lake's in the WP51 directory, and all I found in the WP42 directory was school papers, nothing of any value to the case. And LETTERS held letters to friends, no clues that I could see. But I'll read them again. As soon as I win this game of Alleycat.

The most important discovery, however, was in the directory called TELIX. Kip didn't know what it was, but she was able to suggest that I open it up (you do this by putting the cursor on the file name and hitting ENTER) and see what was inside. One of the files said "Telix.exe." Kip said "exe" was for *execute*. I entered it and a whole new screen came up. It explained the moped.

Earlier, in my reading, I'd unearthed the arcane information that Ursula's *moped* was a modem. And what is a modem? It seems it's something that connects to the computer and your phone line and the world. I don't know. But I *do* know I need to buy a modem. Although one can get almost anything to eat at any hour in New York City, there are no all-night computer stores. So first thing tomorrow I will go to J&R's in the Wall Street district and buy one. What kind? Who knows? Already I feel sorry for the salesperson who will wait on me.

Anyway, this TELIX thing is obviously part of it, because after I hit this key and that key, a phone directory came up with names like XANADU, POSSIBLE FATE, WOMB WOMAN, DEAD CITY, STRANGERS IN THE NIGHT, and LIZZIE BORDEN'S. This last gave me pause. However, the real nightmare is that there are 185 entries in this list!

And you wonder why I'm playing Alleycat.

Chapter

Twelve

I'M NOT a timid person. Maybe I once was ... until about age twelve, but not since then. I couldn't have done what I have in my life, couldn't do what I do now. Still, as I stand here on Park Place, staring, through snow falling like flour, at J&R's across the street, I want to run. I want to turn around and walk back the way I came, away from ... what?

What in hell is the big deal? Last night I thought I had it knocked, the computer phobia a thing of the past. But today, in the sallow light of winter weather, streets soiled by partially frozen puddles, I feel stymied again, as if I have no right to be poking into the mysteries of this alien world — a world that, in some recess of my mind, I still believe is the province of men.

Fury at this galvanizes me, and I cross the street. There are several entrances to J&R's, and after taking a flyer and going in one, I'm told that the computer department has moved down the block. Being a crackerjack P.I., I find it.

Before I enter I try to buoy myself, remind myself how easily I learned what Kip taught me, how I destroyed Alleycat! After all, if Lake could use a modem, why can't I? Millions of people use modems, and probably many are women. I'm being absurd. What does this entail, anyway? I'll simply go to a clerk and ask for one.

Inside, the din is horrendous. Various monitors are displaying action games, and the sound of gunfire and bombs is braided with voices of clamoring customers and harried salesmen. I don't see any saleswomen! There are, of course, women at the cash registers. No wonder I feel as I do. Did!

Looking around for a salesman, I finally spy a short man with a nameplate on the pocket of his white shirt, which says ALLEN TAPPER. He has a square, sharply defined chin that belongs on a bigger face. High cheekbones give his eyes a squint that translates into a leer. No matter. I know that Mr. Tapper will help me.

"Excuse me, I'm looking for a modem," I say authoritatively.

"What baud?" he asks.

Only for a moment do I consider bolting. Recovering, I ask cleverly, "What do *you* suggest?"

Tapper tilts his head to one side, the eyes almost obscured. "Whatcha want it for?"

I run through a list of responses, and nothing seems right. Yet, it's simple, isn't it? I want it to . . . to . . . "Connect," I say.

Tapper does nothing to conceal his look of contempt. "You don't say? That's nice." He grins, showing small, tobacco-stained teeth.

Irritation overrides feelings of humiliation. He's enjoying this. This is what he expects from a woman, and he loves it — lives for it, probably, the twerp. I decide to give him a real thrill.

"I don't know anything about bauds, or modems, for that matter. That's why I'm asking you."

"No kidding."

What happened to "the customer is always right"? What happened to courtesy? "No," I say guilelessly, "I'm not kidding."

"Huh?" His supercilious expression fades like last year's tan.

"I want to buy a modem to go with a Toshiba 3100SX. I don't want to spend a lot of money, Mr. Tapper, but I want something reliable."

"You want a Hayes 2400," he states.

"I do?"

"Yeah. Follow me." He curls a finger as he turns his back.

We thread our way through the store's aisles, pushing past people, and he leads me to a counter that he steps behind. From beneath it he brings up a box. "This," he says, sounding alive now that he knows he has a real dummy on his hands, "is a deal. You know what Hayes 2400 usually sells for?"

"No."

"You look it up. Even at Forty-seventh Street Computer, places like that, mail order, it don't matter, we got it beat. Hayes sells for three, four hundred."

Hundreds. I had no idea. "I can't afford —"

"No, no, no, honey, that's not what *we're* charging. Not for this model. Which is just as good," he hastens to add.

"Oh."

"Listen, sweetie, I —"

"Mr. Tapper," I interrupt, unable to control myself, "please don't call me honey and sweetie, okay?"

"Huh?"

"I'm not your honey or your sweetie." This is dumb to do right now, but my feminist side comes to the fore, unstoppable.

"What're you," he says, laughing, trying to cover what he perceives as a rejection, "a dyke?"

"Yes."

"Huh?"

"Can you please tell me about the modem?"

Tapper stares at me, unwilling to believe that I've said yes to his dyke question. He laughs again, this time as though we're conspirators. He winks, then goes on with his pitch, though slightly less sure of himself, I think.

"This baby is the best. Hayes is the name of the game. It's like Sony in TVs. People are always talkin' Hayes-compatible — why get compatible when you can get the real thing?"

"What does 2400 baud mean?"

"The speed, darling, the speed."

I take a deep breath. "Not 'darling,' either."

"Huh?"

I explain. He shakes his head and eyes me as if he's more willing now to believe in my dykehood.

"Modems come in 300, 1200, 2400, 9600 baud rate. The standard is pretty much 2400. You can access 300 and 1200 with a 2400. It's a good steady speed. Whatcha want it for?"

"Like everyone else," I say.

"Prodigy?"

I recall seeing that name on Lake's directory, and I've certainly seen it advertised. "Yes."

"And bulletin boards, huh?"

Bulletin boards? I don't recall anything on the directory called Bulletin Boards, but that must be the long list of telephone numbers with the crazy names.

He leans over the counter, his big chin practically touching me, his breath tickling my face. "You want to meet people, huh?"

In my mind I leap high into the air, reach the ceiling. *Meet people!* Oh, yes, Tiny Tapper, that's it! I could almost ki— no I couldn't, not him. Trying to remain calm, I ask him what he means.

"Listen, honey, a lotta them BBSs are for tech stuff, downloading files, joining conferences about this and that, but then there're the other ones, the ones where, you know, you meet guys and make dates."

"What ones are those?" I ask prayerfully.

"Ya mean the names?"

"Yes."

"Hey, I dunno. I'm married."

"Is there someone here you could ask?" I know I must sound desperate, but I don't care.

Tapper leans back, crosses his arms over his chest, and sizes me up. "I thought you said you was a dyke."

Politics or practicality? The hell with politics, I'm on a case. "I was just kidding."

"Yeah, I thought so. You're too pretty."

This almost pushes me over the edge, but I have to keep my priorities in order here. "Could you ask somebody for the name of one of those billboards?"

He laughs raucously. People stare. He points a finger at me. "'Billboards,' she says. Billboards."

No one else is laughing, and I fail to see the joke.

"She means *bulletin boards*," he explains to his audience.

Then they *do* laugh. The men, that is. More snickering than outright laughter, but it's not a great enough gag to bond them or keep them occupied for more than a moment, and everyone returns to his own transaction.

"Look, babe, you wanna buy this thing or not?"

"How much?"

"It's on sale. A deal. One twenty-nine including Smartcom software."

I ask what this is.

He grins again, his condescension like a waving football pennant. "It's what you run the modem with, sweetie."

"I have Telix," I say, taking a gamble.

"Telix is good. How come you got the communications software and not the modem?"

"It's a long story. What about a name for one of those bulletin boards you were telling me about?"

"Can't help you. You want this tootsie or not? There's a lot of people wanna buy."

I tell him yes. He writes up my order and dispatches me to the cashier. While I wait on line I wonder whether the long list of names in the Telix phone directory are all dating services. Surely not Lizzie Borden's. On the other hand ... No. A dating service wouldn't have a name like that.

But Possible Fate and Strangers in the Night may well be what I'm looking for.

◆

Even though I'm anxious to begin my modem pursuit, I have an appointment with Helena Bradshaw to keep. There's information I need that probably only she can give me.

As I ascend in the elevator, I reflect on how much she must've changed in the last twenty years. But haven't we all? And where did our marching and protesting get us? We face the abortion question again, and racial prejudice runs riot. The nineties are worse than the sixties because we're apathetic, unwilling to fight the big battles again. Our money is gone, our hearts and minds shattered, cynicism is our master. We will reap the deadly harvest of the Reagan administration for years to come.

Helena Bradshaw answers the door wearing a light-blue jumpsuit, a dark-blue turtleneck underneath. I like jumpsuits and have two. But I find them impractical because when you go to the bathroom, especially if you're not wearing anything underneath, you find yourself almost naked. Besides, there have been times when a sleeve has dipped into a toilet.

She sits on one of her couches and I occupy the other as I attempt to fill in some of the blanks. "Why did your husband leave his money to Lake? Why not you, or at least Mark?"

She touches her face with long lean fingers, playing her cheek like an instrument.

"I can't answer that, can I?" she says sharply.

"Then you had no prior knowledge of your husband's will?"

"No."

"Were you surprised that he left his money to his stepdaughter?"

"Well, yes, I suppose I was."

"And angry?"

"Hurt. But everything Lake had was mine, so it didn't matter much."

"I'm afraid I don't understand," I say, feeling odd, perhaps because I *do* understand, all too well. Blurred boundaries. I know a lot about them.

"Lake was extremely generous. We had joint savings and checking accounts."

I'm stunned. "Whose idea was that?"

"Lake's, of course. She was the beneficiary, after all."

Something occurs to me. "If Lake had all that money, why did she live where she did?"

"I know," she says, waving a hand, and goes on in a gossipy tone. "I couldn't understand it. That girl could've lived anywhere. Sutton Place, for God's sake."

"Why didn't she, Mrs. Bradshaw?"

"Helena," she corrects. "I only know what she told me, which was that she wanted to be like her friends and she thought living in the East Village was an experience. *I'll* say it was an experience. I went to visit her there once." She shivers, as if to demonstrate how uncomfortable it made her.

"Only once?" I ask.

"Were you ever there, Lauren?" she says in a patronizing way.

"Yes." I wonder if I should tell her under what circumstances, decide against it.

"Well, if you were there, surely you needn't ask why I wouldn't go back. Crack people on the streets, other degenerates."

"Why wasn't Lake's father at the funeral?" I ask, purposely changing the subject, a technique I learned from the Bureau.

"Whitey? Oh, well, if you knew him." She smokes; a stream whirls above her like a lasso.

"But I don't." I omit that I plan to try to meet him. "Did you tell him about Lake's death?"

She hesitates for a moment. "I wouldn't know where to find him. I'm sure he's heard about it from television or the papers, but Whitey hasn't seen Lake for . . . well, since I left him."

"Why not?" I feel a swell of anger thinking about this man who neglected his daughter.

"I suppose he simply wasn't interested," she says.

"And Lake? Was *she* interested in seeing *him?*"

"Funny, but she was. I mean, funny because it was only lately that she talked about trying to visit him. Lake thought of Harold as her father; she doesn't . . . didn't remember Whitey."

"Then *she* knew where he lived?"

"I don't know. She suddenly started asking me lots of questions about him."

"How long ago?"

Helena thinks, her eyes toward the ceiling. "About three weeks ago."

Since the rape. I won't ever know for sure what Lake's need was here, but it's easy to see that she had one. I feel I understand. After my own rape I wanted to be with my family, and even though my father was a man, I needed his support, his love. As much as Bradshaw may have been a father to Lake, he was dead and her real father was alive. That she didn't make the connection with him tells me she was ambivalent, perhaps clear on not trying to get oranges from a hardware store. On the other hand, perhaps she *did* see him. I ask Helena about this possibility.

"Oh, no, no, no. She would've told me."

I don't remind her that Lake didn't tell her about the rape, but I note Lake's interest in reuniting with her biological father.

"Where was Whitey living when you last saw him?"

"In Hurley, Pennsylvania."

"Is it possible he's still there?"

"That was over twenty years ago," Helena says, incredulous.

"Then Whitey wasn't someone who'd stay put?"

"Well, actually, he was. It never occurred to me that he might still be in Hurley." She shakes her head, astonished, as if the idea of living in the same place for such a long time is unique.

I write "Hurley, PA" in my notebook.

"Let's get back to the money. How about Mark? How did he react to his father leaving Lake all that money?"

"I think he was shocked, and angry, too. Especially because his relationship with Lake was strained, to say the least. He always resented her. Harold made such a fuss over her and was so cold toward Mark."

"Why didn't Mark's mother get custody?"

"Oh, don't you know about that?" She purses her lips disdainfully. "The mother is a lesbian. Or was. Well, I suppose she still is. Anyway, one couldn't have one's son raised by two of *them*."

She waits for my concordance. Naturally, I don't give it to her. This is when silence strangles. But I remind myself why I'm here, why I'm talking to this woman, and put my resentment on the shelf, noting, once again, that we *are* everywhere.

"What's Mark's mother's name?"

"Why?" she asks suspiciously.

"I have to know who the players are, Helena."

She likes this, and her light-blue eyes take on a sheen, as though newly polished.

"Yes, that makes sense," she says. "Her name is Mal."

"Bradshaw?"

"God, no. Harold was far too angry to let her keep his name. She went back to her maiden name, Cleaver."

I wonder whether Mal went back to her own name because Harold Bradshaw wouldn't let her keep his (something I doubt he could legally do) or whether it was because she *wanted* to be rid of her married name.

"You said something about *two* lesbians. What's the other one's name?"

"Now you're reaching. I mean, this was what, over twenty years ago? People like that don't stay together." She viciously stubs out her cigarette.

I have to stop myself from pointing out that she's been divorced. What good will it do? I might win the battle but never the war. "Do you remember the other one's name?"

"If only they *would* stay together, maybe we wouldn't have all these people dying from AIDS," she says, ignoring my question.

Color rises in her cheeks, and I can sense a homophobic diatribe coming, so I quickly change the subject, uncertain how long I can prevent politics from overpowering priorities.

"Does Mark know that Lake was so generous with you?"

She sits up straighter, lights another cigarette. "What do you mean, 'so generous'?"

"The joint checking and savings accounts," I remind her.

"I don't see anything so generous about that," she says truthfully. "I *am* . . . I *was* her mother."

"Not every daughter would do what Lake did."

"Harold was *my* husband. The inheritance should have been mine. Lake didn't have a choice, did she?" Her eyes flash furiously.

At last I've hit the right note. "In fact, Lake *did* have a choice. She could've kept all the money for herself. She could've cut you out completely. There was nothing you could do legally, was there?"

For a moment the gorgeous face contorts, making her ugly, then almost at once she sheds the expression like an unwanted skin and is back to being beautiful.

"No," she says softly. "There was nothing I could do legally. Mark tried. He took Lake to court, but as he'd been left a pittance, he didn't have a leg to stand on. Harold did leave me this apartment and our country house in Connecticut, but no cash."

"You don't work?"

"No, I don't work," she says defiantly, as though I'm a spy from NOW. "I hope you understand that I'm terribly afraid. I don't for a moment believe that this so-called rapist killed Lake, and I'm sure I'll be next."

"Because of the money?"

She nods.

"So we're back to Ursula and Mark."

"I suppose we are."

"What if they should die before you?"

"What do you mean?"

"What happens to the money then?"

She rises, signaling that our meeting has come to an end. "I don't care for your implication."

I point out that I've implied nothing, but simply asked a question.

She smiles. It's dazzling. "Then you don't mean to suggest that I killed my daughter and want to kill Mark and Ursula so that I can do whatever I want with the money?"

Actually, I haven't thought of that, but it's a damn good motive. And what is it that she wants to do with the money? Something. Is there someone else in the picture? Someone unknown, unnamed. A lover?

I decide to take a risk. "*Did* you kill Lake, Helena?"

"If I did, would I tell you?"

I nod in agreement.

"Just for the record, I didn't. I loved Lake. We were like twins." There's mist in her eyes. "Do you have children, Lauren?"

"No."

"Then you can't understand."

"I can imagine."

"No, you can't." She walks me to the door, opens it. "Only *I* understood Lake. Harold thought he did, but he didn't. And Ursula. She thinks they were friends, but Lake despised her. I'm the only one she cared for. Sometimes I didn't know where I left off and Lake began." Helena shuts the door behind me.

My psyche staggers.

◆

The sniveling snow has turned to rain that comes down in sheets, like plastic wrap. I take refuge in the Burger King on Sixth Avenue. I order coffee and sit at a table next to the window.

My breath comes in small stabs. There are pains in my shoulder and back, my tension announcers.

Looming large on my interior screen is my mother. Unlike Helena, she's never put into words her muddled vision of her and me, her trespass through my life. Though it had all been sleight of hand, it had happened, and even now, remembrance of her intrusion creates anxiety.

Flashes keep appearing of those Friday nights when my father played bridge and we were alone. There was nothing heinous — no incest, no abuse. To an observer she was a devoted mother, always interested in what I did, playing with me whenever I wished. But now I know the truth: the games were for her as much as for me. Perhaps more.

The major game seems innocuous enough: Girlfriends. We would meet for dinner (in the alcove of our kitchen) and we'd talk about our boyfriends. Then one of us would pretend to stay overnight. We'd climb into her big bed and watch television together. I would fall asleep, and when my father came home he would carry me to my own bed.

Her life was so intertwined with mine, so empty except for me, that she needed me to keep her going, to keep her entertained.

We made a silent pact: I would be hers if she would keep *him* at bay.

She tried, she really did. Occasionally she won me my freedom. I wouldn't have been allowed to cross simple streets alone, or go to the movies without a parent, never dated, had it not been for her. Still, I paid a hell of a price:

I was her hostage.

And I fell in love with my abductor.

Was any of this present in Lake and Helena's relationship? Certainly it was there for Helena. I would never know about Lake unless Ursula or Mark had been an astute observer. But Ursula never lived with Lake, nor did Mark. Is it true that Lake despised

Ursula? It didn't seem that way to me. Why would Lake tell Ursula about the rape and then agree to see me if she didn't care for her half-sister? And what plan does Helena have for the money? There's no reason to knock off Mark and Ursula unless Helena has a particular beneficiary in mind. But even so, she can do whatever she wants with the money now. Except if she really is at risk.

I finish my coffee. The weather has not changed, and I'm reluctant to leave this safe, dry harbor, even with its odors of fatty fries and greasy meat. I decide to wait a little longer and go for another coffee.

The sullen girl behind the counter, her lower lip jutting out like a landing field, is staring blankly at the large woman ahead of me.

"Do you have mushrooms?" the woman asks.

"Huh?" the girl says.

I know she's heard, but this is the beginning of a typical transaction between seller and buyer in the restaurants and stores of New York. Maybe everywhere. Passive-aggressive. I watch and listen as the drama unfolds.

"Mushrooms," the woman repeats, and drums her fleshy fingers on the yellow plastic countertop.

"Musshroons?" the girl asks, her brown eyes the only spots of color in her pallid face.

The woman takes a beat, pondering whether to correct the pronunciation or not. She wisely decides against it. "Yeah."

"What?"

"What?"

"What 'yeah'?"

"*Mussshrooooms*," the woman hisses.

"What about musshroons?" the girl says, and there isn't a flicker of hostility in her eyes, but neither is there life.

The woman slaps the counter, a crack crying out for help, and turns toward me. "Can you believe this?" she asks me.

"Yes," I say.

"What?"

She's confused because my line is supposed to be *No. No, I can't believe this*. But I can. "I believe it," I add.

The woman glares at me. "What's *your* problem?"

Uh-oh! I don't wish to have her hatred transferred to me. But there's no answer I can give now to get out of this. I try a smile, an innocent shrug, and the woman, disgusted with me, turns back to the counter girl.

"Haven't you ever heard of a mushroom?" she says through clenched teeth.

"You think I'm stupid or somethin'?" the girl asks.

The possibilities for reply are legion.

The woman says nothing, but I note that her body has begun to quiver with rage.

As another counter girl passes behind her, the first one turns and says, "This customer wans to know I know what a musshroon is."

The second girl gives a shriek of laughter.

A slow turn back to the fat woman, a look that says: *You are an asshole and why should I answer you but I will anyway you stupid piece of shit.* " 'Course I know what a musshroon is. But we don' have none. Nex'." She looks at me.

"Coffee."

The woman whirls on me. "Just a goddamn minute, Miss. I was first. What the hell d'you think you're doing?"

I know better than to reply, and consider leaving. But just then the girl places my container of coffee on the counter.

"Fifty cents," she says.

"Wait a minute here," the fat woman yells. "Wait one fucking minute."

When the *fuck*s start, it's time to leave. But I'm not fast enough: the woman bats my coffee off the counter, and it splashes over the counter girl's uniform.

The girl screams, and the fat woman picks up the closest thing to her, which happens to be a napkin dispenser, and brings her hand back to throw it at *me.*

My .38 is pointed at her, and calmly I say, "Do it. I'd like a change." This is my version of "Make my day."

People are yelling. I announce that I'm the law and pray.

The roar of fear subsides, the woman lowers the dispenser, her eyes like two slivers of granite. "You're a cop, and you let this happen? What's your badge number?"

"Put that down," I say softly. "Put it back on the counter."

She realizes the inequity of our armor and does what I ask. But she's flaming with indignant fury. I can't blame her, but the situation has escalated to a point where the only thing I can do is ask her to leave.

"Go across the street to Third," I urge gently. "There's a McDonald's there."

"Blow it out your ass," she says, and stalks toward the door.

When she's gone the crowd erupts, clapping their hands, cheering. I return my gun to my bag, pay for the coffee, and leave before anyone questions my authority.

The rain is now a drizzle. I pop open my umbrella and head for my office, where I've left the laptop. But before I get started on the modem, I need to sit down in quiet and make a chart of all the people in this case. The modern malignancy of divorce makes family trees a must. The truth is, I don't know who the hell is who!

Chapter

Thirteen

WHEN I RETURN to my office I'm surprised to see Joe Carter, wearing his Wolverine sweatshirt, swabbing the hall. He nods to me.

"Where's Gordon?" I ask.

"Don't know," he answers.

"How come you're cleaning the hall?"

"I'm the super," he says, as if this is a given and I'm very stupid.

"Since when?"

"Since today."

"What happened to Gordon?"

"Told you, I don't know. Best guess is he left or was fired, because I got the job now." He goes back to his work.

"But I just saw him the other day, and he didn't say anything about leaving."

Carter shrugs, I think. After all, how is he to respond to my statement?

"How'd you get the job?"

He stops mopping, stares at me with insolent brown eyes. "What's your problem?"

"I just can't understand Gordon's leaving without saying something to me," I explain, as if Carter has the right to speak to me this way.

"Super usually checks in with you when he's leaving?" he asks, parading a salacious smile.

Why do I feel as if he's caught me at something dirty? "He has a book of mine," I say in stupid defense.

"No kidding?"

I'm suddenly angry. "How did you say you got the job?"

"I didn't."

Neither of us says anything for a moment. Then Carter's eyes soften, and I see something simple, artless.

"I was on a list," he offers.

"A list." He means a list for the job of super. Of course. I give what feels like a sickening smile and say, "See you."

"Yeah," he answers noncommittally.

Then I say, "Madison, Wisconsin?"

"Huh?"

"I thought you might be from Madison, Wisconsin. I'm usually good at accents." I've often wanted to say this to him.

He looks almost frightened. "Not this time."

I point to his sweatshirt. "Michigan?" I know from Kip that the Wolverines are the University of Michigan's football team.

He bunches the front of the sweatshirt in his big hand as though he wants to mutilate the letters. "Got this in a thrift shop."

I wait for him to tell me where he *is* from, but he goes back to work, so I let it go.

As I climb the stairs I continue to wonder what happened to Gordon, dwelling on his promise to return the book next time. Of course, if he was fired, he wouldn't know he wouldn't be back. But why would he be fired? As far as I knew, he did his job well.

I unlock my door and hang up my wet coat, open my tan umbrella and place it on the floor. I don't believe that opening an umbrella inside brings bad luck ... or is that only in a theater dressing room?

Sitting down at my desk, I twirl my Rolodex to T, quickly flip through the letter until I come to THOMPSON, J., the manager of the building. I punch in the number.

"Thompson and Churchill," a woman says.

I tell her I want to talk to someone about this building. She asks what it's about, and I tell her it would be best if I talked to one of the managers. She insists I tell her what I want, so I do.

"Oh, I wouldn't know anything about that," she says, maddeningly, and puts me on hold. The music that comes over the line is a rumba. God forbid anyone should remain in silence, left to think for a moment.

Six months later I hear another female voice on the line, and the speaker identifies herself as Margaret Mitz, Thompson's secretary. I go through the same routine until she finally switches me over to Thompson.

His voice is like a lawn mower. "Who are you?"

Pleasantly, I tell him. "I'd like to know what happened to Gordon Peace?"

"Who?"

I give him my address.

"Oh, the super."

"Yes."

"What's wrong with whatshisname?"

"You mean the new super?"

"Yeah."

"Nothing. He's fine, I —"

"Okay, then."

I feel him starting to hang up. "Wait."

"Yeah?"

"I don't care about the new one, I want to know what happened to the old one."

"Why?"

I realize I don't know why. "Did he quit?" I weasel.

There's a long silence, then, "Could say that. The slob didn't show up at any of the buildings he's supposed to do. I give this guy a good job the homeless give their right nut for, and what do I get in return? He shits on me."

"Did he ever do that before?"

"Shit on me?" he asks seriously.

"Just not show up."

Another long silence. "What is this? You his old lady, or what?"

"I'm concerned because he didn't say anything to me, and we always talked." I know how weak this sounds.

"Who *are* you?" he asks again.

And again I explain.

"Listen, lady, I'm sorry if Peace dumped you but I'm a busy man don't have time for broken hearts so good-bye."

I put the phone back in its cradle. I tell myself I'm being stupid. What's the big deal? So Gordon Peace walked away from his job without notifying me. Is there any reason he should have told me? None. So why do I feel like I'm sitting in a dark cellar in a wet bathing suit? It's the book. No matter what, Gordon would've returned the book.

I open the Manhattan directory, hoping to find a number and

address for Peace, but there's nothing. Either he doesn't have a phone or he lives in another borough, I decide. I have to confess that I never think of other boroughs, of people living in them. To me New York is Manhattan. Even so, I have directories for the other four boroughs. I look through them all. Peace is not listed anywhere.

I feel worse.

Then I remember that he said he lived nearby. My spirits climb again, only to drop when I face that I still don't know *where* he lives. Obviously Gordon Peace doesn't have a phone, or maybe he lives with someone and the phone's listed under the other person's name. The hell with it. I'm being neurotic. Always thinking doom and gloom. Wonder why.

I take out a lined yellow pad and begin to make a family tree. There's one name I don't know and will have to fill in later. Making this tree is simpler than I thought it would be:

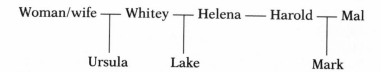

I should speak to as many of these people as I can. I don't know yet whether it's important that I find out what happened to Whitey's first wife, Ursula's mother, the woman in the photograph. It's a long shot, but she might be angry at Whitey and want to get back at him by hurting the daughter he had with Helena.

As I write these questions down in my spiral notebook, I realize I'm seriously speculating that the rapist and the murderer may be two different people.

Why *would* the rapist kill Lake? He's got his letters, and he doesn't know that she talked to me. Killing her would have to bring the police into it and make his chances of being caught greater rather than smaller. If he was afraid of her reporting him, why didn't he kill her at the time of the rape? It doesn't make sense.

So I'm almost positive that the rape and murder were committed by two different people. I put the family tree I've made in my purse.

The disappearance (as I now think of it) of Gordon Peace still troubles me. What would Catherine Saylor do?

I phone Thompson and Churchill again and ask to speak to Margaret Mitz, Thompson's secretary. I find it interesting that the receptionist puts me right through without a question. Secretaries aren't worth an interrogation, put Charles Manson through to them, who the hell cares?

Mitz picks up, and I tell her I called earlier and, taking a chance that she's not crazy about her boss, say that I got a less than satisfactory answer from him. And I go on, using love as my collaborator.

"The thing is," I say, trying to sound pathetic and desperate, "Gordon's left me in a mess. I think he must be married because he wouldn't tell me where he lived or give me a phone number."

"Bastards," she says, indicting all men.

Now I know I have an ally and that I'll get what I want if I keep pressing the "shitty man" button. "I have to find him," I snivel.

"Pregnant?" she whispers.

"Mmmm."

"Bastards."

"Margaret, could you . . . would you give me his phone number and address?"

"I shouldn't," she says tightly.

"I know," I say, like I understand her position. "But I don't know what I'm going to do. Even if I find him, he probably won't help me —"

"— but at least he'll know," she says, finishing my sentence with venom.

I smile, and she gives me his address and phone number.

I let Gordon's phone ring twenty-two times before I give it up. Then I call Cecchi.

"Anything new?" I ask.

"Three murders, four rapes, six child abuses, nine burglaries, six stolen cars, twenty-four drug abuses, three muggings, two suicides, and a partridge in a pear tree." He sighs.

These are the statistics for one twenty-four-hour period in New York. He doesn't always give them to me, but sometimes, when he's overwhelmed by it all, he can't help himself.

"Forget the suicides," he says.

"I can't." Cecchi and I have different opinions about suicide. He believes it's a person's right to take his or her own life. I used to agree, but since I've been with Kip I've learned that if a potential suicide waits — sometimes only a day — the problem will usually pass, or at least change, and the person can go on. Cecchi and I have debated this point for hours.

"What about the Huron case?"

"Stalled. You?"

"Nothing. There're a lot of people I need to talk with. Like Whitey Huron. Helena Bradshaw says she doesn't know where he is now, but his last known address was in Hurley, Pennsylvania."

"Want me to run a make on him?"

"Yes. And while you're doing that, could you run one on Gordon Peace?"

"Who's he?"

"The super of my building."

"What's he got to do with this?"

"Nothing. It's personal."

Cecchi doesn't press me for more details. He accepts that I disclose what he needs to know.

"Okay," he agrees. "How do you spell the last name?"

I give him the particulars, and we hang up.

I sit at my desk and stare at Peace's address doodled on my pad. I feel I should look for Gordon now, but I don't know why. I refuse to call it women's intuition. We can't have it both ways.

I punch in William and Rick's phone number.

William answers. We tell each other how we are, and then I ask him if he's ever heard of Gordon.

"Gordon Peace. I think I'd remember that name if I'd heard it before," he says dryly.

"You're a riot."

"Then why aren't you laughing?"

"I am, but it's silent laughter."

"I've always wondered what that was. Try and picture it."

Now I *do* laugh. "Ask Rick if he knows him?"

"Rick doesn't know anyone. Hold on."

The joke is that Rick knows *everyone*. Sometimes it's almost frightening. Mention a name, and Rick will have met the person seventeen years ago at a fat farm (he has an eating problem, unlike everyone else in America) or, more amazingly, gone to grade school in Denver with him or her.

"Of *course* I know him," Rick says. "He claims he's a writer, but no one's ever seen anything he's written." For years Rick was a writer of sitcoms. Now he's doing his first novel, which he's already sold for a tidy piece of change.

"Is he gay?" I ask out of habit.

"You're not going to believe this."

"What?"

"I don't know."

"I don't believe it."

"I knew you wouldn't. But the good news is I can find out if you give me an hour."

"Great."

"Why do you want to know?"

"Can't tell."

"I *hate* that."

"I know you do, but that's how it has to be."

"Mmmm. So what are we renting tonight?"

I take a beat too long to answer.

"Lauren, I think you'd better do something about your memory."

"Like what?"

"I don't know, have it dry-cleaned or something. Susan told me you forgot a lunch date with her three times."

"I'm preoccupied."

"You're kidding," he says sarcastically. "We're going to order in Chinese and watch a movie."

"Right."

"Oh, sure, when I mention the food she remembers. I'm not watching any horror movies. Last time I had nightmares for a week."

"That's the whole point."

"What about a comedy or a musical or an oldie?"

"Anything's fine with me, except Sherlock Holmes." Rick loves all the old Holmes movies.

"How about *Caged Women*?"

"How about *Trapped Men*?"

"Very funny. Are you in the mood for a Lana Turner?"

"Perfect."

"Where should I call you when I find out more about Peace?"

"My office. Leave it on the machine if I'm not here."

"S'long." Rick hates drawn-out good-byes.

The phone rings immediately. It's Cecchi.

"The address on Whitey Huron is still in Hurley, Pennsylvania. Phone number is 717-555-4372. No arrests, one speeding ticket. Nothing at all on Peace."

"Could you give me Terrence Ford's number and address?"

"Kid's clean, Lauren."

"I'd still like to talk with him."

"Sure." He gives me the info.

I punch in Huron's number. After four rings it's answered. The man sounds sleepy.

"Mr. Huron?"

"Yes?"

I tell him who I am. "I wonder if I could meet with you?"

"What about?"

This is the delicate part. But surely he knows. "I'd like to talk to you about your daughter."

There's a long silence.

"Mr. Huron?"

"Yeah, I'm here."

"Could I come and see you?"

"When?"

I look at my watch. "Tomorrow?"

"I don't know . . . you want to talk to me about Lake?"

"Yes."

Another long silence. "All right," he finally says.

He gives me directions, and I say I'll be there by early afternoon tomorrow.

Next I call Terrence Ford. He agrees to see me at his place in an hour. Then I make an appointment with Mark Bradshaw. He condescends to meet me around five-thirty at Kemeny's, a slick Yuppie bar on Cornelia Street.

Gordon's address is on the desk, under my hand. I'm itching to get to the modem, but something nags me. It's that damn book. He wouldn't leave town without returning it. I should work on the Huron case. No one is paying me to look for Peace. What would Nyla Wade do?

Me, too.

◆

Gordon Peace lives at 33 Greenwich Avenue. The entrance is on Tenth Street, a block down from Three Lives. I wonder how Peace can afford to live here. The building's made of a drab white brick, built in the early sixties, and has little character. A new awning covers the span from midsidewalk to the glass doors. I can see a man in a gray uniform, no hat, standing inside, waiting to do his job. I'll give him a whirl.

He pulls open the door as I approach.

"Help ya?" His face is almost maroon, a good color with the gray uniform.

"Gordon Peace," I say.

"Name?"

Will Gordon recognize my name? I have no choice, and tell the doorman who I am.

He goes behind a little desk, lifts a receiver from a house phone, and pushes a button. I peer into the lobby. Orange couches line one wall, and something that passes for a painting hangs above them. The carpet is gray, as are the freshly painted walls. The owners are probably trying to sell the apartments as condominiums and have given the place a facelift. It doesn't work.

"No answer," the doorman says.

"Have you seen Mr. Peace lately?"

He thinks for a moment. I know this because he squints his rheumy eyes and turns his forehead into a miniature mass of logs. "Can't say I have."

"When's the last time you saw him?"

He does his thinking number. "Can't remember."

I tell him I'm a P.I. and would like to see inside Peace's apartment. He just laughs at me.

"Gowan," he says. "A shrimp like you, a *girl*, is a dick?" Then, realizing what he's said, he bursts into horrible barking laughter; his maroon face deepens alarmingly. Tears form in the corners of his closed eyes.

I wait.

At last he chugs to a halt and wipes his eyes with a wrinkled handkerchief. "Sorry. So yer a . . . shamus, huh?" He winks at me.

I don't wink back.

"A girl gumshoe," he goes on. Paroxysms of laughter.

I've been subjected to this, and worse, many times. I know I have to wait it out, let the asshole say all the dumb things he can think of, get it out of his system.

Just when I think it's over, he says, "A shapely sleuth."

"Actually," I say, "I'm a dyke-dick." But he's lost in his laughter and doesn't hear me. Just as well. Finally it ends, and I suspect this is due only to his vocabulary.

"I can't let ya in Mr. Peace's place. I mean, yer not official."

He's right, of course. I open my purse, take out my wallet, and start to remove some money, but he stops me with a meaty hand on mine.

"Don't bother. This ain't the movies. You don't have enough fer me ta take a chance. Tell ya what I could do, though. I could leave Mr. Peace a message sayin' you wuz here."

I start to put my wallet away, but he touches my hand again and signals me with his eyes that for *this* favor he can be bought. It irritates me because I know that part of his job is to take messages for tenants. But I've goofed, so I hand him a five. He looks at it as if it's an insult. I add another five to that one. He nods, and I give him my name and my office number.

"Soon's I see him."

"Thanks. One other thing: do people own their apartments here?"

"Nah. They tried that, but no go."

"How long has Mr. Peace lived here?"

"I've been workin' here ten years, and he wuz here when I come."

So Peace's rent must be low. There's a restaurant across the street on the corner. I go in, order a Tab, and call my machine. There are two messages. The first is from Kip, who tells me that a lab report awaits me. I've recently had a physical (nagged to do so by the hellion I live with — she says she worries about my health because of my diet). The second message is from Rick.

"Gordon Peace is a het," he says. "And he goes to swinging bars. His favorite is something called — get this — American Pooldoodle, on Twenty-second between Eighth and Ninth. In case the clever name hasn't explained all, it's one of those pool bars. Have fun."

Playing pool has become respectable, even chic. What Rick doesn't know is that if I don't find Peace before tonight, he, William, Kip, and I will be going to American Pooldoodle. I know they'll all be thrilled.

Chapter

Fourteen

═══════════════

TERRENCE FORD lives at One Fifth Avenue. This is a semilarge apartment building that has, on the ground level, an Art Deco restaurant and bar whose entrance is on Eighth Street. When Kip and I were looking for something to buy, we considered an apartment here. Although the places were nice and the prices were okay, we both felt that it was too sterile, too institutional in feeling. Besides, there was a lobby and a doorman, and neither of us likes that atmosphere.

The entrance to the apartments is on Fifth, and the doorman here is definitely a cut above the one at 33 Greenwich Avenue.

His uniform is brown with gold braid. He has a slightly waxen face, as if he's ready for Madame Tussaud's, and when he speaks, nothing but his lips moves.

"May I help you?"

I tell him who I've come to see.

"And you are?" he asks imperiously, face and eyes inert.

After I give him my name, he lifts the handset, pushes a button. When he turns back to me, there's a look of surprise in his eyes, as though he wasn't expecting Ford to admit me.

"Five-L," he informs, and points me toward the elevators.

Ford is standing in the doorway when I get to his apartment. He slouches, trying to look casual but failing. He wears a pair of gray sweatpants and matching sweatshirt, a green polo shirt underneath. And there's something else, something I didn't notice before. One ear is pierced, and in it is a diamond stud.

He ushers me in. The place is a one-bedroom; Ford has money, because I know what these apartments cost ten years ago, when he would've been twelve or thirteen.

The decor is black and white. White walls, black velvet couch and chairs, black lacquered tables, white rug over a blond floor. Even the pictures are black-and-white photographs. All adornments are one or the other.

When we're seated and I've declined a drink, Ford tries to lounge on his couch but succeeds only in looking uncomfortable, unused to relaxation. He has small brown eyes like cloves in a ham, and his wispy blond hair is combed straight forward, no part. His lean lips are pale in his acne-scarred face. Ostrichlike, this man seldom looks at me: perhaps I won't notice his complexion if our eyes don't meet.

"How long have you been in love with Lake?" I begin aggressively.

He twitches. "What's that have to do with anything?"

"Mr. Ford, can we assume, for the sake of brevity, that I have a reason for everything I ask you?"

Deliberating, he lights a cigarette. I stifle a lecture but, as usual, wonder what's wrong with young people who have the information we didn't and still continue to smoke.

"Check," he says.

"How long?"

"About four years."

"How long were you lovers?"

He takes a deep drag of his butt and fills the air with exhaled smoke. "About three," he mumbles, looking into the ashtray he holds in one hand.

"Why did you break up?"

"Wasn't working."

"Why not?"

"Listen," he starts.

I anticipate his reluctance and interrupt. "I have my reasons."

"Check."

I wait.

"Irreconcilable differences." He looks at me quickly, defiantly, a shot of smugness before his eyes depart mine.

"Terrence," I say, "you agreed to see me, so what's the point in playing games?"

"I shouldn't have said yes to you. It was stupid. You caught me in a moment of . . . weakness."

There's something about the way he says the word *weakness* that impels me to ask, "Were you high?"

A downward turn of his mouth passes for a smile. "You're pretty good," he concedes.

"Did Lake smoke, or is it snort?"

"She didn't do either."

"Which is it for you?"

"Why, you want some?"

"Coke or crack?"

"Whatever you want." He uncurls his body, stretches out, legs forming a wide V. And now he looks at me, eyes insolent with the kind of contempt one drug user can have for another: in his view I'm suddenly no better than he.

I decide to let his mistake stand. "Which is your drug of choice, Terry?"

He laughs. "Drug of choice? What're you, some rehab type, a narc?"

Oops. "No, I'm not," I assure him.

"Check," he says sourly.

"Really."

He leans forward, his hands flat on either side of him as if in preparation for springing up. "Then you'd like a line?"

"No."

"What the fuck is this?"

"Did you and Lake break up over your addiction?"

He's furious; his face contorts, then he sighs. "Shit. What's the point? Yeah, that's why. Lake hated the stuff. Hated anything that had to do with drugs."

"Yet she stayed with you three years?"

"I didn't get into it until last year . . . not much at first, well, you know how it goes, don't you?"

"Yes. So what happened?"

"My habit got bigger, and I moved on to crack. Lake was afraid."

"Afraid?"

"No, not afraid."

Oh, yes, *afraid*, I think. I ignore his retraction. "Afraid of what?"

"I said she wasn't," he snaps.

"You were lying. Did you sometimes get violent, Terry? When you were high on crack?"

A year and a half later he answers. "I hit her once."

"Is that when she broke up with you?"

"It was just once," he emphasizes, as if somehow this diminishes the act.

I repeat my question.

Slowly, he nods. "I promised her I'd never do it again — hit her — but she wanted me to give up crack, too."

"And you wouldn't?"

"Couldn't," he whispers, ashamed.

"When she broke up with you, did it make you mad?"

"Sad."

"But not mad?"

"Listen, I didn't kill Lake."

"Who said anything about killing? She hung herself, didn't she?" I'm not sure how much he knows.

"No. Lake wouldn't have killed herself. She had no reason. Christ, she had money and looks and anybody she wanted."

"Oh? What do you mean, 'anybody she wanted'?"

"Guys. Tons of guys hit on her. And it wasn't more than a few days after we broke up that she went out with some creep to a . . ." He trails off, stands abruptly, paces.

"Want to finish that sentence?"

"No." His back is to me, and I see his shoulders rise as he gulps in air.

"How do you know who she went out with and where she went?"

"I didn't say —"

"You started to. Did you follow them, Terry?" I ask, trying to sound sympathetic.

He whirls around, faces me. "Just because she dumped me doesn't mean I stopped loving her. Christ, she didn't even wait a week before she was on some dude's arm, the . . ."

Slut? Tramp? Bitch? Whore? I try to finish the epithet for him, knowing that even if I don't come up with the exact word, I'm on the right track. This man is a rejected lover, violent, possessive. He's unused to being rebuffed, in spite of his pitted skin. Money and position have always assured him of acceptance. I probe further.

"How many girls have broken up with you, Terry?"

"You kidding?" he asks arrogantly. "None." The word lifts his upper lip into a sneer. "I don't know who the hell she thought she was."

I don't point out that she was a woman who had the right to

decide who she wanted to be with, because I know this will be meaningless to this despotic man. But I do pursue my earlier line of questioning.

"Did you know about the new man because you were watching her, following her?"

"So what?" he says by way of an answer.

I know what this means. Lake was his. He had a right to follow her, if he chose, because he loved her so much. Richard Herrins, Joe Pikul, and all the other killers of the women who scorned them come to mind, and an acrid smell, like that of egos burning, makes me nauseated.

"Can you describe the man you saw her with?"

"Check." He gives me the same description I got from Lake.

"Think you could pick him out of a lineup?"

"Check."

I take a left. "If you were no longer seeing each other, how did it happen that you went to her place the day she died?"

His color deepens to a reddish hue. "We stayed in touch."

"Wasn't that hard on you?"

"Check."

"Then why —"

"I needed money," he says candidly.

"Was she expecting you?"

"No."

"Had she given you money before?"

"No. I never asked before."

"But you asked that day?"

His mouth twists smugly. "No, Miss Laurano, she was dead that day."

"And where were you when she was killed?"

"Walking. Trying to get up my nerve to ask her."

"Anyone see you?"

He shrugs. "I've been all through this with the cops, and they believe me."

"I didn't say that I don't believe you."

"But you don't," he states.

I'm not sure. He has a motive: jealousy. He's been violent, and he doesn't really have an alibi. Still, Cecchi said he was clean, and he hasn't been booked. Yet. I get up to leave, walk to the door. He follows me.

"Why don't you put yourself into Hazelden or Smithers?" I suggest.

"What for?"

"To get rid of your crack habit," I say impatiently.

"What for?"

And that, of course, is the bottom line. Terrence Ford likes his addiction, his way of life — if you can call it a life.

"I'll be seeing you," I say.

"Check," he says.

◆

I sit at the long, curved mahogany bar at Kemeny's, sipping a club soda and lime. I'm early. I always like to be the one waiting; it gives me an edge.

The place is sleek, suave, all chrome and glass save the bar; the lighting cool. People are trickling in: suits with briefcases, both sexes. They are groomed to perfection, most of them tanned. No one wears glasses, and no one looks happy. Around me the conversations are about money and real estate. No one sounds happy.

I've talked to Cecchi about Ford, and he says although Terry doesn't have an airtight alibi, he believes him. Besides, they have nothing concrete. Cecchi respects the taxpayers' money and doesn't book anyone unless he's got something solid. We both know Ford's motive is amorphous yet possible. Cecchi still thinks the rapist killed Lake, but I don't. Terrence Ford's not out of the running. He's on my mental A-list with Ursula and Helena. On my B-list are Mark Bradshaw, Whitey Huron, and Whitey's first wife.

In the mirror behind the bar, Bradshaw's reflection appears, his ringlets plastered to his forehead, his expression dour. He's breathing heavily, as if he's been jogging. I say hello.

He doesn't greet me, says, "Shall we get a table?"

I follow him to a small one in a corner. When we're seated, he glances at the half-finished drink in front of me.

"Want another?"

"I'm fine."

He signals a waiter and asks for a martini straight up, his breathing normal now.

"I don't know what you want from me," he says defensively. "I don't know anything about this rapist. Killer."

I note the statement but ignore it. "When your father died and left all his money to Lake, how did you feel?"

His eyes take on an owlish expression, as though he's been startled by possible prey. "What the hell kind of question is that?"

Ridiculous responses run through my mind: *It's Chinese. It's mathematical. It's the kind you bake at 350 degrees!* There's no way to answer him literally, so I persist.

"If I were you, I would've been damned mad."

"I *was* damned mad," he says before he can stop himself. Then his expression goes from anger to fear as he realizes he's stepped in it. Scrambling, he goes on. "Well, who the hell wouldn't be? I mean, she wasn't his, even though he made a damn fuss over her all the time. It wasn't fair." His mottled cheeks look like cherry-vanilla ice cream.

"No," I say sympathetically, "it doesn't seem fair."

"Well, it wasn't." He pouts.

The waiter puts his martini in front of him, and Bradshaw sucks on it as if it were a pacifier.

"And now the money goes to Helena," I continue.

He grunts.

"Do you like her?"

"Helena? She's all right."

"And Ursula?"

"What about her?"

"Do you like her?"

Bradshaw looks at me, sips his drink. "Yes," he says deliberately. "I like Ursula, so what?"

"Did you like Lake?"

"I hardly knew her. I told you that the other day. Why are you asking me all this stupid stuff, anyway? What's this have to do with the rapist-killer?"

I hit him with it. "I'm not positive they're one and the same."

"Meaning?"

"I think it's possible that someone else killed Lake," I explain unnecessarily.

"Like me?" he asks, and gives a short bark of laughter, as though he's been goosed.

I don't answer.

"Or maybe Ursula?" His eyes are bright, whether from what he thinks is amusing or the martini, I can't tell. "Helena, huh? Maybe

Helena killed her own kid? Well, come to think of it," he hints, raises an eyebrow.

"*That* you believe is possible?"

He shrugs. "Like you said, she gets the money now."

"But if she should die, you and Ursula get the money."

"Yeah. So what?"

"So it gives you a motive. Ursula, too."

He finishes his drink and waves for another. "Okay, let me lay this out. You think either Ursula or I killed Lake and that one or both of us are going to kill Helena for the money? Is that it? Have I got it right?"

"It's certainly conceivable."

Beads of sweat pop out on his forehead like hives. "Well, I was with Ursula when Lake . . . hell, you *saw* me there."

"I saw you there later that day, Mark."

"Well, I was with her right up to when the call came from the police."

"You were?"

"Yeah." He checks a smile but still looks like he's trumped my ace.

But I take the trick. "That's not what Ursula says."

His face falls like a ruined soufflé. "What do you mean?"

"She says you were there afterwards."

"Then she's lying."

"A harsh accusation."

"Harsh or not, it's the truth. Why don't you call her now and ask her again?"

I sense something shady, and Mark is relegated to the A-list.

"C'mon," he says, rising. "Let's call her."

He pulls me up by my arm. I don't like it and wriggle free.

"C'mon, over here," he insists.

Bradshaw leads the way to a telephone booth, fishes a quarter out of his pants pocket, drops it in the slot, and dials. He listens, holding the phone away from his ear so that I can hear the ringing, too.

"Hello?" It's Ursula.

"Here," he says, shoving the phone at me. "Ask her, go on."

I take the phone and identify myself. "Do you remember when I asked you if you could prove where you were at the time of —"

"I'm so glad you called," she interrupts. "I remembered."

"Good."

"Mark was with me. I don't know what made me think he'd come later. He was with me right up until the call came from the police."

I thank her, hang up the phone. Of course, she's lying. Not only have they phrased the alibi *exactly* the same way, as if they'd planned it (which I'm sure they have), but if their story were true, then Mark's not accompanying Ursula to Lake's apartment that day would make no sense.

I'm sure now that they're lovers and that they killed Lake together. But there's no proof, and worse, they're each other's alibi. I have to find out more about them. Whitey Huron's a good bet. He must know something about his daughter Ursula. A frisson shuttles down my spine. Unless I pull this thing together, Helena will be right.

She'll be next.

Chapter

Fifteen

KIP HAS COPIED Lake's Telix program onto the hard drive of her computer with a program called Laplink, so that I can work on this thing both at my office (on Lake's portable) and at home. I could carry the Toshiba back and forth, but Kip says I'll be happier using her computer, an Epson Equity 2+ with a 20mg hard drive and an Evervision fourteen-inch EGA monitor. How do you like them apples? EGA, I've learned, stands for Enhanced Graphics Adaptor. Her monitor (screen) displays beautiful color.

A small office off the front room is where the thing is set up, and I enter this sanctum cautiously. Kip is with a patient. I'm on my own.

I have been forewarned about spillage, so I'm careful with my mug of coffee. Unwrapping the J&R package, I feel excited, as if I were opening a pint of Ben & Jerry's Coffee Heath Bar Crunch. I take out the modem and remove it from its cellophane bag. I can't believe that this is it!

About six inches by five inches by four inches at its thickest: I can hold it in the palm of my hand. It's light gray, and on the front, in big letters, it says HAYES. Near the bottom there's a small rectangle with POWER labeled on one side and ANSWER on the other. On closer inspection I see that the rectangle is in two parts: the POWER side looks green, the other maybe yellow. Below this it says "Personal Modem 2400." On the bottom, where it's about two inches thick, there's a darker gray thingamajig, from which extend one phone cord and one cable that must go into the computer. The back of the modem sports a regular two-pronged plug.

I sit down, take out the installation guide, and begin to read. As I sip my coffee, I wonder if I'll go insane from this.

To my surprise what I read is simple. I attach the cable cord (with its nine-pin adapter) to what's called the serial port, on the rear of the computer. Then I remove the phone line from the jack and put in the modem's line. Finally, I plug it in. The rectangle on the modem lights up! Two different shades of green. I finish reading the little guide and realize I'm ready. Why don't I *feel* ready?

I take a certain amount of pride in the fact that I've been able to set the modem up so easily . . . but what if it doesn't work?

Hovering over me, like a lynching party, are my parents. It never ends. I shoo them away, turn on the computer, and get myself into the Telix program. It's much nicer in color: blues, greens, purples. I hit the ALT key and the D, then the ENTER key, and there is the humongous dialing directory, all alphabetized and waiting for me. What will happen if I connect with one of them? This is almost more frightening than if I don't. Maybe there's a book I can buy that will explain this telecommunication business, this world of bulletin boards? I consider shutting down, going over to Software Etc. on Eighth, looking for a book.

Stalling.

The colored cursor bar is on number one, called Always Home — a good or a bad sign, depending on your point of view. Along the bottom of the screen, in a light-green strip, is a series of words, the first being DIAL. Daringly, I hit the D key. The screen changes, and a rectangular box comes up with the name of the bulletin board, its phone number, the count of seconds ticking by. Then suddenly it flashes BUSY.

Relief roars through me like a runaway train. Okay, it's busy — not my fault. But there are 184 more entries I can try! Still, I like the sound of Always Home. It's comforting. I hit the D key again.

This time, after twelve seconds have ticked by, I'm startled when bells tinkle and the words CONNECT 2400, HIT ANY KEY appear at the bottom of the box.

My fingers dangle over the keys, shaking. The bells keep jingling until at last I tap the space bar. The rectangle disappears, and on my screen it says YOU HAVE REACHED THE ALWAYS HOME BBS, and then a lot of other stuff slowly scrolls down the screen until it finally stops with a question: DO YOU WANT GRAPHICS Y/N? Why not?

I gasp as a terrific picture of a skyline appears in various colors. When it's completely formed there's some more information (something about a Sysop, whatever the hell that is) and then it asks me my first name. I type in LAKE. Last name? HURON. Password?

PASSWORD? What the hell have I reached, the Pentagon? I don't know what to do. I hit ENTER and the same question appears. I hit ENTER again; it asks me again. One more time. Now it says ACCESS DENIED, and gobbledygook symbols and letters crowd the screen, ending with NO CARRIER. I am disconnected!

I try not to take this personally, but rejection skitters around my edges. The Critical Parents appear. *I am not doing this right!* I slump. My first instinct is to quit. It's too damn hard. And then that thing in me (the extra chromosome?) rises up, lionlike, and I press on.

This time when I get through to Always Home I type in my own name, and the line NOT FOUND IN USER FILE, TYPE N FOR NEW OR RE-ENTER appears. I type N. Then it asks me for my name again and to choose a password, informing me that dots will ECHO. I try to imagine the sound of dots echoing, but it's beyond me. A password? Something about this makes me panic, and my mind goes blank. I glance at the real bulletin board on the wall behind the computer, and my gaze falls on a snapshot of Rick and Kip. I choose KIP for my password and type it in. But I don't see the word KIP on the screen. What I see is three dots . . . and now I know what "echo" means. I'm learning, and I feel damn good!

◆

"That's it. It's over," Kip says.

We are looking at my medical report. "What's over?" I ask, knowing but not wanting to acknowledge that I do.

"The way you eat," she says with relish, and waves the medical report in my face, slaps it down on the kitchen counter, and points to the incriminating line with a manicured nail. "Face it, Lauren, you're forty-two years old, and things are beginning to change. Just look at this cholesterol count."

It's 258. Dangerous to my health. I find it hard to believe, even though I'm looking at the numbers. How can this be true? And why can't I take it seriously?

"This is serious," she says, as if reading my mind. "Don't you love me?"

"Of course I do."

"All right, I believe you."

"Oh, thank God," I say, and drop to the floor, flinging my arms around her thighs. "Thank God, she finally believes that I love her, and it's only taken eleven years."

There's no response.

I slowly look up at her. Glare, glare, glare.

"It's not funny, Lauren."

I stand up. "Of course it's funny. 'All right, I believe you.' Do you mean until this moment —"

"Don't."

I sigh.

"It's bad enough that the profession you've chosen puts you in danger, but —"

"You were the one who helped me realize what I wanted to do with my life," I remind her.

"Lauren, that has nothing to do with it. Do you think for one minute that I don't worry about you when you're on a case?"

"Who are you, my father?"

"I'm your lover, and I fret when I don't know where you are or what you're doing."

" 'Fret'?"

She tries not to laugh. "Concern. I feel concerned. Distressed. Upset. Okay?"

" 'Fret,' " I say again.

"Stop it. You're not going to get me off the track. When you're on a case there's always this underlying nagging feeling. When the phone rings I'm frightened to pick it up, frightened not to. I'm afraid somebody will tell me you're in the hospital . . . dead."

"Eleven years, and you've never told me this?" I'm incredulous but not speechless. "Why haven't you ever said this before?"

"Precisely because of what you said a minute ago: 'Are you my father?' "

I don't know what to say to her. Somewhere I must've suspected that she felt this way — *I* would if the tables were turned — but I haven't let myself think about it because my own fears are enough to handle.

We look at one another. I go to her and we put our arms around each other and hold tight. "I love you," I whisper.

She gives me a slow hard squeeze, and I return it.

"Lauren?" she whispers back.

"Yes?"

"Knock off the high fat in your diet."

It's one long honeymoon!

◆

Kip, Rick, William, and I have polished off a take-out Chinese meal (I eschewed the pork dish in deference to Kip) and finished viewing Lana Turner's stunning, hysterical performance in *Portrait in Black*. We are sick from laughing. It's ten-thirty, and I've not been able to locate Gordon Peace. Kip gets up, ready to leave.

"I need help," I blurt out.

"You're telling us," William says.

William is six five and has a great body — if you like great male bodies. They don't turn me on, but aesthetically I can appreciate good ones. He has gold-streaked light-brown hair, a mustache and full beard. His blue eyes are lit with intelligence like Fourth of July sparklers. When he was a youth, people said he looked like the young Ingrid Bergman. (Even though he didn't know William then, Rick insists that people must have meant Ingmar!) At forty-one the Bergman look-alike has turned into a handsome man.

He wears one of his ubiquitous plaid flannel shirts, the sleeves rolled up to the elbows, and a pair of jeans. On his feet are light-tan suede boots. His only jewelry is a silver wedding band. He has beautiful hands, long fingers, but his nails are small, like those of an adolescent.

William is a nonfiction writer. He has a column in the *New Republic* and does interviews with celebrities for various publications. He hates this, but it allows him to work on his biography of Stendhal, which he's been laboring over for seven years. He has trouble getting to his real work because he doesn't enjoy writing, but he can't not do it.

"It's about Gordon Peace," I say.

"I thought we did Gordon Peace," says Rick.

"What's that, l'il honey?" William says, smiling. He calls Rick by this endearment to be funny.

Rick is at least a foot shorter than William and goes up and down weightwise. At the moment he's on the up route. He has reddish-brown hair, which he almost never combs, cherubic brown eyes, a strong nose, good mouth, and a cleft chin. Tonight he's wearing his fat clothes: a large black turtleneck shirt, black pants, and black loafers. William says sometimes he feels like he's living with a mortician. The jewelry Rick sports is a silver wedding band and a fortieth-birthday gift his editor gave him: dog tags engraved with the name of his book and the words FORTY YEARS.

"So what about Gordon Peace?" Rick asks.

"I can't find him," I say.

"I told you where to find him . . . oh, no. Not me, Lauren," Rick says.

"Please," I beg.

"What is it?" Kip asks.

Rick says, "She wants us to go to a place called American Pooldoodle."

"Called *what?*" William and Kip chorus.

With eyes closed and eyebrows raised, Rick nods repeatedly, as if this is his answer and will convey to the others the essence of the club — which, of course, it does.

Kip looks at her watch. "I'm going to bed."

"I have to go there, and I can't go alone," I explain.

"And I have an eight-o'clock patient."

"She probably wants you to cancel it," Rick says. "All right, we'll go with you."

"Who's 'we'?" William asks. "At eleven o'clock I have to interview Stepfanie Kramer."

"Who?" we all ask.

"The star of 'Hunter.' "

We look at him.

"I've never seen it either," he says. "Anyway, I have to meet her at the Plaza at eleven A.M."

To William this is the middle of the night. In contrast to Rick, who rises at six, William is hardly ever out of bed by noon unless he has to be.

I'm grateful that Kip and I have similar inner clocks. Basically, bed by eleven, up by seven-thirty. The idea of going to American Pooldoodle at this hour does not enchant me either. Especially since I have to drive to Hurley tomorrow. Still, I feel I need to look for Gordon.

"And if you stay home," Rick says to William, "I suppose you'll be in your jammies before we hit the street, hmmm?"

"Well, no." William never goes to bed before one. "But I don't know if I can go to something called American Pooldoodle."

"What *is* it, Lauren?" Kip asks.

Rick says, "It's a nightclub that features pool."

"I bet you could've figured that out by yourself if you'd given it another moment," William mocks merrily.

Kip smiles. "I don't want to play pool. I'm going home." She starts for the door.

"Oh, come on," Rick says. "It'll be fun."

"We won't stay late," I promise.

"Are you going, William?" Kip asks.

"Of course he's going," Rick answers.

"I am?"

"You know you wouldn't miss it."

"What about Stepfanie Kramer?"

"Fuck Stepfanie Kramer," Rick says.

"At the Plaza? But we're going to be in the Palm Court."

We all laugh.

"Kip," I say, "I really understand. Since the guys are going with me, you don't have to go."

There's a sudden droop to her eyes that I call her Beagle Look. Kip can't stand to miss anything.

"How late do you think you'll be?" she asks, and I know she's coming with us.

◆

It's viciously cold. Winter wields its gelid baton, and fingers freeze through heavy gloves. Leg warmers and layers don't help much either.

American Pooldoodle is in Chelsea, which is the area between Twenty-third and Thirty-third streets and Seventh and Ninth avenues. It's another upwardly mobile neighborhood. A lot of the streets are lined with refurbished brownstones, newly planted trees, and smart shops. Yuppies like to call Chelsea home.

This block is dark except for the club. There's a long line waiting to get in, but Rick goes up to the man who decides the fate of potential customers, talks to him for thirty seconds, then waves to us to come from the end of the line to the door.

"L'il honey," William says, "you've done it again." He turns to me. "A hundred dollars says he meets twelve people he knows before we get a drink."

"No bet," I say, because it will probably happen.

Inside, the lighting is dim and I feel as if I'm in a bunker. The music is loud, pulsating, and awful. People are dancing, and the smell of smoke and sweat permeates the room. I don't see any pool tables.

After we check our coats, we push our way through the throng. Rick says hello to this one and that. When we reach the bar, William shouts to me, "Thank God you didn't take the bet — he only knew eleven."

The bar is softly lit and peopled with men and women in their twenties and thirties who, despite an attempt to appear scruffy and indifferent, look costumed and desperate.

Three years pass before one of the bartenders takes our drink orders.

"I can't believe I'm doing this," Kip screams, crushed between William and me. "Why do I let you talk me into these things?"

"I didn't talk you into this," I say.

William and Rick nod in agreement.

"Then how did it happen?" she asks.

"If you don't know," Rick yells, "I think you'd better see a shrink."

Kip opens her mouth to say something, but there's a blast of music like a demolition ball crashing into a building. We can no longer talk at all.

I look around for Gordon Peace and feel a wave of depression come over me like a heavy black hood. Not only does it seem unlikely that I'll find Peace in this tangled, writhing mass, but the whole scene is dispiriting, and I begin to understand why Lake played her dangerous game and why some of my single friends do the same.

I can't help wondering, in this age of herpes and AIDS, if these people still go off with one another for one-night stands, as they did in the sixties, seventies, and early eighties.

I tap Rick on the shoulder, and he leans down, his ear to my lips. "Where are the pool tables?"

Now he puts his lips to my ear. "It's against the law in New York to serve alcohol where pool is played, so there's a separate billiards room."

We reverse mouth and ear positions again.

"Is there music in the pool room?"

"Softer."

"Let's go."

We tell the other two where we're going. Kip knows what Peace looks like, so she says she'll keep an eye out for him here. William stays with her.

Maneuvering through the undulating crowd, which has grown to twice the size it was when we entered, is a nightmare. I feel like I'm on the subway at rush hour, and I can't imagine why anyone would *choose* to do this. The smell of perfumes turns my stomach. I am allergic to any scent except Chanel No. 5. When I was a child, riding in a closed car, the heater on, my mother's sickeningly sugary perfume would make me melancholy and then nauseated, often culminating in a stop with me vomiting at the side of the road.

Wearing perfume is something Kip has sacrificed for me, as she hates Chanel No. 5. I know she misses it, but there's nothing I can do. Whether my reaction is physical or emotional I don't know, but it doesn't make much difference.

I try not to breathe, and put my hand over my mouth and nose as if I'm about to view a decomposing body.

Rick leads me to a red door with the word BILLIARDS painted on it in big block letters. As soon as the door swings shut behind us, the decibel level falls, though I can still hear the music.

We go up six stairs and through another door. Inside are the pool tables, the sharp green felt like separate small parks. There are twenty or so. The music *is* much softer here, the constant clicking of pool balls the dominant sound. People are talking, but the words seem muted since no one needs to shout.

A heavyset man with a face like a peeled egg, wearing a red sweatshirt with the yellow words AMERICAN POOLDOODLE emblazoned on it and stonewashed jeans, comes over to us. It's obvious that he's also wearing a toupee. I marvel at the denial men must go into to wear these things, and wonder, as always, why we can come up with the technology to make fusion in a bottle but are unable to fashion a toupee that looks real. This one, for instance, resembles a dead badger's tail.

"How are you, Teddy?" Rick says, offering his hand.

Teddy pumps it as if the well's run dry.

"Fine," Rick says, and pulls from Teddy's grip.

"There's a wait about half an hour for a table." Teddy glances at me, and I can see that he thinks he's sized me up.

"We're not going to play. We're looking for someone," Rick says.

"Who?"

"A guy named Gordon Peace."

"Hey, yeah. Now you mention his name, I realize I haven't seen the dude for a few nights. Always here. Every night, but I didn't think about it till you mention it, son of a bitch."

"Does he go to any other clubs?" I ask, praying he doesn't.

Teddy gives the answer to Rick. "Don't think so."

"He hang out with anyone special?"

Again, Teddy answers Rick. "Yeah, maybe. Yeah." He looks around the room, then points to a woman who's about to take a shot. "That one wit the big hooters."

The woman misses and swears. Conveniently, her game is over, and she takes something from the pocket of her suede-fringed jacket and slips it to her opponent. Signs around the room caution against betting, but it's clear she doesn't heed the warning. The woman and man replace their cues in the rack and start toward us.

"Excuse me," I say to her.

She eyes me as if I'm a predator and steps possessively in front of the man. Her blond hair is professionally coiffured, face carefully made up: blush, mascara, eyeliner, lipstick. Besides the jacket, she wears a sapphire silk shirt and a black mini that hugs her flesh like a second skin. There's an icy sheen to her blue eyes, and I can only read hostility.

"What?" she asks in a throaty voice.

Teddy says, "It's okay, Blanche."

She appears not to believe him and scrutinizes me in a challenging way.

"Do you know Gordon Peace?" I ask her.

The fiery flash in her eyes tells me she does.

"Why?"

"It's okay, Blanche," Teddy says again.

"I'd like to talk with him," I explain.

"What about?" I think I detect the drawl of a Southern accent.

"Teddy says you know him. I thought you might be able to tell me where to find him, because he seems to have disappeared."

"He sure does," she says bitterly. "He stood me up night before last."

I'm certain now about the accent, and I think it's Virginia. "You had a date?"

Blanche looks over her shoulder at the man behind her. "Why don't you get our coats, George, and I'll meet you at the door."

George nods and lumbers past us.

"Yeah," she says, "I had a date with him. We were gonna have dinner and then come here for a game or two. Gordon's good at pool, and he's been teachin' me."

"Were you meeting him, or was he picking you up?"

"Actually, *I* was pickin' *him* up, but he wasn't home, and he didn't show for half an hour, so I left. Never called me, neither."

"So the last time you saw him was when?"

"Like I said, three nights ago. Aren't you listenin'?"

"Sorry. Just making sure."

"Anythin' else? I'm keepin' my date waitin'."

"Do you know anything about Gordon's habits? Where else he might go, other things he does, friends?"

"I only know about pool. Never went anywhere else with him. First time we were even gonna have dinner was the night he didn't show."

"Any other women?" I ask with trepidation.

"Probably tons. Ask around. I gotta go now."

"Thanks," I say to her back. "Charlottesville?"

Blanche whirls around. "How'd you know that?"

I shrug. "It's something I happen to be good at."

The look she gives me is meant to wilt, as if I've tried to put something over on her. Inherent in it is a warning: *Don't come around me ever again.*

Rick and I question people about Gordon, and though many know who he is, no one seems to really *know* him; no one claims him as a friend.

We leave American Pooldoodle, and I feel slightly depressed. I've learned nothing except to confirm that the man is a loner and appears to be missing.

◆

It's late and Kip and I are exhausted, but neither of us can go to sleep without reading, no matter what time it is. She opens her book about Mary Todd Lincoln, and I open my mystery by Sarah Shankman.

"Honey?" Kip says.

"Hmmm?"

"I just wanted to thank you for a fabulous evening."

"Really?" I say, surprised.

"Absolutely. Standing around a bar with William, where I can't hear or speak, is definitely ... my idea of something to do." She sings the last six words.

"Great," I say. "We'll go again tomorrow night."

"Just try it!"

We kiss goodnight and return to our books. The portentous feeling of gloom and doom about Gordon hangs on, and I vow to myself that when I get back from Hurley, I'll get into Peace's apartment.

Chapter

Sixteen

THE PREDICTED SNOW has not begun, but when I step into the garden I see a lowering sky. I wonder if I should cancel my trip to Hurley. What if I get snowbound there? With Whitey Huron? What if on the way there there's a blizzard and I can't see and have to pull off the road and I freeze to death? Or I can't see and skid into another car and am paralyzed and blinded? Am I my father's daughter? You bet.

The phone rings, and I come back in. It's Kip's mother, Carolyn. She sounds odd.

"Anything wrong?" I ask.

There's an ominous pause. "I . . . is Christine available?"

I'm always thrown by Kip's real name. "She's with a patient."

Another pause. This is unlike Carolyn, who is usually chatty with me.

"Carolyn," I say, "what is it?"

Pause.

"Is everybody all right?" I'm referring to Kip's two brothers and sister and their families. Donald, Kip's father, died four years ago.

A sigh. "I think . . . I think I'd better talk to Christine about this."

I feel stung. Am I a member of the Adams family, or not? "Okay," I say, trying not to betray my feelings. "I'll tell her to call you."

"Thank you, dear."

Now I'm "dear." We say good-bye. I pour myself a cup of coffee and sit at the table. Supposedly Carolyn accepts me as a family member, as do the rest of Kip's kin. Still, over the years there have been little things that have repudiated this. I've tried to ignore them, but it's hard. Carolyn, for instance, when hearing my taped voice and leaving a message on our joint answering machine, alternately calls herself Carolyn, Mom, or, as recently as a year ago, Mrs. Adams. And then there's the matter of my birthday. She never sends me a card. She never acknowledges it in any way.

I've asked the other Adams spouses if their birthdays are recognized, and all say they are. Except for Sam, who's Tom's lover. Tom is Kip's younger brother, and he and Sam have been together for nine years.

Then there's the Christmas card. Carolyn's is always a carol she's composed, and at the bottom she writes where all of her four children are and what they and their spouses and children are doing. Sam and I are never mentioned. These are little things, I know, but they rankle. Those complaints aside, the Adams family (including Carolyn) is wonderful to Sam and me.

Kip's other brother, Steve, took a while to accept me as his sister-in-law, but now he does. I think he has a harder time with Sam. Judy, Kip's sister, made me feel part of the family immediately. But then so did her husband, Paul, and Steve's wife, Leslie. All of their children refer to me as their aunt. I love this because I have no nieces or nephews of my own.

The thing is, I love the Adams family, all of them — all the in-laws, all the children. They're warm, smart, talented, and incredibly funny. And they're especially remarkable in that they all like each other.

What could it be that Carolyn couldn't tell me? Suddenly I feel a stab in my gut. Is Carolyn ill? Cancer? I didn't think of it immediately because she comes from stock where the women live into their nineties. If she *is* sick, I can understand why she'd want to tell Kip herself. As I ruminate about other possibilities, Kip comes into the kitchen.

"I don't think you should go," she says.

At first I don't know what she's talking about, so lost in my concern for Carolyn, but then I realize.

"Why not?"

"It's going to snow, and what if you get caught in a blizzard, have to pull off, and freeze to death? Or have an accident? Or —"

"Don't be ridiculous," I say.

"But what if —"

"Kip, you never used to be like this."

"I didn't, did I? You've done this to me, Lauren. You and your father. Thanks, toots."

"Welcome. Your mother called and wants you to call her back."

"At this hour? What'd she want?"

"She wouldn't tell me."

"What do you mean, she *wouldn't* tell you?"

"Did I say that in Russian? Gee, I'm sorry, let me try it in English now: She wouldn't tell me," I say snappily.

Kip looks at me.

I look back.

"What's up, Lauren?" She puts her hand on my shoulder. I think about shaking it off but stop myself from behaving as if I'm five years old, and try for seven.

"I don't know how else to explain. Your mother wouldn't tell me what she wanted, and it hurt my feelings."

"I don't blame you." She kisses the top of my head. "I'll say something when I call back."

"No. Don't do that."

Kip looks at her watch. "I don't have time to call her now. Did she say she'd be there all day?"

"She didn't say anything." Carolyn is a professional potter and has a studio in her house on Lake Michigan.

I hear the bell ring.

"Who?" I ask.

"Ms. Curlyhead." She pushes the button to let her in.

Ms. Curlyhead hates her parents and siblings. She's one of Kip's normal patients.

"When are you leaving?"

"Soon."

"You'll be careful driving, won't you? I didn't say that."

I smile and stand up. We kiss. "Don't forget to call your mother," I remind her gently.

"I won't."

"I hope it's not bad news."

"Me too. See you later. Good luck in Hurley."

"Thanks." We look at each other, and then Kip comes back for another kiss.

When she's gone I finish my coffee and the *New York Times*, then get ready for my trip.

◆

Our car is a red Dodge Raider. We keep it in a garage on Tenth and Seventh, once again a block from Three Lives. The price is phenomenal, but leaving it on the street is out of the question. If we did, our new Raider would be our old Raider within days. Cars parked on the street bear signs that read NO RADIO, NOTHING VALUABLE, NOTHING HIDDEN, EMPTY TRUNK, and various other things. It wasn't always this way, and I consider how much worse everything got during the Reagan years. We are a nation of thieves, drug dealers, and addicts. Our values, ethics, and morals are as substantial as cotton candy. We ooze corruption.

Although we've been parking here for several years, the attendant on duty does his passive-aggressive routine which consists of forgetting who I am and sulking.

"Morning, Danny," I say.

He looks at me as though I'm clairvoyant because I know his name, and doesn't bother to return my greeting.

◆

It takes me about an hour and a half to reach the outskirts of Hurley. First I pass over a quaint bridge called Dingman's Ferry. A middle-aged man dressed in a sheepskin coat, a blue knit cap, and jeans stands in the center of the road. His hands are bare, red, and chapped, and he issues puffs of breath as if he's smoking. He smiles as I pay a fifty-cent toll. Does he stand there all day? I wonder. There is a small shelter at the side of the road, but it's not placed in such way that one could stay inside it and collect the toll.

"Am I going right for Sunset Lake?" I ask.

"Sure are. Stay on this road and you'll come to it. Don't take the turn into Hurley by the bank. Just keep going."

I thank him and continue. The sky still threatens to spill snow. I pass the turn by the bank, and in another minute I see the sign for Sunset Lake Estates, two fieldstone pillars at the entrance. I turn in. There are mailboxes and a netless tennis court to my left, where I pull off to read the directions again: one more right and one left.

In the front yard of the house where I make the right turn, there's a plane fuselage, tail exposed, covered with a blue plastic tarp. What could it mean?

The houses are mostly prefabs. They're all stained a reddish brown and have tiny windows. Some have fake lambs on the lawn, which look so real I almost go off the road. There are other lawn ornaments, like the backside of a woman leaning over, her dress red with polka dots. What possesses people to buy things like this?

I make the left. More of the same. I come to the end of the road, where one can turn either way or go across the road and straight down a driveway to a house on the lake. This is Whitey Huron's house; his name's on a post.

I park next to his maroon Range Rover, get out, and climb the wooden stairs. Part of the lake is visible from here, and I guess that were I to keep walking, I would be on a deck. A blind covers the glass portion of the door. I knock and it's opened immediately.

The man standing in front of me is a tall, angular person who looks like he was constructed from an erector set. He wears a brown turtleneck sweater and black jeans. His face is haggard, dark circles underscoring flinty blue eyes. He wears his fading blond hair in a ponytail. But what I find remarkable about him is that he can't be more than forty-six or -seven. It's unlikely that he's Ursula's father. And he's certainly not the man in the photograph I saw at her place.

"You Laurano?" he asks, suspiciously.

I tell him I am, and he allows me to enter.

"Coat?"

I take it off, and he carries it to a closet, hangs it up. The front of the house is all glass; the view is of the lake, the trees naked and vulnerable. It must be gorgeous in summer.

We're in a living room, the kitchen in an open area behind us. Logs burn in a huge fieldstone fireplace. The furniture, a worn brown-and-white-striped couch and matching chairs, surrounds a large white square table, magazines and papers covering almost the entire surface. The white walls are decorated with prints one might find in a motel room.

"You like some coffee?"

"If it's no trouble."

"Hell, no. It's made." From a cabinet in the kitchen area he takes out a mug. On the stove is an old-fashioned iron pot. No Mr. Coffees, Krupses, or Brauns for Huron. Even from this distance I can see that the brew is dark, and I know it will be bitter.

"How d'you take it?"

"Lots of milk and two sugars," I say. I'll worry about my cholesterol tomorrow.

Finally we're seated in facing chairs, our coffees in front of us, steam rising from the mugs like miniature twisters. He lights a cigarette, shoves it into the corner of his mouth, and, as an after-thought, offers me one, which I refuse.

Again I notice the numerous magazines and newspapers. This is not a man who's out of touch with the world, though there's not a television in sight. But I've noted an upper floor and a set of steps leading downstairs. And there's a door off the dining area where a TV might be housed. Surely he knew about Lake's death in time to come to her funeral if he'd wanted to. Stalling, I taste the coffee and am surprised to find it isn't bad, though, as I expected, stronger than I like it.

"Good coffee," I say.

Nothing.

I must begin. "I'm sorry about Lake."

"What for?"

I'm astonished.

He reads my expression. "You think that's callous?"

"Well, she *was* your daughter," I say, trying not to sound too judgmental.

His eyes crackle. He's silent. I wait.

Then, definitively, he says, "Last time I saw her, she was two years old."

"That was when you and Helena separated?"

"Right."

"How long had you been married?"

"We were never married."

This takes me by surprise.

Smoke from the cigarette curls past his nose.

"You're not Ursula's father, are you?"

"Hell, no. Woulda had a been a child groom."

"Then Ursula and Lake weren't half-sisters."

"Nope."

"So who're Ursula's parents?"

"Her mother's name's Marion. Father was Bob Wise."

So there is no first Mrs. Huron, either. "Yet Ursula took your name."

"Didn't like her father," he says.

To my ear Huron is unmistakably from the Boston area, but I don't bother to mention it. I don't like this man. He seems unfeeling, as if to have any emotion is unkempt, slatternly. He rolls the cigarette from one corner of his mouth to the other and squints at me through the smoke.

"Who hired you?"

"Ursula."

"That's the kinda thing she'd do," he says, elucidating nothing.

"Could you tell me what you mean by that?"

"Hell, yes. Ursula was always trying to get to the bottom of things. She was like a ferret. Never able to take things at face value."

"What kind of things, Mr. Huron?"

With his tongue he pushes the cigarette forward, grabs it between thumb and forefinger, and squashes it out in an already filled ceramic ashtray. "I don't know. She was just naturally suspicious, I guess. Always poking in where she didn't belong."

I sense that I'm not going to get an example from Huron, so I abruptly shift my focus.

"Did Lake get in touch with you in the last few weeks?"

"Hell, no. Why'd she do that?"

"She was asking a lot of questions about you ... I guess she wanted to meet you."

"Yeah? Well, I never heard from her."

"How do you feel about Lake's murder?"

He blinks his eyes after the word *murder*. "I'm curious."

I don't bother to tell him this isn't a feeling. "About what?"

He shrugs, his bony shoulders touching the long lobes of his ears. "I wonder who did it."

"Do you have any ideas about that?"

"Hell, no. I didn't know this girl from Adam." Striking a wooden match on the fireplace, he lights another Pall Mall. "Still, there's a connection."

"I'll say." I can't help myself.

Huron sucks on his cigarette for a moment, cocks his head to the side. "Did you know Lake?"

"Very briefly."

"That's still more than I knew her." He gestures to the litter of papers on the table. "To me it was like reading about a stranger. You expect me to get all worked up over a girl I saw last when she was just a kid? Hey, I read about anybody getting murdered, I'm curious who did it. This isn't any different."

"But she was yours and —"

"No."

"What?"

"She wasn't mine. I never said that, did I? You gotta remember what it was like back then. It was Woodstock and Chappaquiddick and the Moon shot and Manson and Flower Power and everybody balling everybody. A whole different world back then."

I was in my first full-time year with the FBI and the hippie things Huron is talking about I observed but didn't participate in. "I know," I say, in a way that I hope will make him believe I was part of it all.

His eyes search mine. "I got some good stuff upstairs," he says softly, testing me.

"No thanks," I say.

"No more, or never did?"

"No more," I lie.

He shakes his head as if to say I'm a disappointment. "It's all gone to hell," he says, more to himself than to me.

"You were telling me about Lake," I prod.

He turns his head and looks through the glass windows. I follow his gaze. It's snowing, large wet flakes. They appear to be the kind that don't stick. I look again at Huron; his jaw juts out like the prow of a boat.

"Can we go back to Lake?"

"Why not?"

"She wasn't your daughter?" I ask tentatively.

"Hell, no."

"Whose daughter was she?"

"Could've been a lotta people's."

"But you have an idea whose she was, don't you?"

He looks at me for a second, and I feel a chill. Then he smiles, the side of his mouth without the cigarette turning up. "You know, you ought to be a detective."

I force myself to laugh. And then I wait.

"Why is this important? I mean, what difference does it make who her father was?"

"It probably doesn't, but you never know."

"It was Zach," he says candidly.

Zach again.

"We were like the three musketeers." Huron seems to slip from the present; his eyes exhibit a sentimental sheen. "Zach was my best friend, and Helena my old lady. Then I caught them together. Shit." He shakes his head, erasing the memory.

"Zach who?"

"Ellroy."

"Where's he now?"

"You kidding?"

"What happened when you caught them together?"

"Nothing. Well, something. Look, is this necessary?"

I try to evade the question. "What do you mean, 'something'?"

Whitey Huron stands up, and I fear that my interview with him is over. I watch as he goes to the glass doors, stands with his arms folded, stares out.

The snow is coming down more heavily. I can no longer see the other side of the lake. I feel anxious because I don't want to be trapped here with this man. I know I should depart before the snowstorm gets worse, but I haven't learned enough to leave yet. I ask him again what he means by *something*.

His back to me, he says, "I joined them."

We're both silent. Huron's humiliation is palpable. Even in the sixties the situation must have hurt him.

"What did you *want* to do?" I ask.

"Kill them," he replies succinctly.

I believe him.

Still staring at the snow, he says, "I had to be cool. We weren't into possessiveness back then. Free. Everybody was supposed to be free. Well, *she* was. I didn't know it at the time, but Helena was balling everyone." He laughs, a crooked sound. "Funny thing was, I was only balling her."

"What about Zach, what did he feel about Lake?"

"He split before she was born. But that baby was his. Hell, she looked just like him. I mean, take away the beard and mustache and you could see it plain as day." He turns around. "You saw her grown up, what do you think?"

"She looked like Helena," I tell him.

"Oh. I couldn't tell from the picture."

"Where does Ursula fit in?"

He takes his time. "She was a runaway. We took her in, me and Helena."

"Why would Ursula say she was Lake's half-sister?"

"Guess she felt like she was. Hell, she lived with the kid for a couple a years. Maybe you better ask her."

"Yes. I assume you have an alibi for the time of Lake's murder?"

"Alibi? Me? How about this for an *alibi*: I haven't left Hurley for more than twenty years."

I believe him because he's clearly a man who's frightened of the world, a man who's stayed stuck in time, like Flower Power. Still, I have to be sure.

"What about that day? Anyone see you?"

"You're something," he says derogatorily. "Yeah, I guess the usual saw me. Down the paper store. Drugstore where I eat my breakfast. Mike Schmutzer, Bill Wilson, Bucky Wolver, Ed Gorman —"

I hold up a hand to stop him. "I get the picture." I can check this out, but I'm sure Huron's telling the truth. His only motive would be to hurt Helena for having this Zach Ellroy's baby, and I don't think Whitey Huron's a punitive person. Besides, he lacks the vitality and imagination. Huron's not my man.

I say, "I think I better leave before the storm gets worse."

"You're going to drive back to New York in this?"

"You wouldn't?"

"Hell, no. You got four-wheel drive?"

"Yes."

"Even so. I can tell this is going to get a lot worse. You're welcome to stay."

I detect an eagerness in his voice: a man who's been alone too long, a man who'd like company.

"Call your old man," he says. "Tell him what's happening here."

He's taken in my wedding band, made his assumption.

"Listen, I'm not into . . . I mean, you don't have to worry about me," he says, his connotation clear.

I believe him again, but I don't want to stay. "I have to get back. Could you give me a description of Zach?"

"What for?"

"I'd like to talk to him."

"Hell, last time I saw him he was, what? maybe twenty-five, twenty-six?"

"That's all right, I'll age him in my mind."

He snorts contemptuously. "You think you can do that? Hell, I didn't know I was going to look like this. I used to be . . . well, different." He looks down at his hands, slightly wrinkled and spotted. "I don't know how it happened so damn fast."

I identify, but I can't get into this now. Every moment I stay, the storm gets worse. "Would you describe him as he was then?"

"Tall. Big chest. Muscles. He worked out, not like the rest of us. Probably what Helena went for. Hell, she went for them all."

"Zach," I remind him.

"Dark hair, lots of it. Big nose."

"What color eyes?"

He thinks. "Damned if I can remember. Helena's were blue. I remember that. But how d'ya expect me to remember some guy's?"

I'm properly convinced that he's a macho man. "Did Zach have any distinguishing characteristics, like a scar or a mole or something?"

"Don't remember."

I know he's lying, and I think I know why.

"Whitey," I say, "what was it?"

He turns back to the windows and the storm. After a few moments he says, "He had a mole on his ass. Left cheek."

I was right. "That all you can remember?"

"That's it. If you're going, you better get. This thing's coming down heavy."

He brings me my coat. I pick up my purse and feel the heavy security of the gun inside. "Thanks for seeing me," I say.

"Helena's a widow now, right?"

"Yes. You want me to give her a message or anything?"

After a long silence he says softly, "Hell, no."

Outside the snow covers me in the few seconds it takes to get from the house to the car. I feel apprehensive about this drive and think maybe I should try to find a motel. The Raider starts right up. With the wipers on I can see somewhat. It will be better, I tell myself, when I get to Route 80. I make my way out of the driveway and retrace the directions.

When I'm out of Sunset Lake Estates I take it slowly, looking for a store. I decide to call Kip to see what she thinks about my trying to make it home.

I pass the turn into Hurley and remember there's a store not too far along. About four thousand miles later I spot the place. It's a combination market and video store. I pray they have a phone.

They do.

Kip accepts the collect call.

"It's not snowing here yet, but it's going to," she says, sounding strange.

"What's wrong?"

"Nothing."

"Sure?"

"Sure."

"It's pretty bad here, and I was thinking about finding a motel or something."

She's silent.

"Kip? What is it?"

"Nothing. I think you should do that."

I can tell she doesn't mean this. "Look, it's not that bad. I'm going to come home."

"No, don't. I'll just worry."

She doesn't sound right to me, but I can see through the store window that the storm is growing. "Well, if you're sure you're okay?"

"Honey, please. I'm fine. I have a patient in a minute. Call me later when you find a place, okay?"

When I hang up I go to the rack of paperbacks. Usually I carry a book with me, but I'd forgotten. The choice I'm offered is not appealing. But it's not the lack of a good book that decides me. It's Kip. Something is wrong. I know her too well. I'm going home.

It's after I cross the bridge and enter New Jersey that I notice and make a connection. There's a blue Honda Accord behind me, and I realize I've seen it before. And when.

On the way here. It was there at a discreet distance until I crossed into Pennsylvania. In my rearview mirror I see the Honda's headlights grow larger as the car moves closer, and I accept that someone followed me here from New York.

And someone is following me again.

Chapter

Seventeen

IS THERE ANYTHING in movies more boring than the obligatory car chase? I hate it. But now I wish I'd paid more attention, picked up a trick or two, because there's no way I'm going to shake whoever's on my tail. And soon, I guess, the Honda will try running me off the road. One thing's in my favor: the snow.

Spiraling down in thick nuggets, it strains my wipers, impairs my vision. I assume the same is true for my pursuer. Have I ever seen a film where a car chase takes place in the snow? I must have. But my mind can only focus on what's happening in the present.

Navigation is hell. Nothing comes toward me. The roads here curve and wind, one bend after another. In my rearview I can see the headlights, sometimes drifting off like fireflies, sometimes so near I'm sure the Honda's going to crash into me.

Rivulets of sweat streak my face and stream down my sides under my heavy coat and sweater. I turn off the heater.

But this is ridiculous! Why should I think this car is following me? I'm becoming paranoid. Becoming? There must be hundreds of blue Honda Accords in New York. And maybe I imagined that there was one behind me coming to Pennsylvania.

Wherever I go, I almost always subliminally file in my mind the cars near me. I try to recall the trip here. The roads were almost empty because of the ensuing storm, so this should be easy. There was a tan Buick, but it turned off for Morristown. A Ford, two Chevys, a Jeep, and the blue Honda. It was there all the way. I didn't imagine it; this isn't paranoia. Why didn't I realize it? Denial. Why was I in denial? What switch did I pull, and why?

While I'm thinking about this, the Honda has crept up on me, and I feel the bumper touch mine. I swerve to the left. There's nothing coming toward me, and I manage to get back over to my side of the road. The Honda's headlights, like owl's eyes, appear in my rearview again. I try to see the license plate. By the color I can tell it's a New York plate. I see a letter: *F*. But then I must look at the slippery road in front of me so that I won't go off it. The last thing I want now is to get stuck in a snowdrift.

A blustering wind sweeps across the terrain, and I have to slow down, but so does the car in pursuit. I check and see that the wind has cleared the license plate; I'm able to get all but the last number. FXX61. I say it over and over, burning it into my mind. I can't tell whether the driver's a man or a woman, can barely see a face.

Who knew that I was coming to Hurley? Ursula. She certainly would've told Mark, even if they're not in on this together. And Helena knew too. Terrence Ford? I didn't mention it to him, but he could have spoken to Helena. I know it's not Whitey Huron, but he's the only one I can exempt.

My Raider is good in snow, the four-wheel drive giving me an edge over the Honda. I decide to try to outrun it when I make the turn onto 521.

For two minutes the Honda keeps half a car length behind me, and then I take a curve. The Raider feels as though it's going to turn over, but it doesn't. As I drive out of the curve I see the Honda skid toward a drift, and then it's out of view. My breath comes in ragged gasps as I wait for it to reappear. It doesn't, and I assume it's gone off the road. I slow down. Should I keep going or turn back, gun in hand, to see who was following me? I decide I'm lucky this time, and gun or no gun, it would be stupid to confront my stalker. I don't care what Carlotta Carlyle would do!

◆

It takes three and a half hours to make the hour-and-a-half trip. I've never been so thrilled to be stuck in traffic in the Holland Tunnel, because there's no blue Honda behind me.

Forty minutes later I emerge. It's dark and the snow swirls in my headlights. I can't remember the last time we had a snowstorm in the city. January is finally behaving like January, and I find this comforting.

After I take the car back to the parking lot, I wend my way down Tenth Street toward Seventh Avenue. There's an unusual hush over the city, as though the world has ended. This always comes with snow in New York, and it can be eerie, but I like it.

My city looks pristine. My city smells virtuous. I try not to think of what it will be like in a few days. Stay in the moment, I tell myself: enjoy the invigorating air. I stick out my tongue and let the flakes fall into my mouth. I love the snow but don't like to have snowballs thrown at me, so whenever children approach, I walk with a limp. It works every time.

Stalled cars have been abandoned at odd angles. People on cross-country skis trek Seventh Avenue as if it's a wilderness. Everyone ignores the traffic lights, and I cross on a red, the beams of an oncoming car in the distance. Walking up the avenue, I reach Perry Street just as the car does. It's a blue Honda Accord, and my detective's heart shatters when I see by the plate that it's *the* car. Slowly it passes me, the windows fogged. I still can't identify the driver and guess the driver doesn't see me. There's a dent in the right rear fender, and my old ticker leaps for joy as I catch the final number of the plate: 5. I can't wait to phone Cecchi to have him run a make on it.

As I turn onto Perry, my exultation diminishes. Am I crazy? This was no mere coincidence. Perhaps the driver hadn't spotted me — my hood up, he/she concentrating on the road — but this killer knows where I live. Of course. Any one of my suspects could easily find out. I want to be off the streets now, so I run the rest of the way, slipping and sliding, once falling on my ass.

I'm covered with snow. When I enter the apartment, the heat hits me and I fear that I'll melt. Removing my coat and boots, I realize that beyond this point the apartment is dark. It's twenty-five after eight. I'm disappointed that Kip's gone out, but remembering the modem, I cheer up. Eager to reach Cecchi, I go into the living room and snap on a light.

A cry clips the air like sharp shears.

It's Kip. Sitting in the dark.

We look at one another as if we're strangers, adversaries, and then she jumps up and we meet in the center of the room, flinging our arms around each other.

"I can't believe you're here," she says, the words muffled in my hair.

"What's wrong?" I ask. "Why're you sitting in the dark?"

"Oh, God, Lauren." I feel her body pitch and roll against mine as she begins to cry, and I hold her tighter, then lead her to the couch.

"What is it?"

"It's Tom," she says. "He's HIV-positive."

My thoughts fall into place then, like pinballs in a chute. Carolyn's call shot me into denial, and once there, I remained in denial about everything. The mind cannot be selective, and I realize that this is why I didn't take in the blue Honda on my trip *to* Pennsylvania.

Kip and I colluded this morning. The possibility of Tom or Sam's getting AIDS is something we've talked about many times. Yet neither of us allowed herself to consider that this could be the reason for Carolyn's call, the call in which she couldn't tell me what it was she wanted.

We both knew, and both rejected it as being too terrible.

Kip's tears run down my cheek. I don't cry. My crying mechanism cuts off when Kip needs me. I wait, stroke her hair, kiss her face. When she can hear me, I'll know.

The time comes. "HIV doesn't mean he's terminal, Kip."

"There's more."

I feel myself sinking.

"He has shingles."

We both know this is an early sign of the disease, have had friends who began their terminal trip this way.

"Is he in a hospital?"

"Yes."

Tom and Sam live in San Francisco. "Do you want to go there?"

"I do, but when I talked to Sam, he said I should wait, that it would alarm Tom if I showed up."

I nod, understanding. "How's your mother?"

She shrugs. "You know Mom. She's trying to put the best face on it she can."

"What face would that be?"

"Oh, all the research that's being done and all the new drugs they're coming up with."

Carolyn's relentless positive attitude is something the family jokes about, even to her. "But she's right this time," I say.

Kip raises her head and looks at me. "Is she, Lauren?"

"Sure. If this were a few years ago, it would be different. But now . . ."

"Lauren, just . . . just *please* don't try to cheer me up or raise my hopes, okay?"

"Why not?"

After a beat she laughs. "You're right, why not?"

"And what I'm saying's true, honey. Things have gotten better."

"I suppose they can prolong life now, but nobody has actually beaten this thing."

"Yet."

We're both bitter about the government's lack of funding, lack of interest in AIDS, and can't help thinking that if it were a heterosexual disease (no drug users, either), incredible amounts of money would have been poured into research by now.

"I can't believe we didn't know this morning," she says.

"Denial."

Kip says, "This is one that should go into the Denial Museum."

We both laugh. And keep laughing for far too long, until we've gone over the edge and are squealing, unable to stop. We're helpless with laughter and don't dare look at one another. Six months later we regain control, wipe the laugh tears from our eyes, slump back into the couch.

"God," Kip says, and gulps air. "I feel a little better. They've known that he was HIV-positive for about eight months."

"Why didn't they tell anyone?"

"Sam said Tom didn't want the family to worry."

"What about friends?"

"No."

"What a nightmare for Sam, carrying this by himself."

"I know."

"And what about Sam?"

"He doesn't want to have the test."

We're silent. If Kip had it, would I be tested, or prefer to live in ignorance? I wonder. Fortunately, I don't have to make this choice. There hasn't yet been a reported case of a woman giving AIDS to another woman. It's perhaps the only time in history that being lesbian is preferable to being anything else.

Suddenly Kip sits up, pulls away from me. "What the hell are you doing here? You're supposed to be in a motel."

"I knew something was wrong."

"You drove in this storm? Are you nuts, Lauren? That's all I need now, you in an accident."

I decide not to tell her about the blue Honda. "Well, I'm here, and I wasn't in an accident."

"Jesus, that makes me mad."

"That I wasn't in an accident?"

"Not funny."

"Tell me you hate it that I'm here."

She turns off the light and starts for the stairs. "That's beside the point."

"I don't think it is."

We head for the second floor. Undressing, we are silent. I think about Tom. And Sam. I try to imagine how he must feel. I'd be nuts if it were Kip. I thank God that it isn't.

When we finally get into bed, Kip turns toward me and asks about my day. After we've discussed it, there's a look in her eyes that tells me she wants to make love. This doesn't surprise me. When Kip is hurting, she finds solace in sex.

We move toward each other, I slide on top of her, kiss her eyes, her face, and make my way to her lips. I know how they will feel after all these years; still, sexy shocks run through me. After a few minutes, all rational thought is vanquished and we surrender to love.

Chapter

Eighteen

THIS MORNING Cecchi gave me the info on the blue Honda. It's registered to a Deanna Alpert, who reported it stolen days ago. Surprise, surprise!

Now I'm in the midst of "talking" to a Sysop (Systems Operator) named Richard, who is very patient and teaching me my way around his bulletin board. The boards use diverse software, though most employ one of about four different types. Richard's is a Wildcat board. All this means is that the menu that appears and the various ways to get from one thing to another are unlike those on a BBS that uses some other form of software.

"We're leaving in fifteen minutes," Kip says, standing in the doorway.

"Shhh. I'm talking."

"Oh, forgive me."

"This is important."

"What about our dinner date?"

"Dinner date? At this hour?" Obviously Kip's confused.

"Lauren, it's seven o'clock."

Shocked, I turn away from the screen, stare at her. She nods. It can't be: I haven't had lunch, haven't gone to the bathroom. It was just eleven A.M.! Back to the screen. Richard is explaining how to join SIGs (special-interest groups), where you leave and get messages on the topic of the SIG.

"Lauren? Come on."

"Go without me."

"Why?"

I don't even know who we're having dinner with, but I don't think that's wise to admit. "I need to do this."

"You need to have dinner, too. We're meeting the Js at Formerly Joe's in ten minutes."

"I'll be there later. You don't understand, Kip."

"Unfortunately, I think I do. I've read about this. How long will you be?"

"When I finish up with this guy I'll be there."

"Yeah, but how long will that be?"

I can't believe how much I want her to leave me alone. She's making me miss instructions. "Fifteen minutes," I say.

"I'll call them, then, and —"

"NO! It might take longer." I want her out.

"See you there," she says.

Formerly Joe's was, formerly, Joe's, and it's on the corner of Tenth and West Fourth streets, in the same block as my office. Once it was an Italian restaurant, and now it's . . . eclectic. I find the three of them in a booth in the nonsmoking back room. When I sit down I see they're drinking coffee. They stare at me, say nothing.

"Glad to see you, too," I say, smiling, wondering why they're drinking coffee before the meal.

Kip says, "Nice of you to join us."

There's something in the tone of her voice that sets off alarm bells in my head; they bring to mind the bells of the BBSs! Surreptitiously, I glance at my watch, having forgotten to check before. Jesus! It's nine-thirty. I don't know what to say.

"I'm stunned by what you're doing," Jenny says hyperbolically.

"I was working," I defend.

Jill says, "I don't get it. I mean, what's it got to do with Lake's murder?"

"Are you in a hurry? I'd like to eat something."

They say they have time, and I order the salmon. "Let me explain. Lake lied to me. I don't know why she said she met the creep through an ad in the paper, but I think she did it through one of these bulletin boards. There are quite a few that are strictly for dating."

"Don't they check people out?" Jenny asks.

"I don't know yet. They probably do the best they can, but it's like the paper — they can only go so far."

"How are you going to know which one she used?" Kip asks.

My very question. "I can't know until I get into them. Well, I do know more than I did, because Richard, this Sysop —"

"This *what?*" A chorus.

"Systems Operator of a bulletin board. Anyway, he taught me how to toggle and —"

"Lauren . . . we don't know what the hell you're talking about," Kip says.

I take a breath. "I hit this word called *toggle* in the communications software — Telix — and it showed me the phone directory in another way. Next to the places Lake connected with, there's a date for the last time she talked to them, and a number for how many times. It's a lifesaver, because I've been able to narrow it down to sixty-five places."

"Whew! Thank God for Richard," Kip says sarcastically. "Only sixty-five, huh?"

"Well, some of them, like New York City Computer Club and BloodStop, are probably not dating services. There are six that I think are naturals, and I'll try those first. I'd like to get into them as Lake — if the rapist uses the board, it might throw him."

"So," Jill asks, "what's the problem?"

"I don't know her password."

Predictably, they all look at each other, disdainful and imperious. I cut them off at their patronizing pass. "Everybody has to have a password to get in."

" 'Get in'?"

"To get access to the various services on any bulletin board," I say slowly, a pointed space between each word.

"Is this to protect you or them?" Jenny asks, looking over the rim of her coffee cup.

"Both, I guess. Anyway, I have no idea what password she used."

Jill asks, "Did you have to give a password for yourself?"

"Yes." They aren't taking this seriously, and I'll be damned if I'll tell them everything. So when Jenny asks, I refuse.

Kip says, "You're not going to tell *us* your damned password?"

"Right." I take a lovely bite of salmon.

"You're kidding," Jenny states.

"No."

"What are *we* going to do with your fucking password?" Kip asks.

She hardly ever uses that kind of language, so I know I've gotten to her. The thing is, I have to have some kind of defense against these doubting Thomasinas. What would Kip think, I wonder, if she knew my password was her name?

"The point here is not *my* password but *Lake's* password."

"Oh no you don't," Kip says.

"Hmmm?"

"You think you're going to get out of it just like that?"

"Out of what?"

In a dangerous monotone, Kip says, "I don't think I've ever known anyone more infuriating."

"Or more adorable," I add.

"Lauren, tell us your password," demands Kip.

"No."

Jenny laughs.

Jill gives her a "shut-up" look.

I order a slice of lemon meringue. The others eye me as though I'm insane. I don't know whether it's about the pie or the password.

"I don't believe this," Kip says.

"Believe it, baby," I say, imitating Bogey.

"How'd you pick your password?" Jill asks. She puts up her hand, palm out. "I'm not trying to find out what it is, I'm just curious about the process. Maybe Lake used the same method."

I look at Jill. I could kiss her. "Excuse me a minute." I go to the phone, dial Ursula. When I get her, I ask if she can meet me at Lake's apartment in half an hour. At first she balks, but I convince her that it's very important. And it is.

◆

Kip was not happy about my hasty departure, but work is work. I wait in front of Lake's building. I'm cold, uncomfortable, and a bit unnerved. I stick my hand in my bag and feel the reassuring grip of my .38. There's always the danger that Ursula might decide to fire me. The permanent way! I wonder if she'll bring Mark, or if he'll follow her, stay concealed until the right moment, and then . . .

A woman in her twenties, a Stewart plaid skirt wrapped around her head, wearing a flimsy green sweater, gray sweatpants, and white open-toed shoes, no socks, stops in front of me. Her face looks like a broken sidewalk.

"You know what I'm going to do?" she asks me in a high-pitched whine.

"What?"

"I'm going to take off the top of my skull and put a glass dome there instead so I can see what's going on inside."

"Good idea."

"You wanna do it, too?"

"I don't *want* to know what's going on inside."

"You don't?" She's shocked.

"I know this concept is hard to fathom," I say, "but that's the way I feel about it."

"Hey, no problem. To each her own."

She wanders off just as Ursula arrives.

"A friend?" she asks.

"An old high-school teacher of mine."

"Ah."

Surreptitiously I look around. No sign of Mark, but that doesn't mean he isn't out there.

"Let's go up. I assume you'll tell me what this is all about?"

On our way up the stairs, I explain as best I can about the use of the modem and my suspicions about Lake's connection to her rapist. Naturally I don't tell her that I suspect rapist and murderer may not be one. Nor is this the time, I decide, to confront her about her lies.

Ursula unlocks the door and we go into the apartment. Oddly, inside there seems to be a strange scent, like a potpourri of melancholy. Ursula flips a switch, and the room lights up. Nothing's changed. Good.

"I still don't understand what you want here, Lauren."

"I'm not sure," I say. What Jill said about my choosing my password, and that perhaps Lake used the same method, makes me feel that if I were in her surroundings I might be able to figure it out. There's no chance of finding it written down anywhere, as the police have removed all her papers.

"Do you know where Lake did her work, where she might have used the computer?"

"I suppose at her desk in the bedroom."

We go there. As I remembered, it's a common student's desk: a board over two file cabinets. These drawers are wooden and old, with open sides. The desktop is empty except for a white phone. Above the desk is a travel poster of France, one corner curling downward. I follow the phone line down behind the desk, but the jack's not there. The line continues around the edge of the room and

ends at a jack next to the bed. Above the jack is a wall outlet. In the
top socket is the plug from the lamp above her bed. Suddenly, as if I
can see it there, I know that if her modem was like mine — briefly I
wonder what happened to hers — it was plugged into the bottom
slot. I also know that Lake made her modem calls from bed!

"What is it?" Ursula asks, registering what must be the look of
triumph on my face.

"Do you mind?" I ask her, indicating that I want to sit on the bed.
She shrugs forlornly.

Carefully, as though I might defile it, I ease down on the tan
quilt, push the two pillows against the wall, and sit stiffly, legs
stretched out. I imagine the computer on my lap.

But it would be much too heavy.

I feel dispirited, but then, in my mind's eye, I remember something I'd seen on a shelf in the closet, casually wondered about, and
forgotten. Now I think I know what it is.

I hop off the bed, open the closet. It's still there. I don't like
having my back to Ursula, so I turn, and she's right there behind
me. I suck in my breath. She looks at me, bewildered by my reaction.

"Scared me," I say automatically.

"Sorry." She backs up, smiling innocently.

Am I wrong about her? I return my attention to the closet shelf.
The thing is plastic, I think, and all I can see from my vantage point
is its edge and underside. I hate it, but I have to ask Ursula to get it
down for me. She does so with ease.

"What is it?" she asks.

I don't answer her but take it with me to the bed and place it over
my legs. A perfect fit. It's a table made from one sheet of plastic,
with no seams, and I'm sure Lake used it for the computer. Probably had it made. I explain this to Ursula then revert to where I was
before I remembered the table.

On the opposite wall is an old poster of Jimi Hendrix in action.
I've seen this before; it's quite famous. On the wall next to the bed
are more posters: David Bowie, Sting, U2. There're no women.

I recall my own room when I lived at home. I was more interested in movie stars than in musicians. The pictures that decorated
my walls were of both men and women — but then, of course, it was
the women I wanted up there; the men were for show!

My guess is that the absence of women on Lake's walls is due
more to the lack of women rock stars than anything else. Leisurely I

look around the room, taking in every detail: the cracks in the plaster, the framed print of Chagall's famous wedding painting, the bamboo blinds.

Ursula taps her foot.

"I know this seems crazy," I say, "but I'm trying to find something out."

"I know, but what?" she asks, annoyed.

How can I explain? And then it hits me because my eyes keep coming back to the same place. My detective's pulse pumps like Schwarzenegger's iron. I can't wait to get home.

I jump off the bed. "Ursula, thanks a lot for meeting me. We can go now."

"But ..."

"If I'm right, I'll let you know." I'm out the door and down the stairs. I hail a cab, put Ursula in, then hail a second one for myself.

◆

When I get home, Kip's in bed reading Virginia Woolf's last diary. She's wearing her new reading glasses and looks at me through the plain half.

I don't want to be here, I want to be downstairs with the computer, but I think it's politic for me to check in with her first, considering how I left her. I sit on the edge of the bed.

"Hi." I touch her cheek with the back of my hand. Still smooth.

"Hi." She lowers the book to her blanketed thighs.

"Sorry I ran out like that."

"Mmmm."

"You're mad."

"Mad? I don't know ... no, not mad."

"What, then?"

"Hurt, I guess."

"God." I feel like hell. I can't stand hurting Kip. She's the most precious part of my life, after all. I lean over and kiss her; our lips, trying to dispel pain, effect amity rather than engaging in anything ardent. "I get wrapped up," I say.

"Obsessed," she corrects.

"Okay."

"Look, if I haven't gotten used to your compulsive, obsessive, addictive behavior by now, then —"

"Hold it." I sit up.

"What?"

"I'm not one of your patients," I say indignantly.

"I'm sorry."

"Okay. My work sometimes makes me . . ."

"I know." She stretches out both arms, and I come into them like a bird to her nest.

We lie this way for a while, neither saying anything but feeling close again, loving. Then I feel Kip's lips on my neck as she plants a trail of tiny kisses up to a point right below my ear. She stops, then whispers.

"Come to bed, darling."

The words I usually love to hear have turned into the words from hell! Now what? The only thing I want to do is go to the computer and try out my theory. But how can I explain this to my lover, who has just called me compulsive, obsessive, and addictive, all of which I've denied? Besides, I don't want to reject her. Still, the modem and computer loom like giants in my mind.

"Darling, did you hear me?"

"Yes. It's kind of late, isn't it?"

"To come to bed?" she says facetiously.

"Well, no . . . I mean . . . well, we just did it," I say lamely.

"I didn't know there was a quota system, toots."

"It's not that, I . . ."

"A quickie," she suggests.

I want to ask *how* quick but check it. Kip and I learned after the first romantic years that sometimes making love doesn't have to be a Hollywood production number — sometimes it can be short and to the point, so to speak — and that that doesn't make it any less meaningful.

Okay, I say to myself. So I'm not in the mood. But I will be. From experience I know that once I've begun, I'll get into it. I also know that we're talking about fifteen to twenty-five minutes, and that it's now eleven or so. I smile at her, and as she begins to undo the buttons on my shirt, I calculate that by 1:00 A.M. I should have my answer.

"Where are you going?" she asks.

I'm at the bedroom door in my pajamas and robe. I thought she was asleep. I think about lying, dismiss it. I think about telling the truth, dismiss it. What's left?

"Lauren?" She turns on her light.

"You're awake," I say stupidly.

"Where are you going?"

It's no use. "I have an idea . . . I have to try something out."

"On the computer?"

"Yes."

"Oh. Well, see you in the morning. G'night, honey."

The woman's a national treasure!

I log on to DYP (Dial Your Partner) by entering Lake's name, and when it comes time for the password, I type in what I think it is. As usual, only dots show. Holding my breath, I hit the ENTER key.

WRONG PASSWORD, TRY AGAIN.

Shit! I type in my second choice, dots echoing, and hit the ENTER key.

It works! I feel as if I've found Judge Crater. The first password I tried was *Jimi*, the second, *Hendrix*. Sitting on Lake's bed, looking at that poster, I reasoned that when she was asked for a password, she might have, like me, selected the first thing that came to mind — and like me, she might've looked up to think, seen the poster and chosen his name. And she had!

Lauren, I say to myself, have you ever thought of becoming a detective?

Chapter

Nineteen

I SIT in my office, at my desk, drinking coffee. My eyes are slits in a sea of puffy skin. I've been up all night, logging on to boards as Lake. My suspicion that she used the same password everywhere has been confirmed. On every BBS, in the message center, I've left a letter to ALL that I've been away and now I'm back, ready to date again, or words to that effect. Now I have to wait and check back in for my E-mail (*E* for *Electronic*) in a day or so.

I've also discovered the boards with teleconferences, where many people can be on at once. You type in what you have to say and get a response immediately. At three and four in the morning there weren't too many people on, but I did get into a conversation with someone who called himself The Demon. This, I've learned, is a handle. Lake's handle turns out to have been *Hendrix* on these boards, her password *Jimi*. I kept getting bumped until I figured out that combination, but detective supremo that I am, it only took me about fifteen minutes.

Anyway, The Demon and I talked for a while. He seemed to know me (Lake), so I had to fudge a few things, pretend I knew certain references when I didn't. Still, I got by.

One of the extraordinary things I discovered was that even though I made only local calls, I could talk to people from all over the country or leave messages for them by way of something called RelayNet. But even if Lake's rapist doesn't live in the New York area, it's doubtful that he lives in Colorado or Michigan or some-place like that. He's more than likely within easy flying distance.

The Toshiba is sitting on my desk. I've brought the modem with me, just in case. It's ridiculous. Although I've still got many boards to check out, I've been at this thing all night, and I've got paperwork to do.

I open my desk drawer and take out the outstanding-bills file. I flip back the manila cover and start to leaf through the papers. I need to send out second letters to the people who owe me money. It's extremely important. I close the file, put it back in my desk, shut the drawer, turn on the Toshiba, and plug in the modem. Just for an hour.

◆

Cecchi calls. There's been another rape.

"Twenty-five years old. Name's Jane Chapman. The guy wore an Easton ring, so I'm taking her up to the school today to see if she can I.D. him from the yearbook pictures. Want to come?"

I shut down the computer, leave my office.

Jane Chapman has platinum hair. It's dyed and cut so that there's a little tail in back. She has large brown eyes like the bottoms of Hershey's Kisses, and wears a long black and white sweater and gray sweatpants. Her right cheek is bruised and cut, the skin around her left eye ebony and purple. Still, I can see that she's pretty. It pains me to look at her.

Chapman's place is a studio apartment. The first thing I notice is an Epson computer. On the desk next to it is a modem, different from mine. I've seen this kind advertised. It's more expensive and has lights and a speaker so the user can hear the thing dialing and ringing.

Cecchi and I sit on a light-blue futon couch. Jane sips an herb tea that smells swell but tastes, I know, like colored water. It's all she has, so we stay dry. And silent.

Minutes pass. At last she puts down her mug, which says JANE'S on the side. She bites her upper lip, moves the mug against her breast, over her heart, as if it will protect her from further harm. The gesture touches me, almost renders me speechless, but I clear my throat and forge ahead.

"Ms. Chapman," I say, "do you think you can talk about it now?"

She speaks softly. "I'll try."

I smile sympathetically, trying to impart understanding. I don't want to tell my story again. Besides, even though Cecchi knows, I feel it'll embarrass him to hear it in front of a third person.

"You found this man through a bulletin board?"

"Yes."

Cecchi looks at me, surprised. I know I have to tell him about Lake's computer and all that goes with it. He'll be mad that I've withheld info, but we'll get through it.

"Which board?" I ask.

"B and GT."

"How's that?" Cecchi asks.

Jane flushes. "Boys and Girls Together," she says sheepishly.

"What name did he use, what handle?" I ask.

"Paul Brown. It could've been real, you know what I'm saying?"

I nod. Smith. Brown. I wonder if Jones will be next. "What made you respond to him in particular?"

"When we chatted — you know, typed — on the board, he talked about his feelings. Most men don't have feelings." She glances at Cecchi, then back to me. "What I mean is, most men don't want to show their feelings. Living in New York, you might as well be on the Isle of Lesbos as far as meeting men is concerned."

I try not to be paranoid.

"Especially when most of your friends are married," she continues. "It gets lonely. They don't include you, you know. An extra man at the dinner table, swell. An extra woman, forget it. It doesn't matter they don't pair you up with the extra man, because he's usually gay anyway. 'I've got to fix you up,' they say, but they never do. And bars are out, you know what I'm saying? Too dangerous." She laughs, realizing the irony of what she's said.

"Ms. Chapman —"

"Call me Jane. Why should we stand on ceremony after . . . oh, hell."

"Jane, can you describe him?"

"Yes."

She sips her tea while we wait.

Eventually she says, "I hate talking about him."

"I understand," I say, and ask her again to describe the rapist, anxious to tie him to Lake's.

"He was tall and thin."

"How tall?" I ask.

"Six two, maybe taller."

"How old?"

"Thirty-two, -three."

My detective's heart is beating faster. "How about his hair?" I prod.

"Blond."

"Are you sure?"

"Of course I'm sure," she answers, miffed.

I can't blame her, but Lake's rapist had brown hair. Is this a different guy, or . . . ?

"I know this is a strange question," I say, "but do you think he wore a wig?"

"Oh, no. No wig."

"Was his hair long or short?"

"It was a modified crew. I didn't like that about him."

I think, I must ask Lake if it's possible that the guy wore a wig. Then I remember with a thud and press on. "Eyes?"

"They were brown," she answers, certain.

Brown? I hesitate to ask if she's sure, but I must. "Not blue?"

"Brown. I'm not color-blind." She's indignant.

My detective's heart sinks. "Anything else?"

"What do you mean?" she asks coldly.

I fear I'm losing her. "I know it's irritating when I ask if you're sure, but I have a reason. Don't take it personally." I appreciate the stupidity of this. How else can she take it? Understandably, she says nothing. I try to be more specific. "Any distinguishing features?"

"Is a mustache a distinguishing feature?"

"Sure." Tentatively I ask, "Do you think it was a real mustache?"

"Yes."

"Why?"

"I don't know. I just do. I mean, isn't it obvious if someone's wearing a fake one?"

"Not always," I tell her.

"I'm sure his was real."

"What kind of mustache was it? Full, new, handlebar?"

She smiles when I say "handlebar," then puts a forefinger between mouth and nose. "It was straight — called a toothbrush, you know what I'm saying?"

"Full?"

She closes her eyes, trying to picture it. "Yeah, it was full," she says, with obvious distaste. I know now that he kissed her. I wonder how long it takes to grow a full mustache.

Recalling Lake's description, I say, "Would you classify him as regular-looking, ordinary?"

"Yeah, I guess you could call him that."

I'm relieved. At least this tallies. "You wrote letters to each other before you met, correct?"

Her cheeks redden. She's remembering reckless words. "Yeah, we exchanged letters. E-mail, you know."

"Did you print his out?"

"Sure."

"You have them?"

Her bottom lip quivers with the prelude to tears, and she shakes her head.

"Where are they?" Cecchi speaks for the first time in what seems like days and looks at me suspiciously. I think he's beginning to realize that I know something I haven't told him.

"He took them."

"When?" I ask.

"You know," she says, childlike.

"After he raped you?"

She nods.

"Where did you go on your first date?"

"We met at a restaurant. I thought someplace on neutral territory ... I thought it'd be safer, you know what I'm saying?" This time she doesn't laugh. She looks at me earnestly, as though it's important that I see she's a responsible woman.

"Who chose the place?" I know the answer.

"He did."

"Do you remember the name of the restaurant?"

For the first time there's a gloss to her eyes, as though they've been buffed.

"I'll never forget it. I thought it was so romantic." Her expression freezes as she acknowledges the paradox. "Donadello's. It's on the East Side. In the Sixties."

"An Italian restaurant?"

"Before we met we found out that we both loved everything Italian."

I almost smile. French for one, Italian for the other. Cynically, I wonder what cuisine will be next.

"Did you go anywhere after dinner?" A Fellini double bill? I almost ask.

"We walked. It was a nice night, and we didn't want to go inside. Later we stopped and had coffee."

"An Italian coffeehouse?"

"What else?" She shrugs. Then tells me what they had and that he phoned her around midnight to say, in Italian, how wonderful the evening had been.

◆

We wait for Dean Barry to call us in. Mrs. Barnett has informed him of our arrival, but he's with a student, she says, her look meant to impart how bad this kid is, how much he needs discipline.

On the way here Cecchi whispered to me that we needed to talk, and I agreed, acknowledging that I had something to tell him.

Barry's door opens, and a small, stringy boy comes out. He keeps his head down so that we see only the crown of his brown hair. He passes by, and I imagine I can smell the obscure odor of remorse.

Mrs. Barnett's phone rings. She picks it up, nods into it as if the caller can see her, replaces the handset in the cradle. "You can go in now," she says to us.

We file in, Jane between Cecchi and me. I make the introductions. Barry adjusts the wire-rim glasses, reseats himself. On his desk, in a stack, are five yearbooks. He pushes them toward us.

"These are the years you asked for," Barry says unnecessarily.

I hand the top one to Jane, who takes it with shaking hands, as if the yearbook will rape her. This is one of the subtle ways she'll approach life now.

As she opens it, we all look at each other. We're uncomfortable, embarrassed, as though we're watching something we shouldn't be. Something intimate.

Barry clears his throat, shifts in his chair, adjusts his tie. Cecchi and I look at each other.

"I'll be right back," Barry says, rising. He leaves.

The room is quiet except for the slow swishing sound of turning pages. Occasionally Jane glances at us apprehensively, as if she's wondering whether she's doing this right. I smile encouragement.

It's during her perusal of the third yearbook that she emits a sound like the cry of a distressed bird. Cecchi and I sit up at attention.

"What is it?" he asks.

She doesn't answer. I see that her whole body is assaulted by tremors. I reach out and put my hand on her arm. She jumps. I should know better.

"Jane," I say softly. "Have you found him?"

Slowly, she nods.

Cecchi and I both stand up, lean over to see the face and name of the picture Jane is pointing to.

He is innocuous-looking, a child. But this was years ago. His hair's cut short and appears light in the black-and-white photograph; the ordinary face is oval, and the eyes are dark. His name is Harrison Webster. Of course it is.

"Are you sure, Jane?" I ask.

"Yes," she whispers. "He's different now, but this is him."

The address is on Central Park South. His family's home. It's unlikely that Harrison still lives there, but perhaps his parents will know where he *does* live. This is exciting, the first real lead we've had.

Mead Barry comes back. I tell him about the I.D.

"That's impossible," he sputters.

"Why?"

"The Websters are a fine old family," he says stupidly.

"So?" Cecchi asks.

"They simply couldn't be involved in a thing like . . . like this."

I want to rap him one. Tweak his fat nose, at least.

"Do you remember Harrison?" I ask.

"Wonderful boy." Barry says this defiantly.

"Terrific boy," Cecchi mutters.

"Are you going to take the word of this . . . this girl and embarrass the Websters?"

"This girl," I say, my hand resting gently on Jane's shoulder, "is a woman. And I have no reason to doubt her I.D." Barry, I assume, is offended by Jane's platinum hair and faddish tail and has made an assessment that tells him, erroneously, that no Webster would rape someone like her. He no longer considers the violent act itself but rather uses his spurious evaluation of Jane as his guideline. He makes me sick.

"Do you know where Harrison Webster is now?" Cecchi asks.

Barry shakes his head.

"The family?"

"I imagine they still live at that address. I just don't know."

Cecchi says, "We'll have to take the yearbook."

No one shakes hands. We leave Barry's office.

In the car I sit in the back with Jane, my hand on her wrist. I can tell she's grateful for the touch.

Again I'm whirled back to the time of my own rape. I know Jane will never be the same. She won't ever completely trust again, though she won't know this. For a long time she'll look over her shoulder as she walks the streets, even in daylight. There will be other, subtler things, too. And then there will be the nightmares.

I remember waking up and seeing my parents at my bedside, their faces frozen in horror, unable to change their expressions as they tried to soothe me.

But Jane lives alone. When the nightmares wake her, who'll be there to hold her hand, stroke her cheek? I think about urging her to stay with a friend, leave the city, go home to her family if she has one. I can't do this, because we need her, and I feel guilt run through my veins like a corrosive stream. It's times like this that I'm not proud of what I do.

"What will happen now?" she asks.

"We'll try to find Webster."

"Will I have to see him? You know what I'm saying?"

"You may have to identify him, but he won't see you."

"You mean through a one-way glass?"

"Yes."

"Will there be a trial?"

"I hope so," I say, already worrying about our antiquated legal system, the possibility that Webster will slip out of the charges like a greased pig.

"Then I'll have to testify."

I nod, pat her hand. "Don't worry about that now. One step at a time." But I know how she feels.

I remember, as though no time has passed, sitting in the courtroom, West and Bailey at the defendant's table, the baleful looks they gave me, the shame I felt. And the fear. I wish I could tell Jane that Webster will go away for a long time, but it's a promise I can't make. He may not go to prison at all. For the millionth time I wonder how men can rape women, sometimes kill them, and live to walk the streets again, perhaps repeat their crimes, while Jean Harris sits in jail year after year.

We pull up in front of Jane's apartment building on Sheridan Square.

Cecchi turns, looks over his shoulder at her. "Don't worry, Jane, we've got people watching the place."

She nods, her skin tone ashen. "If you find him . . . if you find him, will you tell me?"

"Right away," Cecchi says.

"Want me to go up with you?" I ask.

"Would you?"

We take the elevator to the third floor, walk down the hall. She unlocks her door, I signal for her to wait. I take out my gun and, combat-style, enter the apartment. It doesn't take me long to determine that no one's there. I wave Jane in.

"Don't open the door to anyone you don't know," I caution. I ask her if she has food, and she says she does. I'm tempted to say that everything will be all right (this, or a form of it, is said in every movie ever made), but I check myself because I can't be sure it will be. Instead, I squeeze her shoulder and tell her that I'll see her soon. I also say, "You're very brave, Jane."

A smile skims her lips and is gone.

I wait while she locks the door behind me, puts the police lock in place.

Back in the car, Cecchi asks, "You want to come to the Websters'?"

"No, Cecchi," I say, "I thought I'd go to the movies."

He laughs because he thinks I'm scared.

I laugh because he's right.

Chapter

Twenty

ON THE WAY UPTOWN I tell Cecchi about Lake's computer, the bulletin boards, and what I've been doing. Initially he is, as I'd expected, pissed. When he calms down, I agree to turn over her laptop to him, and he agrees that whatever I do on my own is all right with him, as long as I don't make a date with Webster without telling him. I promise.

The Websters' Central Park South apartment is in one of those old, ornate buildings that face the park, where the residents have owned their places for years, long before it became a New York necessity.

The doorman seems shrunken in his blue uniform, the gold braid across the shoulders signifying nothing. The blue cap with its shiny visor sits on his head at a rakish angle, as if to contradict the evidence of his dying face, telling the world there's life left in him yet.

He approaches us with the annoying authority that people in jobs they deem beneath them often assume.

"Help you?" he asks. His brown eyes, like small starry specks, look us over disdainfully.

Cecchi flashes his shield. "Webster," he says.

The doorman takes a step back, as if the shield might be radioactive. "She expecting you?"

"No."

Appointments again.

He grunts, picks up the house phone, pushes a black button. "Millie," he says. "People to see Mrs. Webster. Cops." He nods, hangs up the phone. "Penthouse," he says. Reluctantly, he opens the door for us.

The main lobby is marbled: floors, walls, ceiling. Plants in huge urns are in countless locations. In the middle of the expanse there are three maroon velvet divans, yards away from each other. I feel as though I'm in a hotel.

There is, of course, an elevator man. But he's as young and healthy as the doorman is old and sick. His uniform is maroon with gold piping, his tie black.

"Penthouse," Cecchi says as we get in.

With no expression the man cranks the door shut and starts us upward, the only sound the whirring of the elevator. After a rocky stop, he opens the doors. We step into a hallway, and the elevator door closes behind us.

We are *in* the apartment, though a door separates us from the main part of the place. On the wall hangs a Monet, and I know it's real. A black woman in a black, white-laced uniform comes through the door. She takes our coats.

"Follow me," she orders.

Room after room is furnished with antiques and more paintings I can't bear to look at for fear of envy. At last she opens a glass door, and we enter a solarium.

This room has comfortable chintz-covered chairs and chaise longues, an anachronism in this house of wealth and pomp.

Lying on a chaise is a woman whose age is difficult to determine with the January sun shining through the glass into my squinting eyes. I put a hand over my brow as though I'm saluting.

"Come in," she says. "Sit down."

We do. I see her more clearly now. She's probably in her mid-fifties. Her blond hair is fine and kinky, and she's let it grow its own way so that it stands out from her head like a fuzzy halo. I take an educated guess that when she goes out she wears it differently.

Mrs. Webster has sorrowful blue eyes, as though something or someone has overwhelmed her capacity for joy. She has a long, thin nose in a narrow face with high cheekbones. Her mouth is generous, the lower lip thrust forward, which gives her a sensual rather than a sulky appearance.

A long lithe body is clothed in a cerise satin dressing gown, her feet shod in matching slippers. She's been reading something in the collected works of Jane Austen. Placing a silver bookmark in the volume, she says, "There's nothing good to read anymore. I find myself going back to the tried and true."

I hate this attitude about books. Sometimes, I agree, one longs for the pure language of an Edith Wharton or the power of a Dostoyevsky, but then along comes a Don DeLillo, an Alice McDermott, a Mary Gordon, a Russell Banks, and faith is restored. I find the idea of completely giving up on contemporary writers a kind of snobbishness.

"Well," she says, getting no response to her pronouncement on literature. "How may I help you?" Plucked blond eyebrows arch.

Cecchi says, "Do you have a son named Harrison, Mrs. Webster?"

A thin hand flies to her heart and flutters there like a moth. "Has something happened to Harrison?"

"No."

She takes a deep breath, sighs. "Then?"

"We need to question him in connection with an investigation. Purely routine. Can you tell us how to get in touch with him?"

"Why, yes, of course. What's it about?"

"Confidential," Cecchi says, for probably the millionth time in his career.

Mrs. Webster's eyes appear to shrink as the lids lower. She doesn't believe him. "What division did you say you were with, Detective?"

Cecchi takes a beat. "I didn't say. Homicide."

The pale brows arch again, so high this time they almost meet her hairline. "Homicide," she repeats. "What could Harrison have to do with that?" She swings her legs over the side of the chaise and sits up straight.

Cecchi glances at me. I need to speak so that it will appear that I'm there officially.

"We don't know yet, Mrs. Webster. That's why we have to talk to him. We wouldn't have bothered you, but he's not in the book, and doesn't have an unlisted number."

"Of course not," she says smugly.

We wait.

"Harrison lives in Cleveland."

I know that Cecchi is surprised by this, but knowing what I do about RelayNet, I'm not.

Smoothing his gray temples, Cecchi says silkily, "Could you give us his address and phone there?"

She stands. An expression that I'm unable to decipher crosses her face. Pushed, I would say it's pain. Mrs. Webster wrests a long filtered cigarette from a glass box, ignites it with a crown-shaped silver lighter. She exhales a cloudy fume and appears to have forgotten that we're there.

Cecchi clears his throat. "Mrs. Webster?"

She turns — twirls, really — and I think of Loretta Young, the entrance she used to make on her television show, which aired on Sunday nights when I was a child.

"Harrison's phone and address," he reminds her.

"Well, he — he doesn't have a phone. Harrison likes his privacy."

I'll bet. This is becoming more interesting.

"And his address?"

"He — he has a post-office box."

My detective's heart soars. Harrison Webster may not live anywhere *near* Cleveland! Cecchi asks her for the box number, and she reluctantly gives it to us.

"How long has it been since you've seen Harrison?"

"He was home for Christmas," she says, smiling, looking as if she's bested us.

"Do you have a recent picture of him?" I ask.

"Picture?" she stalls.

"A photograph," I interpret unnecessarily.

"Well, no, I don't. Harrison doesn't like to have his picture taken." She tries a girlish giggle, as if to suggest that her son's a bit eccentric, but it doesn't work.

"Why not?" Cecchi asks.

"He just doesn't," she answers coldly.

"Has he changed much since high school? Since his high-school graduation picture, for instance?" I ask.

She eyes me with a wintry scrutiny. "How do you know what he looked like then? What is this? I'm his mother, I have a right to know," she insists.

We can't tell her, take the chance that she'll alert him somehow.

"Thank you for your help, Mrs. Webster," Cecchi says, and he rises, turns to leave. I follow.

"Wait," she commands.

We do.

Her eyes are softer now, made so by the tears that have gathered there. "Please," she begs pathetically. "If my son's in trouble, I should know."

"Why do you think he's in trouble?" Cecchi asks.

She points at us.

"We told you," he says, "it's a routine thing."

She straightens up, the blue eyes inclement now. "I am not a stupid woman, Detective. You may think I'm a cosseted creature, reading old books, lounging in my solarium, but I'm much more than that."

I'm beginning to like her, or at least I'm gaining respect for her.

"Do you have children?"

They always ask this.

He says yes, and when she looks at me I shake my head. She turns back to Cecchi.

"How would you feel if it were your son?" she asks.

But Cecchi has been here too many times and is unmoved. "It's not," he says simply. Then, "Tell me, what does Harrison do for a living?"

"He's a doctor," she says.

It doesn't matter what they do, their education or lack of it; they're all capable of rape, perhaps murder.

"What kind of doctor?" I ask.

"A psychiatrist."

Why did I know she was going to say that? We thank her again and leave.

◆

Psychiatrists are often connected to hospitals, so Cecchi has asked for a rundown on Harrison Webster at all the hospitals in Cleveland, even though we're almost positive that his name will not turn up.

We decide to have lunch at Woody's, on Seventh Avenue, in the Village. Years ago this place was a gay bar called Page Three. In the back, where we sit in a wooden booth, there used to be nightclubtype tables, those small round ones that hold two drinks and an ashtray. And they had entertainment. Where there is now a fake fireplace there was once a small stage. Tiny Tim, among others, played here. What ever happened to Tiny Tim? Hell, what ever happened to gay bars?

Not specialty bars like they still have for men, but regular, ordinary gay bars where both men and women went to drink, dance, talk, meet someone. What happened to them? The names tumble through my mind: The Grapevine, John's, Lennie's, The Bagatelle, Seven Steps Down, The Prego, The Provincetown, The Sea Colony, Club 28, Bonnie and Clyde's, The Laurels, The Duchess. Some of them were before my time, but some I frequented, and a feeling of nostalgia almost sinks me. Where do women go now to meet each other? I wonder. They don't. They answer personal ads and talk over modems. The circle closes.

I order my favorite meal here: quesadilla with chorizo. Afterwards I'll have the mudcake. In deference to my cholesterol count, I'll skip the whipped cream.

Kip's on her lunch break too, so I call her to see if she's heard anything new about Tom. She has.

"Sam wants to talk Tom into coming back to New York when he gets out of the hospital."

I wonder if Tom *will* get out. Some don't. Some AIDS patients go very fast.

Kip says, "They still have their place on Saint Marks. They sublet it month-to-month."

She tells me this as if it's information I don't know. I say nothing, let her go on talking. It's what she needs to do.

"I hope they'll come back. I . . . I . . ." Kip begins to weep.

I feel helpless. Her crying, though I know it's good for her, hurts me. When she sniffs and I sense the major tears are over, I ask her if she'd like me to come home.

"Oh, darling, thank you, no. I have a patient. A new one. Got to pull myself together."

"Let's go out tonight," I say.

"Only if you promise you won't eat anything bad for you."

"Who're you, the food police?"

"Sorry. Where do you want to go?"

"You pick a place. Let's go somewhere nice."

"Actually, Lauren, I'd like to go somewhere awful," Kip says, her sarcastic self again.

I laugh. "I love you," I say.

"Me, too . . . you."

Suddenly I get an idea. "Kip, have you ever heard of a psychiatrist named Harrison Webster?"

"Yes, why?"

My detective's heart skyrockets. "How? Where?"

"He's fairly well known."

"Well known in connection with what?"

"He's a leader in his field, works with sex offenders."

It's almost impossible to describe what I feel. But beyond the shock, there's the thrill of the chase, the excitement of closing in. "Does he work in New York?"

"Boston," she says.

"Boston."

"I can look him up if you want me to."

"Look him up?" I ask, like an idiot. Why hasn't this occurred to me before?

"Yeah, here it is." She gives me his phone number and address. I barely say a civil good-bye before running up the stairs to the restaurant.

"Cecchi," I say, sliding into the booth. "I've found him."

He's shoveling in a forkful of Huevos Rancheros. "Found who?"

"Webster."

Head bent over his plate, he raises his eyes, his brows two peaks of wonder.

I tell him.

He puts down his fork. "Sex offenders," he says, shakes his head.

"It makes a kind of sense."

"*What* kind?"

"It's complicated."

"What is it with these shrinks? They're all fucking nuts! Except Kip," he says quickly. "Except her."

I smile. "I think they're all nuts, too. Except her." I look longingly down at my quesadilla. "Should we go?"

"Go where?"

"To Boston."

"For what?"

"To pick up Webster."

"On what charge, Lauren?"

"Oh, right." I'm somewhat relieved because now I can eat my lunch, which I begin to do.

Cecchi says, "I'll have my guy in Boston run a make on him, but I don't expect anything. Then we have to wait."

"For what?"

"For him to try to kill Chapman, rape somebody else, or make a date with you."

"Terrific choice," I say.
"Eat."
I do.

◆

After lunch I mention my anxiety about Gordon Peace, and Cecchi goes with me to the building on Greenwich and Tenth. A different doorman's on duty, and after Cecchi flashes his shield we're led to 2G by the super. A familiar odor, though not rank, infiltrates the hall, and we exchange knowing looks.

"It's a studio apartment," the large man says, as if this will explain everything, including evolution. He shoves a key into the lock and opens the door.

The smell hits us immediately, and I put a hand over my nose and mouth.

"Jesus!" the super says, gagging.

Cecchi takes out his linen handkerchief and puts it to his face. We all know approximately what we're going to find. The super steps to the side and lets Cecchi go first. I follow.

Gordon is lying on his back on the bed. If not for the smell, the knife stuck in his chest, and his black face, you might think he was asleep. My book's on his night table, but I know I can't take it now.

"Didn't anybody complain about the smell?" I ask the super, whose face is whiter than a stripped stick, his meaty hand still clapped over his mouth and nose.

Holding his breath, he says, "Yeah. Da people nex door. I taught it was a dead mouse in da wall, a rat maybe. Happens a lod."

"Let's get out of here," Cecchi says. He tells the super to lock up and not to let anyone in until the forensics team and the M.E. arrive.

In the lobby Cecchi makes the essential phone call.

"How the hell did you know?" he asks me.

"I didn't."

Cecchi asks me why I suspected something, and I tell him about the book. I feel terrible. It's bad enough when anyone is murdered, but when it's someone you know, even as slightly as I knew Peace, there's a feeling of disintegration, collapse, the planet whirling out of its orbit. Somehow, though you know the world's not a safe place, especially if you're in my business, and especially in New York, you get through the day by relegating that knowledge to a secluded corner of your mind. And here we are, back at denial again. My good old friend.

I don't want to stick around for the procession of lab people, forensics, photographers, and all the rest who go hand in hand with murder. And chiefly, I don't want to watch Gordon being carried out in a body bag, another anonymous corpse.

I tell Cecchi I'm leaving. He understands and reminds me to get the laptop to him ASAP.

I go back to my office. When I open the door and step inside, I immediately feel that someone's been there. But I'm wrong. Someone *is* there. And by the time I realize that, it's too late. The blow to the back of my head registers painlessly, but I see stars, like the ones in cartoons, and as I'm falling, I think of Elmer Fudd.

Chapter

Twenty-one

MY EYELIDS are glued shut. I push them open. What I see is dust and red-brown wood. It only takes me three or four months to realize that I'm lying down . . . on the floor . . . in my office.

The back of my head feels as if it's caved in. I lift an arm that weighs six hundred pounds and reach around to touch where it hurts. My fingers slide, as though they've discovered an oil spill. But when I bring my hand back to where I can see it, there's blood on my fingers, not oil. This startles me and also makes my stomach lurch. Although I'm lying down, I swoon. I'm not good with blood.

I hate this about myself because it's such a cliché. Still, I can't help it. I didn't always feel this way. It happened for the first time when I saw Lois lying on the ground, blood seeping from her mouth, blood staining her yellow blouse where my bullet had struck. Since then I've felt woozy at the sight of blood, especially my own. But even Cecchi doesn't detect my phobia. Only Kip knows.

Kip. I want her. I need her. I'm not sure I can get up. Slowly, I turn my head on the point of my chin, and it feels like I'm weighted down by sandbags. Even from this humble point of view I can see that my office has been tossed. Papers cover the floor, and I can imagine the rest.

I must get up and get to the phone. I look at my watch. Kip's in session and won't pick up. I think about who I'll get on one try because I'm not sure I have more than that in me. What day is this? Will Jenny or Jill be at the store or at home? Or will they be on one of their day trips, looking for a house to buy? I count the days, and when I think I have it right I'm almost sure that one or maybe both of them will be at work.

What would Pam Nilsen do now? The trick is to get up and to my desk, where the phone is. This is not easy. Not when Roseanne Barr is sitting on you.

I want to sleep but resist. Instead, I send a command to my legs, and unhurried, they creep into a kneeling position. Next I recruit my arms, pull up so that I'm on my elbows. Elbows and knees. This seems like a fine position, and I think I'll conduct my life from here. The trouble is, I can't reach the phone.

I lift my head. Whoa! The world spins, but I hold my pose so I don't drop to the floor again, as this would be disastrous. I fix my gaze on a wall stain until my dizziness abates, then begin the crawl to my desk. Now I know how Admiral Perry felt.

It is the year 2065 when I touch the leg of my chair. The haul up is long and arduous, the pain thunks in my head. I make it. Sitting at my desk, I see the room swirl again. I wait it out, eyes closed. When at last I feel still and open my eyes, the room is as I imagined: in chaos. Every shelf is swept clean, every drawer emptied, all my files are on the floor, and the Toshiba is gone.

Fortunately I have a memory phone, and I push the button for Three Lives.

"Three Lives," a voice says.

"Jill?"

"No. Who's calling — Lauren?" It's Jenny.

"I need help. My office." I drop the phone, and out I go.

◆

The emergency room of any hospital in New York City is a nightmare. Saint Vincent's, in the Village, is no exception. I lie on a gurney, where I've been for the last ten years.

Jenny and Jill are not allowed to be with me and are in the waiting room. At least, one of them is. The other has gone to get Kip.

The noise level is almost beyond bearing. A variety of nauseating smells assaults my nostrils, but I've smelled worse. Gordon Peace smelled worse.

There are several battered women here. Perhaps because I'm lying down I'm able to look at their bleeding, bashed-in noses, blackened eyes without fainting. I notice that these women don't look at each other but sit slumped in their chairs, guilt splashed across their pummeled faces, as if this horrifying state is their fault.

A young white girl sits in a corner, her head between her knees. She wails. No one pays attention.

A black man sprawls in a chair. There's a long, bloody cut through his khaki shirt from shoulder to waist. No one pays attention.

A Hispanic woman holding a baby that never stops crying has burns covering her arms. No one pays attention.

A drunken white man vomits. No one pays attention.

Except the white woman he has vomited on. She jumps up. "Oh, God," she screams. "Oh, my God, will you look at this." From the elbows, she holds up both arms, hands at her shoulders, fingers wiggling like worms in hot ashes. A dark-green leather bag hangs from the crook of one arm.

Her tan-slacked thighs are covered with vomit. I take a good look at her. She's in her late twenties, with brown hair worn in an old-fashioned pageboy. Gold jewelry adorns her neck, gold loop earrings hang from her ears; an expensive watch is on her left wrist, a bracelet on her right. Her face is carefully made up, nothing smeared. I wonder why she's here. There's no blood, no burns, nothing out of place except for the vomit that runs down her pant legs.

"Jesus," she goes on. "Somebody do something."

No one pays attention.

She looks at the vomiter. "Do you see what you did?" she asks him.

He stares.

"Do you see?"

"Yeah," he says, head bobbing as if it's a buoy.

"How could you do that?"

He stares.

"What am I going to do?" she asks him.

"Huh?"

"Are you crazy, or what?" she says. "You barfed all over me."

"Barfed," he repeats, and I see that he's going to smile.

"It's not funny," she whines. "What am I going to do?"

"Shut the hell up," someone yells.

The young woman becomes enraged as she looks in the direction of the yeller. She walks toward the voice and out of my range of vision. But I can still hear her.

"Are you out of your mind?" she says to him. "You're telling *me* to shut up?"

"Yeah. Shut the fuck up. And get away from me. You stink."

I hear a huge intake of breath, like shock, and I know it's the woman. "*I* stink? *I* stink?"

I wonder why she finds this so incredible. Surely she must know that the vomit smells.

"Don't you know that that — that drunken maniac did this to me?"

"Still stinks," the man says, sensibly.

"This is an outrage," she screams, and now she's back where I can see her. Her face is red; eyes bulge.

"Is there a doctor here, or what? I mean, what is this, anyway? What kind of place *is* this?"

"It's a fuckin' 'mergency room, lady," someone says. "Where ya think ya are, Bloomindale's, somepin?"

There's a smattering of listless laughter.

She goes back to the perp. "Why have you done this to me?" she asks, in what passes for a reasonable tone, even though it's an unreasonable question. Her arms remain up; the bag still swings from her arm.

The drunk looks at her, surveys his damage. " 'Why?' " he says. "Huh?"

She looks wildly around the room for someone to speak with, a person in charge. But there's no one. She bursts into tears. I would like to choke her.

"Miss," I call out, hurting my head. She doesn't hear me, so I try again. This time she hears and sees me, stops crying, and takes tentative steps in my direction. She stands back, obviously afraid that I'm going to do something to her. The smell reaches me. I raise a hand and crook a finger, urging her to come closer because it's difficult for me to raise my voice.

She stands her ground. "What is it?" she asks suspiciously.

"Go to the bathroom and wipe it off," I say.

"What?"

I repeat this wisdom, but she still can't hear me and won't come any closer.

A man next to me says in a loud voice, "She said, 'Go to da batroom and wipe it off,' fer Crissakes."

The woman looks as if she's been told something totally outlandish. "*I* should wipe this off? *I* should do it?"

"No," the man says, "you should get Sly Stallone to lick it off, you stupid bitch."

"How dare you?" she says haughtily. "I come in here with a toe that's probably broken, and no one cares. Then I'm barfed on, abused, ridiculed and —"

From behind me a woman yells, "Go fuck yourself!"

The vomited-on woman screams as though she's been mortally wounded and runs from the room.

There's weak applause.

Now that the woman's gone, I feel the pain again and wish she was back, distracting me. I run some thoughts through what's left of my mind:

Who tossed my office?

Why?

Who slugged me?

Does it have to do with the rapes?

Does it have to do with Lake's murder?

Is it significant that the laptop was taken?

Does it have to do with Gordon Peace?

Are they all connected, or all separate?

And then a doctor approaches me and starts to do his job.

◆

When I open my eyes, it is raven-dark. It takes only moments for me to realize I'm in a bed, sheets crisp, comforting. As I become accustomed to the lack of light, I begin to see. A chest of drawers, a television, a chair — I'm home!

Someone is in the chair. "Kip?"

"Yes, darling?"

I pat a place on the bed and she sits. Her cool hand strokes my brow, gently pushes hair off my face. I feel her lips lightly brush mine.

I say, "I don't want to ask what happened, but what happened? I mean, I know what happened, except for a piece of time between the hospital and here. No. I remember leaving the hospital with you, Jenny, and Jill. And I remember coming home . . . and I remember your undressing me and putting me to bed."

"Then you remember it all, honey. You've been sleeping since then."

"How long?"

"About six hours. It's four now."

"In the morning?"

She says yes, and I ask her what she's doing up.

"I've been out dancing and I just got in, so I thought I'd look in on you for a sec."

I smile in the dark and wonder if this is like a tree falling in the forest when there's no one present.

"How's your head?"

"What head?"

"Do you know who did it?"

"No."

"Cecchi says your office was tossed."

I love it when Kip uses words like *tossed.*

"What would anyone want in *there?*" she asks.

"You don't have to make it sound like the La Brea Tar Pits."

She laughs. It's a lovely sound, and my lover's heart trips over itself.

"I think you should go back to sleep."

"I'm not sleepy. Why don't you get into bed?"

She rises and walks around to the other side. I feel the bed exhale as she joins me. Our bodies touch; we hold hands.

Kip says, "Do you have any idea what the person was looking for?"

"None. But it must have something to do with the rape and murder case." I tell her that I think they may be separate situations and who the suspects are. Now that Whitey Huron and his nonexistent wife are out, there are five: Helena, Ursula, Mark, Terrence, and the rapist, whom I can't exclude because I could be wrong.

"I'm scared," she says seriously.

Here we go.

"Someone tried to kill you, Lauren."

"Believe me, if the person wanted to kill me, I'd be dead. I walked in on someone looking for something, and he or she had to conk me or get caught."

"Somehow this doesn't put me at ease."

"Kip, we've been over this so many times. It's a dangerous business, but the point is I'm okay now."

"You're not okay. You have a concussion and you have to stay in bed."

"For how long?" I ask warily.

"Let's go to sleep," she says, dodging ineffectively.

"How long?"

"At least a week."

This is impossible, but I don't say anything now because it'll serve no purpose, rile her up. I grunt to show I'm upset; otherwise it won't ring true.

Now *I* try a dodge. "Why are therapists all so nuts?"

"Thank you very much."

"Except you," I amend quickly.

"I've told you before, most therapists go into it because they're neurotic to start with. Read Alice Miller."

"I don't want to read Alice Miller. Kip, remember Harrison Webster I asked you about?"

"Yeah?"

"We're almost positive he's the rapist."

I feel her shock as she sits up. "Are you serious?"

"Very."

"Jesus Christ! I've heard him speak. He's brilliant. Why do you think he's the one?"

I tell her about the connection to the Easton School and Jane Chapman's I.D.

"She could be wrong, of course," Kip says. I understand her desire to protect one of her own.

"Could be, but I don't think so."

"And . . . Lake's murder?"

"I'm not sure."

"Harrison Webster couldn't be a murderer, Lauren."

I note that she doesn't say he couldn't be a rapist, and I point this out.

"It's different," she says softly, as though those words might be enough to condemn him.

"Why? My rapists were murderers."

I see the faces of West and Bailey, smug, arrogant, angry. I was theirs to do with as they liked. I imagine it's the same with Webster. He takes what he wants. What's yours is his. There's no regard for a woman's right to her own body. Power is the key. And taking a life is all those things and one more. To take a life is to . . . conclude. The victim of a rapist, though damaged, goes on; the victim of a murderer is eradicated. It's the paramount power, the ultimate act, irrevocable. Still.

"Tell me why you think Webster isn't a murderer," I say to Kip.

"I can't. It's a feeling."

I trust Kip's feelings. Besides, it fits my theory, so it must be right!

"Do you want anything?" she asks.

"No."

She slides down next to me again. "I hope you're wrong about Webster. I mean, I want you to catch the rapist, but I hope it isn't him, hope your perp isn't a therapist. Or your murderer. We have such an awful rep as it is. I don't relish hearing about this hour after hour for days, weeks, months. You can't imagine how gleeful patients are when a therapist turns out to be less than perfect. They love it. And use it. It's a goddamn nightmare. I could joyfully have punched out Janet Malcolm's lights."

"I remember," I say.

"You'd better get some sleep," she says.

"You too. What time's your first patient?"

"I canceled them all."

"You didn't have to do that." Now she'll be watching me all day, and I won't be able to get to the computer.

"Yeah, I did. Sure you don't need anything?"

"Sure."

"Good night, honey."

"Night."

I lie there on my back, my eyes open.

"Lauren?"

"What?"

"Close your eyes."

"How do you know?" I ask, amazed.

"I know. Close 'em."

I do.

"Now turn off your mind."

"I can't."

"Yes, you can. Use what I taught you."

She's referring to self-hypnosis. It's often been helpful, and I can't think of a better time to use it. Carefully, as if my head were made of paper, I turn onto my side and close my eyes. Kip spoons me. Then I say to myself, over and over, *Puppy, puppy, puppy.* Okay, so this isn't the way Sharon McCone puts herself to sleep. I can't help it. *Puppy, puppy, puppy.*

◆

At two in the afternoon, Cecchi comes to see me. I'm in bed because the warden has insisted.

"You look like hell," he says.

"Thanks."

"You know what I mean. How do you feel?"

"Like hell."

"Right."

"Find out anything?"

"Some latent prints in your office match prints found in Lake's apartment. They're not on file. And get this: we found the same prints at Gordon Peace's place."

"I knew it," I say. "So there *is* a connection."

"I don't get it."

"Neither do I. But we will, Cecchi."

"Then there's the other set of prints."

I start to arch an eyebrow, but it's too painful. He understands anyway.

"Both at Lake's and at Chapman's. No make on them either."

"They're probably Webster's."

"Probably. But we can't pull him in, print him on a *probably*."

"Right."

"Can't pull *anyone* in yet. By the way, the laptop wasn't in your office," he says.

I'd forgotten. That's what he/she wanted. This points to Webster again, and I say this to Cecchi.

"I know. So now you don't even have the list of places, huh?"

I explain about Kip's computer. He asks for a copy of the Telix directory, and I tell him where the backup disk is. We agree that catching Webster in the act is the best way to get him and to keep him behind bars. Even Chapman's I.D. won't be enough. Cecchi agrees to let me go on trying to make contact with Webster while he puts a twenty-four-hour watch on him, if he can enlist the help of the Boston cops, which he's sure he can do. Meanwhile, other people in his office will work with the Telix directory. This irritates me, but there's nothing I can do.

After he leaves, the phone rings. I pick it up.

Susan says, "I suppose you think getting knocked out and having a concussion is an excuse for skipping lunch?"

"Oh, no," I say.

"Oh, yes. Today. One-thirty."

I still haven't met her for lunch. At least this time it's not my fault.

Susan goes into a riff, imitating the voice-over of a movie ad: "They tried to have lunch. *Neeneeneenee, neeneeneenee,*" she trills. "*Something* kept them from it. *Neeneeneenee, neeneeneenee.* Everything was in place, the date was made. But over and over and over again . . . *something* changed their plans. What was it? *THE LADIES WHO DIDN'T LUNCH*. Coming soon to a theater near you." She hangs up.

I laugh.

If Ursula and Mark are in on this together, why would either of them have killed Gordon? Maybe he saw something. But what? Unless he actually witnessed the murder, he wouldn't have been a threat to them. And that would apply to Helena and Ford, too. I rule out his having been a witness to murder; it doesn't jibe. Christ! It comes back to Harrison Webster.

Gordon must've seen them together and . . . but Webster wouldn't know Gordon, wouldn't know that he'd seen them. Unless Gordon tried to blackmail Webster after reading about the rape and murder. How would Gordon have known where to find him? He wouldn't. My mind is mush. Webster has to be caught so we can rule him in or out as the murderer.

I have to get back to the bulletin boards; they're the best chance I have of setting Webster up. I'll stay in bed for two days.

Compromise in marriage is everything.

Chapter

Twenty-two

―――――――――――

"YOU HAVE modem hair," Kip says, standing in the doorway of the study, staring at me.

"What?"

"And you probably have modem breath."

It's eight in the morning, the fourth morning after the attack on me. I've been back on the boards for a day and a night, and I can see Kip's still smarting from the fracas we had over my refusal to stay in bed longer.

She's wearing a gorgeous burgundy suede suit, a light-gray silk blouse, and high dark-gray boots. Even through my bloodshot eyes I see that she looks smashing.

"What's modem hair?" I ask, numbly.

"It's like hospital hair."

"Oh." I know what she means: flat in the back, unkempt. "I don't have modem breath," I protest.

"I'm not going to check it out," she says.

"Why are you dressed like that?" I'm terrified that it's really eight in the evening and we're supposed to be going somewhere.

"You honestly don't know, do you?"

It can't be night; I see light through the Levolor blind. I want to defend myself, try to make her understand that I've been working. But what would she think if she knew I'd been playing Galactic Wars with Larry ("Knavenut") Gomillion for hours? Should I pretend I know, or admit the truth?

"It's slipped my mind. The knock on the head," I dissemble.

"It's nothing to do with the knock on your head. It's because of your *modem* mind."

I ignore this slur. I also position myself in such a way that the monitor is hidden. On it is a piece of software that I've d/l'd (downloaded — had sent to me from a BBS through the telephone wires via modem), a graphics demo, totally useless but beautiful.

"What are you hiding?" she asks.

"Hiding?" I make the word sound as if she's insane.

"What's on the screen? Oh, never mind. I have to go."

Cute. She's not going to say where she's going. Okay, I can live with that. I'll find out tonight when she comes home. She's staring at me.

"Why are you looking at me like that?"

"Because I find it incredible that you don't know."

"Know what?"

"Where the hell I'm going."

Condescendingly, I say, "Does it really matter, Kip? I mean, is where you're going the be-all and end-all of my life?"

"Right." She turns away.

I jump up. "No. Wait." I don't want things to be like this between us. It's true that aside from my days in bed, we haven't seen much of each other lately, but I don't think we've been fighting.

She stops, stares at me again with those piercing eyes.

I come up to her — not too close, in case of modem breath — and touch her arms with the tips of my fingers. "Okay, I admit it, it's incredible that I don't know where you're going."

"Do you care?"

"Of course." Do I?

"Why don't I believe you?"

"Because you're a paranoid schizophrenic serial killer."

"Lauren . . . I think you need help."

I laugh.

She doesn't. "I'm not joking now."

"Because I called you a para—"

"Because you're addicted."

"To what?" I'm indignant.

"To the goddamn modem. I don't have time to go into this now, and I admit it's the wrong time to have brought it up, but I want you to think about it while I'm away."

AWAY!!!!!

"I've got to go, I'll miss my plane."

PLANE!!!!!

I follow her to the door, where I see her suitcase. It's the smaller one, so she can't be going for weeks or anything, though Kip knows how to pack light. Wait — it's coming back — a conference.

She picks up her bag. How long will she be gone? I realize I'm feeling as though I'm having an affair and being given the freedom to conduct it without the need for any machinations.

"I'll see you Friday," she says.

FOUR DAYS!!!!!

New Orleans! Yes, that's where she's going. To a conference on incest survivors, in New Orleans. Thank God, I'm not totally out of it.

Slyly I say, "I hope the weather in New Orleans is good."

She smiles, but I can't read it. "Thanks, toots."

We hug and kiss each other on the cheek (obviously both still worried about modem breath).

"I'll miss you," I say automatically.

"Me too. And Lauren," she says before closing the door, "don't forget to feed the cat."

"I won't."

It's minutes later, when I'm dialing The March Hare BBS, that I remember we don't have a cat.

◆

For three days I fend off friends. I sleep in spurts, two hours here, three there. My uniform is sweatpants, sweatshirt, leg warmers, and slippers. And I don't know why, but I've taken to wearing a Detroit Tigers baseball cap that's Kip's.

As for personal hygiene ... I brush my teeth. This morning I forced myself to take a shower. Tomorrow, before Kip returns, I'll wash my hair.

It's not that I don't miss Kip ... it's that I don't miss Kip. I've always enjoyed my time alone when she's gone away before, but this is different. Except when she calls me, I don't think about her. Fortunately I know this doesn't have anything to do with whether or not I love her. I know I love her. I just don't have time right now to miss her. No, it's more than that. I'm glad she's not here. If she were here I'd have to do things, like talk to her and have meals and be normal. I have only one day left, but I try not to think about that.

Food is a whole other question. I don't seem to get hungry anymore. Hours pass while I'm on the boards, and I realize I haven't eaten. When I remember, I find things in the freezer that I nuke in the microwave, or sometimes I just eat ice cream out of the container.

I've spent these past days sometimes as Lake, sometimes as me. Yes, I've registered at new places as myself. One BBS number leads to another. Sometimes people leave names and numbers on the boards as ads; sometimes someone suggests one in a chat or in a message. And then there are the 120 BBSs where Lake did not register. Most of these are always busy, so I can't get into them either.

But I've found my own places. There are several gay BBSs, but no women are on them. Still, the men are very nice to me and glad to have me aboard. WHERE ARE THE WOMEN? Except at the dating BBSs, women generally don't participate in this way of life because they're afraid of computers and modems. I'm disgusted at this, and then I remember that it was only weeks — days — ago that I, too, was computer-illiterate and frightened. I wonder if I should write a book about this. I see myself on "Oprah" and "Dona-hue." Obviously I haven't had enough sleep.

The software I've downloaded is extraordinary. Games, data bases, graphics, and other stuff. And then there are the new people I've met. Only hours earlier I had a long and interesting conversation with a new friend, The Major, about DNA printing. Later, when I looked him up in the Members' Registry, I discovered that he was twelve. So what?

But I've gotten no closer to finding Harrison Webster. I'm beginning to think that he doesn't stay on the boards where he's already made contact, like B&GT, where Jane Chapman connected with him.

He's not fooled. The mail to Lake is not from him. So I've been leaving messages as myself. Well, not exactly myself. I had to give my real name to the Sysop, but on the boards I'm Gilda, in honor of one of my all-time favorite Rita Hayworth movies. I'm also twenty-three and roughly fit Lake's description. I've made my interests close to hers, and I'm waiting. In fact, it's time to check into a few of the dating BBSs to see if Gilda has any mail.

I bring up my phone directory on my monitor.

And then I hear it.

A loud banging on the door. I try to ignore it, but I am the owner of a building. It's probably one of the PITAs with a complaint. I discern a touch of grief as I leave my computer and creep silently toward the front door. The banging continues, and then I hear his voice.

"Lauren, will you open up, I know you're in there." It's Rick.

I unlock the door and let him in. He stares at me.

"Why are you wearing that cap?" he asks.

I've forgotten that I have it on. "What's wrong with it?"

"Nothing. All this time, and I didn't know you were a jock. It comes as a stunning revelation."

"I hate baseball."

"So why are you wearing that?"

"It's too complicated to explain."

"You look horrible."

"Thanks." It seems people are always telling me this — a person could get low self-esteem!

"What're you doing, and why didn't you want to come to dinner last night? William made your favorite."

"It's not that I didn't *want* to come," I lie.

"Oh, it was that the President forbade it. I understand." Then he sees what I have laid out on the dining-room table. From the various BBSs there are reams of printouts of file directories (lists of available programs), rules and regulations, directions on how to use the individual boards, colored folders that will hold the information for each BBS, Scotch tape, stapler, pens, paper clips, and Magic Markers.

"Playing office?" he asks.

"I'm working."

"Lauren, you've become a computer nerd. Face it. You're losing your friends, your lover doesn't know what to make of you, and you have no life."

"Do you want to see it?"

"Your life?"

"The modem."

"What's to see?"

I try not to laugh in his face. I know Rick very well. "Follow me."

Three hours later, Rick is leaving. "Do you think I should go to J and R or Forty-seventh Street Computer? But I want a fax-modem . . . we don't know if J and R carries that, do we?"

"We don't," I say.

"I'll call around."

"When will you get it?"

"Today, of course."

When he's gone I experience guilt . . . I feel like a dope dealer . . . but it only lasts a moment.

◆

My monitor lights up the room like fireworks and I realize that it's night again. I log on to the Strangers in the Night BBS as me. I've stopped logging on under Lake's name because I realized that if Webster did murder her, this might tip him off that someone's on to him.

After I go through the usual procedure for logging on, words come up informing me (Gilda) that I have . . . *NEW MAIL*.

****NEW MAIL****

The two most exciting words in the English language.

I take the steps to retrieve it. There is only one letter, and I feel slightly dejected — but one is better than none. I hit a key, and the text appears before me.

```
Dear Gilda,
    I think we have a lot in common. Looking over
your dossier in the registry I was particularly
attracted by your interests in concerts, litera-
ture, spicy food, and tennis. They're my inter-
ests exactly. If you look me up you'll see my
profile, so I won't bother to tell you here what I
look like. Suffice it to say I don't think you'll
be disappointed.
    I'd like to begin a correspondence with you
that might lead to more. Sometimes these things
can move very slowly, and that's fine, but if you'd
like to speed things up I won't be adverse to that.
Naturally, we'll write to see if we really do have
mutual interests, but once that's established I
hope you'll want to meet. I know a wonderful Indian
restaurant on the Lower East Side, an excellent
place for cappuccino, and a theater that always
plays foreign films. I hope I hear from you soon,
Gilda. With high hopes, I am,
                              Valentino
```

I go to the users' directory and look him up.

Real Name: John McKenzie   Sex: M Age: 30
Handle: Valentino
City/State: New York, NY
Voice Phone #: N/A
Comp. Phone #: N/A
Favorite Movie: The Seventh Seal
Favorite TV Show: "Masterpiece Theatre"
Favorite Music: Opera & Classical
Instrument played: None
Favorite Foods: Italian, French, Indian
Favorite Sport: Tennis
Hobbies/Interests: Reading, films
Summary: I'm a professional, unmarried and looking
    for someone unafraid of discussing feelings

I reply immediately, agreeing with everything he says and expanding on the mutual interests.

And now I have to wait.

And it makes me crazy.

Because I know it's him.

Chapter

Twenty-three

VALENTINO AND I have moved as quickly as possible, and we are to meet this evening at The Ganges, an Indian restaurant on East Seventh Street. We have established the Indian connection. This man, if nothing else, is eclectic.

I haven't confronted Ursula about her lies yet, but I've kept her apprised of developments in the case, and she seems pleased at the progress. She doesn't know that I'm to be a decoy.

And neither does Kip.

We never lie to each other. It's not that we share every thought — each of us has her private musings and reflections, a necessary part of any successful marriage — but there's no duplicity. When dishonesty designs the frame of a relationship, the relationship is bound to crumble. Deceit breeds betrayal, and this becomes an end in itself. I've seen it many times. Kip and I have built what we have on verity and candor.

However, The Warden doesn't know about the meet.

I've chosen a fashionable gray wool dress and gray leather boots with pointed toes.

Kip comes into the bedroom between patients. She looks at me as if I'm insane. "Why are you dressed like that?"

"I felt like being in drag."

"Will you stop it? I'm serious. What are you up to?"

Obviously I have to tell her I'm going out. But where, and with whom? Oh, God. Lying tempts me momentarily.

I look her over. She's particularly attractive today. Her hair is the perfect length, half an inch above her shoulders, and she wears a blue-striped Gatsby shirt with dark-blue slacks. As always, she's employed subtle eye makeup, a blush, and a touch of lipstick. I both admire and desire her.

I think of Burl Ives giving his mendacity speech in *Cat*. I have to tell her the truth.

"You're not going to like this, Kip."

"Really?" she says, in mock shock.

"I'm meeting Harrison Webster for dinner."

She stares at me.

Neither of us says anything.

Kip sits on the edge of the bed.

"At least I think it's Webster. I have to," I state.

"How long have you known about this, Lauren?"

Uh-oh. She's heading toward a disloyalty charge. "A day or two."

"A day . . . or two?"

"Two."

"Why haven't you told me?"

"I didn't want to worry you."

"Oh, please. Don't give me that old saw. Where are you meeting him?"

I tell her.

"And then?"

This, of course, is the all-important question. Do I dare say "Then nothing," which is a distinct possibility but not the plan? Or do I lay out the probability, frightening as it may be to her? If I lie, it'll be a tear in the fabric of our union, but if I tell her the truth, we'll fight.

During our first years together, she always thought that a fight meant it was all over. And I had difficulty regaining intimacy. But we've both changed and now know that we can get past it, however uncomfortable or hurtful an argument may be. Still, I despise fighting with Kip because it leaves me feeling lonely as well as angry.

"Lauren? What happens after dinner?"

I have no real choice. "I'm taking him back to Jenny and Jill's apartment. Cecchi will be in the closet."

"Oh, Christ," she says.

"The other women waited until the second date to let him in their places, but we want to get this over with. Another cop will be there, too."

"You know there are always variables."

This is true.

"Kip, I have to do this."

"No you don't. Someone else could do it. How about a police-woman, for instance? You *want* to do it."

Right.

"And aren't you a little long in the tooth for Webster?"

"Thanks."

"You *are* forty-two."

"I know how old I am, Kip."

"You still think you look thirty, don't you?"

"I don't look forty-two," I say.

"You know what, Lauren? You do. That's exactly how old you look. Forty-two."

Death, there is thy sting!

"And you look forty," I say childishly.

"*I* know that. And don't try to turn this thing around." She gets up, paces. "Are you really going to put yourself in this kind of jeopardy?"

"It's not like this is the first time."

"Exactly. And I can't take it."

"Oh, so now this *is* about you."

She points a finger at me. "Look —"

"Don't give me *Look*," I say.

Her hands find her hips. "It's a stupid thing to do. Wait until I see Cecchi."

"You say one word to him, and . . . and . . ." I hate it when I can't think of a threat.

But she doesn't notice. "I'll say whatever I want to to Cecchi. I think this whole thing's outrageous."

"It's part of my job. Christ, you take your life in your hands every day with some of your patients."

"That's absurd."

"Is it?"

"None of my patients is dangerous."

"You've had referrals that've scared you," I say, hitting a nerve.

But she barrels on. "And I've refused them. Besides, I have never been knocked out, beaten up, shot at, or raped."

The word *raped* ricochets round the room like a wild bullet.

"I didn't mean that," she says softly. "I wasn't thinking."

I know this is probably true, but I have to ignore her apology or the argument will wilt. "I'm going, Kip."

"I can't stand it, I just can't."

The patients' buzzer sounds.

"For you," I say, as if this is news to her. I approach her. "Please let's not leave things like this. I'll be upset enough."

"Don't you dare," she says, eyes glittering wrath. "Don't you dare make me feel responsible if anything happens to you."

"I need your support."

"The hell you do. You're going to do what you're going to do, whatever I say."

"That's true, but it would be better if I knew you were behind me."

"Well, I'm not."

The buzzer again.

She starts for the door.

"Kip?"

She turns and looks at me, and anger-sparks seem to spray me like pellets.

"I love you," I say anyway.

"Go to hell," she says, and slams out.

I feel devastated. I know this isn't the end, that we will make up, but I worry that there'll be a small chink in the structure of us. There's always that risk, that danger. Too many chips can lead to erosion, erosion to ruin. Still, I have to — want to — go. I must depend on the depth and substance that I know our marriage has.

◆

Harrison Webster/John McKenzie sits across the table from me in the main room of the Ravenna Café. We've had our Indian meal and have come here for coffee and dessert, as Indian restaurants serve only instant coffee.

He resembles his yearbook picture somewhat, but he's disguised himself yet again, and I'm impressed that Jane Chapman was able to pick him out.

Webster/McKenzie is a handsome man who looks his age, mid-thirties. Despite Kip's doubts, my age hasn't arisen. I don't think he cares.

His eyes are green, and I've discerned that he's wearing contact lenses. I remember Lake's telling me his eyes were a "funny blue," and Jane's saying that they were brown. Does he have an endless supply of lenses? How many colors can eyes be?

He wears an expensive pin-striped gray suit, white shirt, and rep tie. The Easton School ring's on his finger. His hair is reddish, and I suspect that he's using a very good wig. No mustache.

I suppose one could say he's charming. It's hard for me to feel this, knowing what I do. And I can sense his psychosis. I have a built-in antenna for this, which may be due to the fact that there is one manic depressive, two schizophrenics, and a few depressives in my family — cousins, uncles, aunts. Whenever I'm around people who are more than neurotic, I feel something across the back of my neck, like a cold breath of air.

The only outward sign of his dementia showed when, at dinner, I refused wine. His eyes flashed, and it brought to mind Ted Bundy during his final interview, when he perceived that a background noise might be interfering with the taping.

Webster/McKenzie has told me he's a lawyer and that he lives in Chelsea, owns a brownstone. So far he hasn't offered his exact address or his phone number. How can he?

Smiling at me now, he looks up from under long, dark lashes, one dimple pleating a cheek. Chilling. I force myself to smile back, to make it seductive.

"I think," he says, in a honeyed tone, "that we seem to have a lot going for us, don't you?"

"It seems so," I say. I stare into his eyes, and though I know it's ridiculous, I feel they resemble the eyes of *my* rapists, both of them. My woman's heart hammers with fear. I know I mustn't turn away, and it takes all I have to keep looking into the soul of this madman. Eventually he breaks the gaze and tucks into his pecan pie. I breathe again and return to my piece of chocolate ganache cake. Even this dessert does nothing for my faltering fortitude.

I catch him taking a furtive glance at his watch. Does he have to make a plane back to Boston?

"Do you read Barthelme?" he asks.

"Which one?"

"Very good," he says, as if I've passed some test.

A rape test?

"Donald," he says.

"No. I prefer Frederick."

The calculated smile again. "So do I."

We discuss the Barthelme brothers while we finish coffee and dessert. Then he calls for the check. I tried to split dinner with him, but he hotly refused, maintaining that he was an old-fashioned

man. I don't go for the check now because he's established the
ground rules.

We leave and start toward Second Avenue. It's a cold night, but
pleasant. Evidence of snow is long gone. When I look at the sky I see
that the moon is full, and I remember that mad people are not
called lunatics for nothing.

"I'll take you home," he says, steps into the street, and hails a
cab.

As we ride toward Jenny and Jill's apartment, I wonder whether
I should invite him in now or wait until we arrive. He sits at a
discreet distance from me and chats amiably. I realize that I'm
frightened that he'll refuse me and I'll have to make another date.
It's possible that he rapes only when it's on his agenda. Still, I must
try.

"John," I say, attempting to sound casual and unafraid, "would
you like to come up for a nightcap?"

Even in the dark of the cab I can see his surprise, which quickly
turns to bewilderment then, as if he's making changes on a computer, clicks into acceptance. A flexible fellow.

"That would be very nice, Lauren," he says evenly.

I wonder if he has to tamp down his excitement at the prospect of
getting me out of the way in one date.

When we pull up in front of the Js' apartment, a wave of nausea
assails me, but by the time we're going up the outside stairs, that
symptom's been replaced by abject fear.

We've had the foresight to put my name in the space above the
bell for the Js', in case he should look. I feel him behind me, like
doom, as I try to put the key in the lock. My hand's shaking, and
there's nothing I can do to arrest my anxiety. Who am I kidding? My
terror is more accurate.

"May I help?" he asks.

I jump.

"You seem to be on edge," he says seductively.

I turn, smile up at him, and hand him the keys. He suspects
nothing, assuming my trepidation has to do with the possibility of
first-night sex — because after all, why else would I ask a stranger
up to my apartment?

Masterfully, he inserts the key in the lock and opens the door.
The consummate gentleman. We step inside.

"Second floor," I tell him, and don't take back the keys.

As we climb the carpeted stairs, I'm sure that Cecchi's not there.

This is based on nothing. And it's absurd. Cecchi would never let me down, never has. But what if on the way here he was hit by a car? Or had a heart attack? But he's not meant to be in the apartment alone. Another detective will be with him so we can have two witnesses. Even if something has happened to Cecchi, the other detective will be inside, or else he would've prevented us from coming into the building. Having thought this through, I feel slightly relieved.

We reach the door, and Webster holds the keys in the palm of what suddenly seems to be an enormous hand and looks at me as if to ask which one to use.

"The Medeco," I say.

He steps up to the door, opens it easily, and stands aside for me to enter. Will he grab me from behind? What if Cecchi doesn't hear anything? I snap on the light and we're in the part sitting room, part bedroom. The bed has taken on behemoth proportions. I wonder why he hasn't made his move, then realize the door is still open. Reluctantly, I close it.

Nothing happens.

I take off my coat and drape it and his over a chair. When I look at him, he smiles. Then, as if from far away, I hear myself say, "What would you like to drink?"

"I need to use the loo," he says.

Is this why he hasn't made his move? I wonder.

I lead him down the hall and show him the bathroom. All medications with either of the Js' names on them have been removed from the medicine cabinet in anticipation of this.

"I'll have a Scotch, neat," he says before shutting the door.

The closet, where Cecchi should be hiding, is opposite the bathroom. "Cecchi?" I whisper.

Nothing.

I try again.

Nothing.

The toilet flushes, and I have to go into the living room and make the drink. I stand at a small counter, pouring the Scotch, my back to the room. Sweat sizzles down my sides; my wool dress prickles me. I hear him leave the bathroom and enter the living room. I don't turn around, so he has the advantage. But out of the corner of my eye I see him sit on the couch.

I walk over to him and hand him his drink.

"You're not having anything?" he asks, a tinge of annoyance in his voice.

"I told you," I say patiently, "I'm on medication that doesn't mix."

"Oh, right," he says, as if he'd forgotten. "Mind if I ask for what?"

And it's then that I understand: I could have the clap, syphilis, herpes, or something as benign as a yeast infection. Dr. Harrison Webster doesn't want to take any chances.

"Antidepressants," I say. "Prozac." I know from Kip that this is one of the newest kinds.

"Oh, an antidepressant." I can hear the obvious relief in his voice as he puts his untouched drink on the table.

Then everything happens at once.

Like a cheetah, he leaps at me, knocking me backward and onto the floor. I think I hear him growl. Cecchi and another man appear, but before they can pull him off me, he rips my dress down the front in one swift, inhuman exhibition of strength.

I lie there, eyes shut, and listen to the delicious sound of cuffs snapping shut around his wrists.

"Lauren?" Cecchi says, alarmed. "You all right?"

I open my eyes and look into his. "Never better," I say, and burst into tears.

Chapter

Twenty-four

IN THE MORNING Cecchi comes round, bearing jelly doughnuts. His eyes are red-rimmed from lack of sleep; he's unshaven and wears the same clothes he wore last night. I pour him a cup of coffee.

"Is this some of your designer stuff?" he asks.

"Irish creme."

He makes a moue but picks up the mug and sips. "This is kid coffee."

"Throw it out and make some French roast."

"Nah."

I know he likes it but refuses to say so. He can be incredibly stubborn and annoying. Like now, drinking coffee, sinking his teeth into a doughnut. The jelly oozes from the opposite end, drops to his plate. And I wait, my coffee and doughnut untouched.

"Cecchi," I finally say.

"What?"

"Very funny."

He tries not to smile. "What? Oh, you mean Webster?"

I don't dignify this with a word, but just then Kip walks into the kitchen. We haven't made up yet.

When Cecchi brought me home last night, Kip was awake but obviously didn't want to talk. She observed my ripped dress, dryly asked if I had had a good time, saw that I was all right, and went to sleep. Or pretended to. Exhausted, I didn't encourage conversation.

"Morning," Cecchi says.

Kip glances at him, deciding whether or not to forgive him. "Hi," she says coldly.

Cecchi looks at me, and I shrug.

"Want a doughnut?" he persists.

"No thanks. Some of us watch what we eat," she says, eyeing my plate with disdain. She shakes shredded wheat into a white bowl, adds skim milk. "Is this private?"

I signal to Cecchi that I don't care.

"No," he says, and pulls out a chair for her.

She joins us, pours herself coffee. "I gather from the state of your dress you were successful."

Cecchi ignores her sarcasm. "There's no doubt Webster's our rapist. He was eager to confess, like he was proud of it."

"Harrison Webster," Kip says. "Christ, is this going to rock the psychoanalytic community."

"What a piece of work this guy is," Cecchi continues. "The way he talked about his victims, like they were nothing, had no feelings."

"And?" I ask, impatient to learn whether he's also a killer.

"He's raped a lot more women than the two we know about. Something like seventy-four, and he was still confessing when I left."

My mouth drops open.

"All over the country," Cecchi says. "Been doing it since he was in high school. Christ, this guy was clever. Says he didn't kill Huron. Or Peace, for that matter. Doesn't have an alibi, but his prints don't match the ones in Peace's place or your office."

"You believe him?" I ask.

"That he didn't kill her?" He puts down his doughnut and sits back in his chair, shoulders slumped. "I'm not sure. But with his prints at Huron's and no alibi, we're booking him for it."

I can tell Cecchi's not comfortable with this, but I know that unless new evidence turns up, Webster may stand trial and the case may be closed. If Cecchi's not totally convinced, then neither am I. *He* may not be able to continue the investigation, but I can. Ursula will call me off now, glad to accept the official version. Even so, I know I'm going to pursue this until I'm satisfied.

"Does he admit to burglarizing Lake's place, taking the letters?"

"Yeah. But not your place, Lauren, like I said. Somebody else wanted that computer for something."

But for what? To make it look like the rapist was after me? Or just to make it look like a burglary while whoever did it tried to see what kind of info I had? Both seem possible.

Cecchi finishes his coffee and rises. "Got to go. I'll keep in touch." He looks at Kip, then at me. "Thanks again, Lauren. See you, Kip, you look terrific."

She gives him a false smile.

"Right. I'm out of here," he says, and grabs his coat.

When he's gone, Kip says, "So you're right. One of the others killed Lake and Gordon."

"Seems that way to me."

"You still on this case?"

"I guess I am. I have to talk to Ursula."

"But she's one of your suspects."

"Right."

"If she's guilty, isn't she going to go along with the police, dismiss you?" she asks hopefully.

"Probably."

"But that won't matter, will it? You're going on with it no matter what, aren't you?"

"Kip, you know how you feel when a patient quits in the middle of treatment, quits at the wrong time, when you're on the verge of discovering something important?"

She sighs. This is tantamount to a concession; she knows I have her, but she won't verbalize it. Instead she says, "Do you want to talk about last night?"

"First tell me about Tom. Any news?"

"He has thrush now."

I know that this is a mouth infection usually found in babies and is also a common AIDS symptom. "Oh, Kip," I say, and reach across the table to take her hand. She doesn't push me away but remains passive.

"What are we going to do?" she asks. Tears fill her eyes and spill down her cheeks.

"Do?"

"I mean, I feel so helpless, Lauren, so goddamn out of control."

"You are," I say gently.

"And you going around putting yourself in jeopardy. I feel overwhelmed."

Now I grasp why she was so adamant last night, and I feel foolish that I didn't understand, didn't realize what she was going through. I get up and come around to her. "I'm sorry, darling." I put my arms around her and pull her to me, her face against my breasts. She wraps her arms around my waist.

"I'm sorry too," she says.

"No. You were right. I shouldn't have added to your worry."

"I was afraid — what if I lost you, too?"

She has leapt ahead, convinced that Tom will die. The evidence suggests that she's right, but he may have a lot more time.

"We have to stay in the moment," I tell her.

"I know."

I sit down, touch her cheek with the back of my fingers.

"I know you have your job, Lauren, but what you did seemed so gratuitous."

"It was, I guess."

"Tell me about it," she says.

I do.

"I guess you weren't ever in real danger," she admits reluctantly.

"No." I don't tell her about my own qualms. "Do you want me to give up the case?" I ask, only because of Tom.

"No. But please be careful. I couldn't bear it if you . . . you died. I wouldn't want to live without you, Lauren."

"That's a healthy attitude for a shrink," I say, smiling, trying to get us out of this morbid mood. But the truth is, I wouldn't much feel like going on without her, either. Oh, I would. And so would she. But it would be agony.

"I know how neurotic it sounds," Kip says, "but I can't imagine my life without you."

"Me too."

We kiss. It's not a sexual kiss — it arouses neither of us — but rather a kiss that says we are all to each other, comforting, reassuring, loving. We embrace for a long while and then, restored, break apart, begin to clear the table, enter real life once more.

As I start for the bedroom to get dressed, Kip says, "Lauren, I'm sorry about saying you looked forty-two. You don't."

"I don't?" I say happily.

"No. Forty-one."

◆

The weather has turned bitterly cold, and I wear bright orange-and-purple-striped leg warmers over my sweatpants, with long johns underneath.

In a doorway, someone lies wrapped in a blanket like a huge moo shu roll, and I thank God that it isn't me. I go for a container of coffee at my local Korean grocery. While I wait in line, an argument develops between a mother and her child.

"Why not?" the kid says. She's small and spindly.

"Because." To me the woman looks too young to have a child, but as I've grown older my perspective has changed; my assessment of age is way off. This woman, wearing a bright-red down coat that makes her look enormous, appears to be about twelve. I know this can't be so.

"Because why?"

"Because you're four years old. Why would ya need a breath spray? Ya have a date, or what?" She laughs, looks around for an audience, finds no one, and, slightly embarrassed, turns back to the kid. "Just shut up, Charlene."

"But I wannit," she whines.

"I said, *shut up*." This is through her teeth.

"Ya never buy me nothin', Ma."

She gives the kid a shove as it becomes her turn at the register. The child begins to whimper, cry, yowl. The mother grabs her by the shoulders.

"Charlene, I tole you to shut the hell up, and I mean it. Ya don't shut up, I'm going to play *Mommie Dearest* on the VCR again."

Through tears the kid says, "I *hate* that movie."

"So shut up."

She does. The woman pays, and then it's my turn.

As I approach my office, I notice a pain in my shoulder that runs down my back and into my right leg. A spasm of fear. The last time I was here, I was attacked. Reason reassures me this won't happen again, but the pain persists.

I open the front door. Joe Carter, wearing his Wolverine sweatshirt, is sweeping.

He nods to me.

I wonder if he knows about Gordon Peace. I ask him.

"Yeah, I heard. They know who done it?"

"No. I guess you were lucky to come around for the job when you did."

"Not luck. Had my name on file. Hear you got broken into."

"Yes."

"Too bad."

I don't know what to say to this.

"Got conked on the back of the head, too, huh?"

"Yes."

"Too bad."

I don't know what to say to this, either, so I tell him good-bye and start up the stairs. When I put my key in the lock, I can't stop myself from feeling frightened. But when I open the door I know immediately that no one's there, no one unauthorized has been there.

Kip and the Js have put my office back in shape, but I need to go through things to see what, if anything (besides the Toshiba), is missing. I take off my coat, open my coffee to let it cool, and start on my files.

An hour later I determine that nothing else was removed, and I feel more than ever that either the break-in was staged to make me think it was the rapist, or the perp was trying to see if I knew anything and, when I interrupted, had to take something.

By now Ursula must know about Webster's capture. I want to hear her reaction, and it's also time to confront her about her lies and her real connection with Mark Bradshaw.

◆

I've invited Ursula to lunch for two reasons: first, I don't want to chance the presence of Bradshaw at her place, and second, meeting in a restaurant is less formal, can put the interviewee off guard.

I've chosen Rose's on Waverly Place, on the east side of the park. It's a comfortable spot, not upmarket, though it's changed in the last two years from a deli to a deli and a restaurant. You can hear who you're talking to, and the food is good, cooked by Rose, one of the owners. Charlie, her husband, functions as a host manqué. Slight, sallow-skinned, he has pointy features but is oddly handsome. We've greeted each other, and now he sits at a table next to me with two neighborhood women, a blonde and a redhead.

Charlie says, "My wife looks at 'Dynasty,' her mouth hangs open. Bullshit."

"All I know is, I wish I was Crystal," the blonde says.

"Bullshit," says Charlie.

The redhead says, "I'd rather be Alexis."

"Nothing but prostitutes and fags," Charlie declares.

I sigh to myself and take a sip of my Tab as Ursula comes through the door. I wave.

"I've never been here," she says, sounding depreciatory, and sits down.

I'm always struck by the way people condemn things they haven't tried. Is it fear? "You'll like it," I tell her.

We peruse the menu. I order another Tab and the chicken salad plate; Ursula orders a manhattan and a small house salad.

"That's it?"

"I'm not very hungry," she says.

I wonder if her lack of hunger is due to anxiety over this meeting. We small-talk until the drinks come, and then I ask her if she knows about Harrison Webster. She does.

"So that's that," she says, too eagerly for my taste.

I shrug.

"You don't think he did it?"

"No."

"Then who?" Ursula unsuccessfully tries to smooth down her permed red hair, goes for her gold cigarette case, lights up her Nat Sherman. She blows smoke straight out into the room. "I assume it's all right to —"

"I remembered. This is the smoking section."

She gives me a tight smile of thanks, takes a sip of her drink, looks around the room, then back to me.

"You asked me who, Ursula. Why don't *you* tell me?"

"I don't know what you mean."

"Let's start with why you told me Lake was your half-sister?"

I wait for her answer. It doesn't come, so I repeat the question.

"She *is — was* my half-sister," Ursula insists.

"No. She wasn't. Are you going to tell me that your father's Whitey Huron?"

She swigs some of the manhattan. "What does the past have to do with it?"

I don't bother to tell her about Lew Archer, just say, "It may have everything to do with it. The fact that you lied to me makes me think so even more."

The food arrives.

Ursula orders another drink. Good. Maybe it will loosen her tongue.

"You can't be Whitey's daughter. I've met him."

A schoolgirl blush rushes to her cheeks. "Whitey was here?" she says doubtfully.

I don't answer.

"He hates New York. I can't believe he was here."

"I went there. To Hurley. Whitey would have been about fourteen when you were born."

Her second drink arrives, and she takes a gulp. "Whitey mowed the lawn. He left town when he was nineteen, but he — he'd always been nice to my mother and me. He knew my father beat us." There's pain in her eyes. And then she says flatly, "I hated my father."

"And that's why you said Whitey was your father?"

"Yes. I suppose it was something I wished were true, even though he wasn't that much older than me. Still, when he was nineteen and I was five . . ."

"I understand."

"Do you?"

A good question. My father's hitting either my mother or me is unthinkable. "Maybe I don't," I admit. "So your real last name isn't Huron?"

"No. It's Wise. Anyway, Whitey kept in touch with my mother. When I was twelve, he invited me to visit him at this commune in Vermont."

"And your parents let you go?"

"My father had left my mother by that time. She let me go."

"I'd like to talk to your parents."

Ursula presses her lips together, and I see a twitch at the corner of one eye. She doesn't like this idea.

"You can't," she says.

"Why not?"

"I don't know where my father is, and my mother . . . what does this have to do with Lake?"

I return her to her story. "So you went to visit Whitey when you were twelve. Tell me about that."

She lights another Sherman. The salad sits untouched on the plate, like an abandoned garden.

"He was living in this commune. It was like a farm. There were cows and pigs, and they grew all their own vegetables. But there were things . . . things that happened in the sixties . . . people did things then . . . it was a different time." She seems to examine my face carefully. "I'm sure you remember."

"Yes." Much about this case is being blamed on the decade of Flower Children.

"What kind of '*things*'?"

She shakes her head, and I know she's not ready to tell me *that* part, whatever it is. So I take her back to where we were.

"What about Whitey?"

"He was . . . was doing his art and was with Helena."

"He met Helena at the commune?"

She hesitates for only a moment. Maybe significant, maybe not. "Yes. There are things I don't remember."

"Like what?"

"How can I tell you if I don't remember?"

True. "So what happened? At the end of the summer you went home, back to your mother?"

Ursula finishes her drink, sighs audibly. "No. My mother went sort of nuts over that summer. Isn't that extraordinary? I mean, the man abuses her for years, and when he finally leaves, she goes crazy."

It's not extraordinary to me, though to some it might seem so.

"Did you stay with Whitey and Helena?" I already know the answer to this, but I want to see what she says.

"Yes. We moved to Hurley, and Helena . . . Helena had Lake. We were like a family. Lake felt like my sister. Why didn't Whitey tell you this?"

"He did. I wanted to see if your stories tallied."

"This isn't a story," she says indignantly. Too indignantly, I think.

I do my abrupt-switch number. "Are you and Mark lovers, Ursula?"

"I told you —" she starts angrily.

"You also told me a lie about being together when Lake was murdered."

"It wasn't a . . . oh, what's the point?"

"There isn't any. Why did you lie about that?"

"We were afraid. Well, actually, Mark was afraid. He knew how suspicious he looked because of his father's preference for Lake — the money, you know."

"And he doesn't have an alibi?"

"No. He was sitting in the park, thinking."

"About what?"

"Oh, God."

"What?"

"It's going to make things worse."

"Let me give you the facts of life, Ursula: right now you and Mark are at the top of my suspect list. It can't get much worse than that."

She looks at me, her eyes like moribund stars. "You still think *I* could've killed Lake?"

"Nothing's changed. Better tell me about Bradshaw."

She considers, acquiesces. "You're partially right. He's in love with me, and he asked me to marry him that day."

"But you're not in love with him?"

"I didn't know then, and God knows, I don't know now."

"What did you tell him?"

"A lot of things. That's why he went away to think."

"What things?"

"Personal things," she says, and her mouth snaps shut, forming a red stripe in her pinkish skin, like something censored. Personal things are going to remain personal things.

"So you didn't say yes to his proposal?"

She shakes her head. "But Mark didn't kill Lake any more than I did."

I'm starting to think this is true. Have I overlooked someone? Maybe my earlier idea, when I thought Ursula's mother was Whitey's ex, wasn't so far off. It seems even more possible now that I know she had a breakdown. She might've resented Helena, felt Helena had taken her daughter from her.

"Where's your mother now?"

"What's my mother have to do with anything?"

I'm tired of Ursula's asking questions. "Is she still in a mental hospital?"

"No." I recognize the expression on Ursula's face as one of humiliation and despair.

"Jail?" I ask.

She shakes her head. "I don't see what my mother has to do with this."

I don't reply.

"She won't tell you anything," she says angrily. "At least, she won't tell you anything pertinent."

"Let *me* decide that."

Ursula laughs, mirthless. "Fine. Finish your lunch and I'll take you to her."

Chapter

Twenty-five

═══════════════════

URSULA'S AGREED to keep me on the case. Although I lean less toward thinking of her as a suspect, I don't exonerate her completely. She's declined to tell me where she's taking me, but I assume that wherever it is, it's within walking distance, as we make our silent way through the park.

Homeless people occupy the benches as if they're apartments, their meager belongings stashed around them: crammed shopping bags, worn blankets, caches of stolen food. Every day it gets worse.

On the other side of the park we walk across Washington Place, and at the corner of Sixth Avenue I glance at the doorway of an unoccupied store. A young man with white hair, wearing an old khaki army jacket, guides a white rat from his shoulder into his breast pocket. I shudder. This is not my idea of a pet.

We pass Eighth Street, where I skip my usual perusal of books, and continue up the avenue. Finally, at Thirteenth, we cross Sixth and walk west. In the middle of the next block, between Seventh and Eighth avenues, is the home of the Gay and Lesbian Center. For a brief moment I think Ursula is taking me there, but we pass by it. A few yards farther on, we stop.

We're in front of a brownstone that looks like a run-down heel.

"She lives here?"

"No. Across the street."

On the other side there are more brownstones and two stores. I'm baffled.

"If she lives over there, why are we here?"

"Do you see the blue door?"

"Is that it?"

"Look to the left, near the garbage cans."

I see the cans and a huge pile of carpets.

"See the rugs? That's where she lives. She's underneath. My mother."

I can't get my mind around this concept and look at Ursula with uncertainty.

"What's the problem?" she asks me antagonistically.

I sense that the anger is shame, and I feel compassion for Ursula. How would I endure this if it were my mother? I can't think of what to say, but Ursula spares me from asking inevitably insensitive questions.

"When she was finally released from the hospital in New Jersey, she had nowhere to go, nothing to do. I wanted to take care of her, but she wouldn't come to New York. Then she disappeared.

"About a year ago I was walking along Bleecker Street, and there was this woman panhandling. I almost didn't notice her because, as you know, they're everywhere. But something made me look at her face. She was filthy, and her hair was totally gray, matted, and dirty. I started to walk by, and then those eyes registered, even though they were somewhat vacant. I stopped. She held out a grimy hand, waiting for money.

"It was strange. I couldn't call her Mom. I said, 'Marion?' She stared at me, looking frightened. I called her by name again, and this time she said, 'Yes. Do I know you?' "

"I'm so sorry." It's all I can think of to say.

"I've tried everything, but she doesn't want to live with me. She says she likes the streets. I keep track of her, bring her food, give her money. I suppose someday she'll freeze to death. Anyway, you wanted to talk to my mother. Good luck."

Ursula walks away.

"Where are you going?"

"Home. Did you expect an introduction?"

In fact, I did, but now realize the stupidity of this. "No, I . . . I'll keep in touch."

"Fine."

Staring at the lump of carpets, I'm unable to decide whether or not I should try to speak to the person under them. What can she tell me, after all? She didn't know Lake. She doesn't know Helena. Ursula was right: her mother has nothing to do with this. I turn to go, stop. Would Kiernan O'Shaughnessy leave without talking to this woman, even if there was nothing to gain? I cross the street and approach the rugs.

It's absurd, but I feel frightened. I have no practice in interviewing homeless people. I pass them all the time, but I never talk to them. I realize that I don't think of them as people with a past, a family, and I'm chagrined at that. Still, making the first approach is daunting.

Do I tap her rug?

Do I speak, in hopes of her hearing me through the layers of insulation?

Do I lift the front and expose her? What if she's sleeping?

Do I have the right to interfere with her privacy because she's a street person?

I'm in a quandary over this question of ethics when the rugs undulate, and she emerges.

Even in this crisp weather, the smell that comes from her makes me take a step backward. She's wearing a worn pea coat with two buttons missing, grubby gray sweatpants, and new-looking black sneakers. I wonder if Ursula gave them to her. There are no gloves on her hands, and the skin's streaked and stained a shade of burnt umber, as is her face.

I can see vestiges of the woman in the photograph in Ursula's apartment. When she looks up at me with her barren blue eyes, I again experience fear. But only for a moment, because an expression of mortification materializes, then almost as quickly as it surfaced, it vanishes, replaced by a hostile facade.

She squints at me. "What d'ya want?"

What *do* I want? "Marion?"

"You have any money?"

I open my bag, take out my wallet. "Is your name Marion?"

"Sure," she says.

There's something almost comical in the reply: *Sure*. If I'd asked her if her name was Dorothy or Sophia, would she've said "Sure"? "What's your last name?"

"Money," she demands.

I give her five dollars.

She's surprised and pleased, and smiles at me, exposing yellow, cracked teeth. I ask her her last name again.

"What the hell do you care, huh? What difference does it make what my last name is, am I going to vote or something, huh?"

"Do you have a daughter named Ursula?"

Is it a flash of recognition I see?

"Ursula," she repeats, with no expression.

"Your daughter."

After a few moments she says, "Go away."

I decide that this is foolish. There's nothing to be gained here. Then for some unknown reason I say, "Mom?"

She flinches as if I'd slapped her.

"Mom?" I say again. The word doesn't trip easily from my tongue since I've always called my own mother Mother.

This time she looks me over, and I feel lousy. Why have I done this? It can only be confusing to her. I open my mouth to explain who I am, but she interrupts me with a word that sounds like *uluna*.

"Ursula?"

"Elena," she whispers.

Elena? Have I heard correctly? "Who?"

Her mouth trembles, and her eyes are glossy. She stretches out a hand to me. This time the name is clear: "Helena?"

Helena. Why would she say her name? As far as I know, this woman never met Helena. Still, she did know her daughter lived with her. But Ursula said her mother was crazy — hospitalized — during the time she was with Whitey and Helena.

"Did you say 'Helena'?" I ask.

Her features twist into a furious visage. "You're not Helena," she charges.

"No. Do you mean Helena Huron?"

"Helena Huron." Contempt poisons the name.

"You don't like Helena Huron?"

"Albert," she says cryptically.

"Who's Albert?" Am I listening to the gibberish of a desperately sick woman, or is there some meaning to these names? Could there be another Helena? Who is Albert, and does he have anything to do with this case?

I'm feeling weary when she says, "Frank." Tears dribble down her cheeks. "Frank, Frank, Frank," she says reverently. Then again, wailing, "Frank, Frank, Albert."

What've I done? I kneel on the sidewalk, wanting to comfort this woman, but how? I'm sure she'll recoil from my touch. I've kicked up something in her past, and the scars from it haven't healed.

"Go away," she begs through sobs. "Go away."

I'm torn. I want to help her, even though I've been the perpetrator of her grief. I know that to stay would be for me, to assuage my guilt. The harder thing to do is leave, but this is what she wants. I take a twenty from my wallet and press it into her dirty hand, close her fingers around it.

My benevolence gags me.

◆

The Vivaldi, on Jones Street off Bleecker, has a handsome chocolate mousse cake. It's incredibly rich, even for me, and I only have it under extreme circumstances.

Like when I'm feeling guilty or depressed, or both, as I am now.

This café is dim, and I'm glad. It suits my mood. I sit at my table in the corner, sip my cappuccino, take a bite of cake. For the zillionth time I question the work I do. Can my prying and probing, my disruption of lives, the pain I cause, be exculpated?

What I do is not dissimilar to what Kip does (not a new thought), but the people she deals with *want* what happens. Or at least they're willing participants.

It's true that I was hired to find a rapist and murderer, and should I succeed, the end might justify the means, but what does causing a peripheral person like Marion Wise so much pain have to do with anything?

I try to tell myself that there might have been some connection between Ursula's mother and Lake's death, but it doesn't work. I have to face that it was my curiosity in an uproar, my selfishness prevailing.

I cannot excuse myself.

Still.

Something nags.

Or am I looking again for a pardon?

No. The names that Marion spoke bother me. Especially Helena's. And who are Albert and Frank?

I take out my notebook to add these names to the list of people connected to this case:

> *Lake Huron*
> *Ursula Huron* (I change it to *Wise*)
> *Helena Bradshaw*
> *Mark Bradshaw*
> *Harold Bradshaw*
> *Terrence Ford*
> *Whitey Huron*

Jane Chapman
Gordon Peace
Joe Carter

Joe Carter. I stare at the name, not remembering having written it. Why would I put his name on this list? It's true that something about Carter has always bothered me, but other than bartending after Lake's funeral, what does he have to do with these people, the Huron/Peace case, as I now think of it?

I take another bite of cake, close my eyes, picture Carter. I review the various exchanges we've had recently, and though I can't pick out the particular sentence, or sentences, I can *feel* that there was something within those conversations that's important. I make a note about this, look back at the list.

Zach Ellroy
Harrison Webster

And now I add *Marion Wise*, *Albert*, and *Frank*. I go to the phone, feed it my quarter, and punch in Ursula's number. She answers on the second ring.

After identifying myself, I ask her who Albert and Frank are.

"I have no idea."

"Where did you live with your mother?"

"Glen Ridge."

"You come from New Jersey?"

"Yes. Why?"

"I . . . me too. South Orange."

"I don't remember much about it."

Lucky, I think. "Why would your mother say Helena's name?"

Silence.

"Ursula?"

"I'm thinking," she says, irritated. Silence. "She must remember her name from when I went to stay with Whitey and Helena."

"But you said your mother went crazy that summer. How soon after you went to the commune did it happen?"

"Are you kidding? You expect me to know the date she went over the line? Anyway, there's a lot I don't remember about that summer. Sometimes . . ."

"Sometimes what?"

"There're whole chunks of time that are like blank pieces of paper to me."

"Why?"

Silence.

"Ursula? Why?"

"I don't know. What did she say about Helena?" she asks, firmly changing the subject.

I'm sure there's something she's not telling me, some important connection, but I know I'm not going to get it out of her now.

"She didn't say anything. Just her name."

I hear breath being expelled, like a sigh.

"I hope you didn't upset her too much."

"No," I lie.

"You can't pay attention to anything she says. She rattles off names. It means nothing. Like Albert and Frank. They're probably people she's met on the street. Maybe she's even met a Helena."

I'm not buying.

"That's probably it," I concur. After promising to keep her informed, I hang up.

I go back to my table, rummage through my notebook until I find what I'm looking for. The year that Ursula went to the commune was 1968. This would be the same year Marion was hospitalized. I have to find the hospital, and I have to see the record for Marion Wise.

Maybe Sue Slate would know why she had to do this, but I don't.

◆

Walking back to my office, I hear a male voice behind me offering, "Blow, crack, crank, anything ya want." It used to be that these offerings were made in the park, and it surprises me to hear this on Bleecker Street.

He keeps up the chant. I turn to look at him.

He's about eighteen, and at first he grins, but then his face collapses like a bellows. "Never mind," he says, running a hand over his spiky green hair.

Never mind? Has he made me as a P.I. so fast? If so, I'm in trouble.

"What do you mean, 'Never mind'?"

"Jus' never mind, ya know?" He shrugs and starts to turn away.

"Wait a minute." I touch his shoulder, and he pirouettes to face me.

"What?"

"I want to know why you said 'Never mind.' "

"Hey, lady, no big deal, okay?"

"No. It's not okay. Tell me."

He shuffles, sneakers squeaking. "You want to buy?" he asks suspiciously.

"No."

"See," he says, as though this explained all.

"No."

"You really wanna know?"

"Yes."

"You prolly ain't gonna like it."

"I'll try to take it like a soldier."

"Okay, you asked for it. From the back — I mean, me seein' you from the back — I thought one thing, but then when you turn around, hey, I knew you wouldn't be no customer."

Back, front — I don't understand, and I tell him so.

"Let's jus' forget it." He tugs on one of the five earrings in his left ear.

"What's the difference between my back and front?"

"Lady, from the back you could be anywheres from sixteen to thirty, but when you turn around, I says to myself, Whoa, man, this here's an old broad, and she won't want no dope. Okay? Happy now?"

No, I am not happy. I watch the retreating dope dealer shake his head from side to side, as if to say, *Not only is she Methuselah, she's dumb!*

Why should I feel so crushed that this person sees me as too old to buy drugs? There's something wrong with my thinking. I want this boy to view me as a prospective customer when he sees me from the front. Sick.

Slightly depressed after this encounter, I continue to my   fice. When I'm settled in at my desk, I call my mother.

"I was just thinking about you," she says, as always. If this is true, it means that my mother never thinks of anyone else but me. Why don't I find this hard to believe? We go through the usual amenities, and then I get to the reason I've called.

"If a person was in a mental hospital in New Jersey in nineteen sixty-eight, what hospital was it likely to be?" I don't think Ursula will tell me.

"Is this a riddle?" she asks.

"Yeah, it's worth five hundred thousand. Of course it's not a riddle. I thought you might know."

"Is this for your work?"

"Yes."

"It could be any one of several places. We're not talking Rhode Island here, you know."

She knows how much I hate New Jersey. "I mean in our area of the state. Someone who lived in Glen Ridge."

"Nineteen sixty-eight. Well, there would be two choices. Craymoore in Morristown or Forest Keys in Newark. But Forest Keys isn't there anymore."

"You know for sure that Craymoore is?"

"Let me look it up."

I wait.

She comes back. "It's still there." She gives me the phone number and address. "Are you going there?"

I knew this was coming. "Probably."

"When?"

I look at my watch. It's four-thirty. "Tomorrow."

"Do you want to come for dinner?"

"I'll probably come over in the morning."

"Lunch?"

"Do I have to decide now?"

"No. I'll be here."

"It'll all depend on time."

"It would be nice to see you," she says, trying to sound casual.

We say good-bye. I feel disturbed. Is it that I know my mother will be hurt if I don't come for lunch? Is it the idea of seeing her that gets to me? Is it that I have to go to New Jersey? It may be all three.

Spending time alone with my mother can be intense. She'll tell me inappropriate things about my father, their marriage, and won't understand if I ask her not to. And she'll undoubtedly be drinking. My coming to lunch will give her an excuse to start early. But I can't worry about that. I'm not my mother's keeper.

I don't know what I'll do about my mother. All I know now is that tomorrow I'll have to . . . cross the border.

Chapter

Twenty-six

THE TRAFFIC flows through the Holland Tunnel at a steady pace. With each spin of my wheels I grow more depressed. Does everyone feel this way when she approaches her home state? My breathing sounds labored, and as I exit the tunnel a pall settles over me, as though I've entered hell.

I tell myself that I'm here on business; that I'm not going *home*; that I don't have to visit my mother later.

I don't hear a thing.

By the time I get to the center of Morristown, my mood is so low that I decide to stop somewhere for a cup of coffee, the natural antidepressant, before I go to Craymoore.

Morristown is an attractive town, but I don't remember much about it from my youth. Occasionally Warren and I would go to the Community Theater for a movie. I wonder if the place is still there.

I find a parking spot and notice that I'm across the street from a luncheonette. The meter costs a dime for an hour, and I slip one in.

The place is called M.J.'s. Inside it's like almost any other luncheonette in America. A Formica counter with vinyl stools, booths, and a few freestanding tables. I take a spot at the counter.

The breakfast crowd is long gone; the remaining customers are all in their sixties and seventies, obvious retirees, reading a paper, doing a crossword puzzle, wondering where it all went and why the dream never happened. Will Kip and I look as lost and bored as these people when we retire? Somehow I think not.

The woman behind the counter has skin the color of a bruised gardenia; her black hair is piled high on top of her head. I order coffee, and when she returns with it I ask her if she knows where Craymoore is.

She eyes me with a sympathetic look. "Mother, father, or kid?"

"Business," I say.

"Sure, honey."

She clearly doesn't believe me. "Really," I say. Why do I care what she thinks.

She nods patronizingly. I have to let it go. She gives me directions, and when I finish my coffee and pay her, she says, "You shouldn't be ashamed. We all got at least one in our family."

I give her a craven smile, take my change, and leave.

The counterwoman's directions are impeccable, and I pull into the Craymoore parking lot six minutes later.

Craymoore is a two-story brick building. It resembles a Lego structure, as if a child had tacked on wings with no regard for style.

Across the front sprawls a porch where, I imagine, patients sit in good weather. The immense doorway opens onto a hall, and to my left is a reception desk. The head of the man behind the desk is bent over a sheet of paper; his crown is smooth and pink.

I wait for him to look up. Seventeen days later I clear my throat and he raises his head. He looks like Milton Berle playing Jack Nicholson playing the Joker.

"I'd like to see the administrator," I say.

He smiles as though he's caught me in a lie. "You don't have an appointment, do you?"

This is what the twentieth century is about: appointments.

I confess that I don't and flash my I.D.

"What's that?"

"I'm a private detective."

"You think *that's* going to cut any ice with me?"

"I'm investigating a double homicide."

"Double, triple — you still need an appointment."

"Maybe I don't need to see the administrator. Maybe *you* can help me," I say, trying to make him feel as though he were the most important person in the world.

"Me?"

"I'd like to know something about a patient who was here more than twenty years ago."

"You're right, you don't need the administrator."

"Do I need you?"

"Maybe. What do you want to know about this patient?"

"I'm not sure. I'd like to see her records or files or whatever you have on her."

"Can't be done."

I figure fifty will do it, and I slip it to him.

"What's the name and the year?"

I tell him.

"Come back in half an hour."

I spend the time in the car reading the new E. M. Broner book. When I return, the man gives me a manila envelope. Back in the car, I take out five photocopied pages. It's on the first page, in the biographical information, that I find what I need to know. Marion Wise was married twice. The first time, in 1943, was to a Francis Albert. Her first child, a girl, was born in 1944. Her name: Helena.

◆

I'm so angered by this revelation that I'm almost paralyzed. Having a client who lies to you is one of the worst things that can happen. Not only is it a waste of time, but it makes you — me, in this case — feel like a fool.

So Ursula is half-sister to Helena. She was Lake's aunt. Why the deception? Did Lake know the truth? No wonder Marion Wise knew Helena's name. And when I asked Marion if she meant Helena *Huron*, she said "Albert," meaning her daughter's last name. I thought Frank and Albert were two different people, but there was only one person: Frank Albert. Suddenly nothing makes sense, and yet I feel sure that this piece of information is key.

I see a phone booth and park the Raider. First I call Ursula and get her machine. I don't leave a message. The same thing happens when I try Helena.

Frustration makes me slam my door.

So deep in thought am I that I don't realize I've driven to South Orange until I make the turn onto my old street. I stop. What am I doing here? Is it some stupid primal urge to be comforted because I've been betrayed? I can still go back. My mother need never know that I was this close. But I don't. I drive up the hill of the dead-end street, turn around in the semicircle at the top, and park in front of my parents' house.

This is a deeply suburban neighborhood. The houses are close together, and everyone on the street knows everyone else, even if they're not intimate friends. My past, from age six through age eighteen, lingers here, ghostly yet enduring. I feel myself sinking into melancholy, but do I leave? You bet I don't. I pull the brake, turn the wheels into the curb the way my father taught me, get out, and approach the house.

It's painted white with green trim. Snow covers the small front yard and bushes. I walk up the brick steps, open the door to the closed-in porch. The inside door is locked. For an instant I think she may not be there, but that thought dies quickly as I remind myself that she's *always* home. I ring the bell.

Moments later I hear her footsteps when her high heels hit the floor, and instantly my childhood feelings of love and longing laced with sexuality erupt. She looks through one of the small panes of glass at the top of the door.

When she opens up, I immediately know she's been drinking. I have come to the hardware store for oranges. It's eleven-thirty; she used to wait until noon. I receive a too-tight hug, a sloppy kiss, and she tells me to sit in the living room. She doesn't want me to go into the kitchen because evidence of her drinking is there, and like most drunks, she thinks she'll be able to hide it from me if I don't see the glass, the bottle.

This house where I grew up is small: upstairs, three bedrooms and a bathroom; living room, dining room, kitchen downstairs. The old claustrophobic feeling skulks around my edges.

"Hungry?" my mother asks as she returns from the kitchen.

"No." She holds a coffee cup in her hand, but I'm sure that what's in it isn't coffee.

"Thirsty?" She raises the cup.

I tell her no and encourage her to sit down. "I don't have much time."

There's a flicker of disappointment in her eyes, but her need to drink overrides this. And it's there, in those hazel eyes, that I observe the absence of this woman, my mother. Was it always so? Was she never totally present?

I wonder about Marion Wise and how present she was for Helena, Ursula. And Helena, was she completely there for Lake? Or do all mothers check out in their own ways? Is it a necessary part of mothering, a defense of some sort? All people need an out from reality once in a while, but for most, seeing a movie or reading a book can suffice. This is different.

"Tell me about your case," she says, then sips her "coffee."

I do — more to listen to it myself than to share with her, because I know she'll only absorb some of it, like eating the skin on a pudding.

When I'm through she says jocularly, *"Cherchez l'homme!"*

" 'Look for the man'?"

"That's my guess," she insists, and downs the rest of her drink.

"What man?" Why am I paying attention to her?

"Now *that* I can't tell you. You're the detective, you'll have to figure that one out yourself." She rises. "Sure you wouldn't like something to drink? I'm going to have more coffee."

"No thanks," I say. "I have to leave." I don't want to stay around for the inevitable disintegration. Besides, I feel the house closing in on me, as if the walls were moving, the room becoming smaller.

"You always have to leave, don't you?" she snaps.

There's nothing to say to this.

"You think your life's so important." Her eyes shrink, squeeze out sparks of spite.

I've already stayed too long. I stand up. "I'm going now, Mother."

"You don't give a damn about me, you never have." She's heading for the pity pot, and I'm not going to play. I walk toward her, try to give her a kiss, but she jerks her head backward. I touch her sleeve. She recoils.

As I pick up my purse from the sofa she says, "Selfish. You've always been selfish."

"Good-bye," I say, open the door and close it behind me.

When I'm in the car I look back at the house and see her at the glass porch door. She motions, inviting me back. Pretending to misunderstand, I wave to her then start the car, turn the wheels, release the brake, hit the gas pedal, and drive down the street.

I detach without love.

◆

Incredibly, I find a parking space on Helena's block. Stuck with an emotional hangover from the encounter with my mother, I search for the rage I felt earlier at being duped by Helena and Ursula and find I'm able to dredge up only irritation. It'll have to do.

I ring Helena's bell.

"Yes?"

I know she sees me on the TV monitor. "I'd like to talk with you."

"Now?"

I check a smart-ass reply. "Yes."

She buzzes me in.

When I get off the elevator, she's waiting in her doorway. She wears jeans, a red and white scarf for a belt, and a black Gap pocket T-shirt. Her hair is loose, and I try to see some vestige of Marion Wise in her face, but it's impossible. Perhaps she looks like her father, Frank Albert.

"You should've called," she says, annoyed.

"I did. Your machine was on."

"If I'm home and the machine is on, it's because I don't want to speak with anyone."

"That's what I figured. But *I* need to speak with *you*. Don't you care about Lake's murder anymore?"

"I thought they'd caught the murderer."

"They caught the rapist. I don't think he murdered Lake."

"You know more than the police," she says snidely.

"Maybe."

Sighing, she steps aside to let me enter. We sit at either end of one of the white leather couches.

Helena lights a cigarette; the smoke weaves around her head. "Well, what do you want?" she asks brusquely.

I feel angry, so I'm blunt. "You don't look anything like your mother, so you must resemble your father."

"What's that supposed to mean?"

"I think that's pretty straightforward. Do you look like your father?"

"What do you know about my mother and father?"

"Let's put it this way: why didn't you tell me that Ursula is your half-sister?"

"You didn't ask."

"I'm not here to play games, Helena. You and Ursula both passed yourselves off as being unrelated by blood. Why? And while we're at it, why pretend that Ursula and Lake were half-sisters? Why couldn't she know that Ursula was her aunt?"

"It's complicated."

"So I'm beginning to see. I need to know the truth. Everything."

She stands up, paces, twists her bottom lip, paces some more. At last she stops in front of me. "All right. My father was killed in World War Two."

"Frank Albert," I supply.

"Yes. How do you know?"

Why do they always ask this? "It's my job," I say for the thousandth time in my career.

"I never knew him. My mother was pregnant with me when he died. And you're right, I do look like him." She unconsciously touches a gold locket on a chain around her neck.

"You want to show me?" I say.

A scanty smile gambols across her lips, and she bends down, flicks open the locket. On one side is a picture of a man, on the other a photo of Lake. Both resemble Helena.

"Yes, you do look like him. Lake too."

She nods, snaps shut the locket.

It touches me that a woman in her forties carries a picture of a father whom she never knew. The need for family is fundamental. "Go on with your story," I urge.

"My mother raised me alone. When I was ten she met Bob Wise." She spits out his name, as if something foul were in her mouth. "Then she married him when I was eleven and had Ursula the next year."

"And he was a batterer," I say.

"Yes. Ursula told you that?"

I nod.

"Then you know everything."

"Not everything," I say, beginning to suspect that more than battering went on. "Helena, I know this is hard stuff to talk about, but did Wise sexually abuse you?"

She twists the ends of her belt-scarf around her two forefingers until the tips are purple. "Why is this pertinent?"

"It might not be," I say truthfully. "Then again, it might."

There's a long silence, and city sounds resonate like a reticent ensemble. Helena stubs out her cigarette, lights another. Finally she whispers that yes, he abused her sexually.

"Was he Lake's father?"

"Oh, no," she answers. "I got out when I was seventeen. Lake was born when I was twenty-five."

"Then Whitey really is Lake's father."

She nods, walks away, looks out the window.

I accept this, deciding to bring up Zach later. "What about your mother?"

"What about her?" she asks, the words like chips of ice.

"Do you see her?"

Helena turns around, face broadcasting fury. "I've *seen* her. And so have you, I'll bet. Did Ursula show her to you?"

"Yes. Why are you so angry with her?"

"Because she knew what Bob Wise was doing and did nothing about it."

Same old story. I don't question her about this because I'm sure it's true, and though Marion was probably afraid to do anything, I understand Helena's rage.

"You and Whitey got Ursula out of that house because Wise was abusing her too, is that right?"

"What did she say?"

"I didn't ask her that."

She hesitates. "Well, yes, that's right."

"And yet you're not friends now. Why?"

She shrugs. "We . . . drifted. I don't know, these things happen," she says vaguely.

"When you left Whitey, Ursula stayed, right?"

"Right."

"Was there something going on between the two of them?"

"Absolutely not," she says emphatically. "Whitey wasn't like that."

"Why did you leave him?"

"I'd been with him since we were kids. I don't think I was ever in love with him, but he was good to me, got me away from Bob, out of New Jersey."

I can understand being grateful to somebody for getting you out of New Jersey.

"And there was Zach Ellroy," I say matter-of-factly.

Her eyes blaze like fired kindling. "I can't believe Ursula told you about Zach."

"She didn't. Whitey did."

I can see her calculating, perhaps wondering whether Whitey told all.

"You saw Whitey," she states, getting used to the fact that I'm an investigator. "What did he say about Zach?"

"He said that he was never sure that Lake was his, always thought she was Zach's."

"Is that all?"

There's no point in telling her I know about the ménage à trois. "Pretty much. Did you leave Hurley to look for Zach?"

"I hated Hurley."

"But you also wanted to find Zach?"

"No."

"You *did* love Zach?"

"Yes, for a while. And then I hated him."

"Why?"

"It's not important. . . . You'd have to know Zach."

"I'd like to. Did you ever see him again?"

She doesn't answer.

"Have you seen Zach Ellroy?"

"No."

"You have any idea where he is now?"

"No."

I know she's lying about Ellroy, but I don't know why.

"Where was he from?"

"Somewhere west, Midwest. I don't remember."

I don't believe this, but it's all she's going to give me about Zach, so I take her back to the chronology of her story. "Okay, so you and Lake came to New York. . . ."

"No. I came to New York alone. I married Harold a year later, and he insisted on our having Lake with us. He'd always wanted a daughter."

"Didn't *you* want her with you?"

"Sure. Of course." She puffs on her cigarette with a vengeance. There's something off here, something I can't nail down.

"Do you know where Bob Wise is now?"

"No. And if I did, I'd . . ."

"What?"

"I was going to say I'd kill him. But that's not true. I don't know what I'd do."

"Have you seen Bob Wise since you left home?"

"No."

"Could he have killed Lake?"

"As far as I know, he didn't even know she existed."

"Do you know where he was from?"

"Vermont. Burlington, I think."

I make a note to have him checked out. "Is there anything else I should know?"

"No."

"You've told me everything?"

She nods.

I rise. "You've told me the truth about it all?"

"Yes. What do you want, a sworn affidavit?" she asks testily.

I don't reply. "I'll be in touch," I say.

"Do you think . . . do you think you'll find him?"

"Who?"

"The killer."

Oh, him. "I'll do my damnedest. The more I know the truth, the likelier I am to find him," I say pointedly.

As the elevator doors close, I see that Helena Bradshaw has begun to blush. Besides the fact that she's lied, there's something else that she still hasn't told me, and my detective's heart knows it's vital.

On my list of names I cross out *Albert* and *Frank* and circle *Wise* and *Ellroy*.

Chapter

Twenty-seven

KIP DOESN'T HAVE an early appointment, so we enjoy a rare breakfast together. Perhaps *enjoy* is the wrong word. I rant and Kip listens while she sips coffee and picks at her healthy bran muffin. Oat bran, as we all know by now, has been declared fraudulent. Still, I hate plain bran muffins, and every bite she takes is an affront to me. Worse, she actually likes them.

In the middle of my diatribe I see *it* in the corner of the kitchen and jump up on my chair.

"Oh, God," I scream, pointing.

Kip leaps up, too. "What?"

"There . . . there."

"What is it? A grasshopper?"

"It's a water bug," I yell. *A grasshopper!*

Kip grabs a piece of paper towel and in one swift motion captures the hideous thing, crushes it, and takes it into the bathroom, where she flushes it down the toilet.

When we're seated again, I laugh with relief.

Kip says, "I will never understand how someone who takes the risks you do can be afraid of a bug."

"Did you *really* think it was a grasshopper?"

"It was the first thing that came to mind."

"You're cute."

"I'm blind," she says morosely. "I think I need glasses, Lauren."

"You *have* glasses."

"Not just to read. I can't see three feet in front of me. And . . . I haven't wanted to mention this, but . . . I can't see my food. I mean, I see it, but it's blurred, and if we're in a dark restaurant I can't tell one thing from another."

"So why did you only get reading glasses?"

She sighs. "Guess."

"Vanity?"

"And denial."

"Let's face it, Kip, the picture doesn't get prettier."

"But I'm only forty."

"I know, honey. Still, the fact that you're forty means you're not thirty."

"I had twenty-twenty vision," she insists.

"You wouldn't want to say when that was, would you?"

No answer.

"Get contacts."

"Maybe." She picks up a piece of muffin.

"Do you know what that is in your hand?"

"Very funny. I also know what's in *your* hand."

"Don't start." I'm eating a salt bagel with cream cheese. We have agreed that Kip can't be the cholesterol police and that this is something I'll have to take care of myself. Since I still can't take it seriously, I continue to eat the way I always have.

"So . . . you were screaming?" she says, suggesting we return to my discourse.

"Was I really screaming?"

"Let's put it this way: you were vociferous."

"Loud."

"Loud."

"Well, it makes me so damn mad. What is it with these guys? When I think of Helena and Ursula's both being abused . . . God, are we the only two women alive who haven't been?"

"Sometimes it seems that way."

"And why didn't their mother do anything?"

"She was probably too frightened. Or maybe it got her off the sexual hook. There could be many reasons. Anyway, she's paying for it now, because I'd bet anything her refusal to act on what she knew was part of what drove her crazy."

"Sometimes I hate men," I say.

"Pretty sweeping," Kip says sensibly.

"Yeah. I guess I mean *some* men."

The phone rings. Kip gets it, and while she talks I realize Helena never explained why it was necessary for Lake to believe Ursula was her half-sister rather than her aunt. Will Ursula clarify this?

Kip hangs up, looking pleased.

"It was Sam. Tom's home from the hospital."

"Hey, that's great."

"He's on AZT, but he can't go back to work yet. Sam said when he's better they'll fly out for a few days."

I get up and take her in my arms. "I'm so happy, Kip."

Though this is terrific news, we both know he's not out of the woods, may never be. Still, he has time. And so do we who love him.

The phone rings again. It's Cecchi. I've asked him to run a make on both Wise and Ellroy. Kip kisses me and goes to work.

Cecchi says, "So far we have two priors on Wise. One in Vermont in 'seventy-four for child molestation. He got five years, served one."

I feel steam boiling inside me. "Naturally."

"The second in New York in 'eighty-five, same charge. He got off."

"Are you serious?"

"What can I tell you, Lauren?"

"That infuriates me."

"I know, I know. Me too."

"Where is he now?"

"Last known address: One oh five Pell Street."

Chinatown.

"Nothing on Ellroy. But he has a car, and it's registered here, to him and a woman named JoAnn Krupinski, at Thirty-four Watts Street."

"What's the date on the registration?"

"Renewed it a few months ago."

I feel excited. I'm finally going to see Ellroy. I know he figures in this; I just don't know how.

"Webster did it, Lauren. You're wasting your time," Cecchi says.

"Do you really believe that?" I ask.

"Doesn't matter what I believe. I'm on a new case. You'll hear about it on Sports, Weather, and Murder." This is what we call the television news shows. "Came in pieces in a five-gallon container."

"A woman?"

"Of course, a woman. Jesus, Lauren, it never ends. Sometimes I hate men."

I smile. "Pretty sweeping," I say.

"Yeah, I guess."

"There's always you."

"Thanks. You be careful."

After I hang up, I look down at my list of names. Wise interests me, even though I'm anxious to see the mythical Ellroy. The possibility that he's in New York solidifies my instinct that Helena was lying about him. One thing I feel certain of is that if he's here, she's seen him. I believe she hasn't seen Wise. So which of them do I track down first? I opt for Chinatown, deciding to work my way up to Watts Street.

◆

Chinatown is spreading like an oil spill. It's moved north in the last few years, encroaching on Little Italy like a raider attempting a hostile takeover. At least, this is how the Italians view the situation.

There are vicious gangs here, and organized crime. Still, the area attracts tourists because of its narrow, winding streets, shops, and its food. Everyone has her favorite restaurant in Chinatown. Everyone thinks hers is the best. Kip and I like the Kam Bo Rice Shop on Bayard. And for Dim Sum (Chinese breakfast) we like the gaudy Silver Palace on Bowery. Along Canal Street there are dozens of sidewalk markets offering produce and seafood. Pell Street winds off Canal and is lined with restaurants and stores. Dead ducks in various states of readiness hang from hooks in shop windows. I love Chinese duck, but the last time I ate it, I paid too high a price — all night.

Number 105 is tucked between an herb store and a Szechuan restaurant. It's a narrow building with an unlocked, flimsy front door; the names next to the bells are in Chinese, except for two in English. One is H. LAINE and the other is R. WINSLOW. R. WINSLOW interests me because often when people change their names, they keep their same initials. I ring the bell. There's no answer, which means that Winslow either isn't home or isn't answering. Or maybe the bell doesn't work. As I stand here thinking about what I should do, a Chinese man opens the street door.

He's taller than most Oriental men and extremely attractive, with slick black hair that falls freely over his eyebrows. He wears a blue and green parka, black jeans, and a green wool scarf thrown casually around his neck.

When he speaks, puffs of breath encase his Chinese words.

"I don't understand," I tell him.

He continues, waving his hands, his face angry. I shrug, then point to Winslow's name on the roster of bells. The man looks at it, nods many times, gestures for me to follow him down the dark hall. I smell the unmistakable scent of Chinese cooking, and I'm ready to eat.

On the third floor, my guide stops in front of a door that has 3A scratched on it. He says something to me, laughs, shakes his head, and goes back down the stairs.

I automatically check my gun in my bag, leave the flap open, and knock with authority. Nothing happens, so I try again. From deep within the apartment I hear a sound like the shuffling of a deck of cards. It grows louder, steadily slapping. When it stops, I can feel a person on the other side of the door.

A gritty voice asks who's there.

"Mr. Winslow?"

"Who wants to know?"

I gamble. "I'm Miss Laurano, your new social worker."

Silence.

"I'm replacing your usual one." If this doesn't work, I'm out of luck.

In a moment I hear the tumblers turning in the lock, and the door opens. I don't know why I'm stunned by what I see; I should have realized. The stooped man with thin gray hair looks to be in his middle to late sixties. I hadn't aged him and had expected someone in his midthirties.

"Wadda ya want?"

"May I come in?" I remind myself that this man may be R. Winslow and not R. Wise.

He opens the door wide enough for me to slip through and locks it behind me. I feel a stab of fear. Winslow's wearing a pair of faded green work pants and an extra-large gray sweatshirt that makes him appear puny. High, blunt cheekbones partially eclipse his eyes, and there's a glut of lines deeply embedded in his saffron skin.

The place smells stale and gamy, like bad breath and dirty feet. He leads the way, and I see that the slapping sound comes from his run-down slippers hitting the heels of his feet and the floor.

This is a railroad apartment, with the rooms all in a row, one leading off the next. We go through a kitchen whose only contents are a claw-foot tub, an ancient icebox, and a broken chair; the next room has a bed with grayish sheets, an uncased pillow, and a thin, colorless blanket. The final chamber is his living room, the furniture a card table and two legless armchairs spewing stuffing. On the table are discarded containers of food, filled ashtrays, a half bottle of cheap whiskey, a filmy glass. Newspapers, magazines, and books are stacked everywhere, in precarious piles.

When Winslow opens his mouth to speak, I see he's missing teeth.

"So wadda ya want?"

"Are you Robert Winslow?"

He blinks. "Ronald. What happened to whatshername?"

"Transferred. Mr. Winslow, is your name really Robert Wise?"

His slack face takes on a tightness that gives me pause.

"What the hell *is* this?"

Although he's a shambles of a man, I place my hand on my purse. "Were you married to a woman named Marion, and did you have a daughter named Ursula?"

The names seem to frighten him, and he takes two steps back from me, bumping the rickety card table.

"Yer no social worker."

"No, I'm not. I'm a private investigator looking into a homicide."

"Hey, lissen, lady, I'm no killer. I mean, I know I got a sheet, but I'm no killer."

I don't believe he is, either. I think this man is ill and incapable of doing anything requiring physical strength. But I persist. "Are you Robert Wise?"

"Yeah. Can I sit down?"

I almost laugh. This batterer, this molester is asking my permission to do something. It must rankle, and I'm delighted. I nod. He shuffles to one of the chairs and eases himself into it.

"I'm a sick man," he says.

"Have you ever heard of Lake Huron?"

"Sure. It's in —"

"No, not the lake. A person's name." It's become so familiar to me now that I forget how it must sound to someone who's never heard it.

"A person's name?" His face changes, and I guess he's smiling. "No, I never heard . . ." He trails off.

"Do you remember Helena?"

"Huh?"

"Helena. Your stepdaughter."

He nods grimly.

"Did you molest her, Wise?"

"I don't have to answer you," he says, but there's no power in his words.

"Did you molest Ursula, your daughter?"

Unexpectedly his expression changes from one of fear into one of anguish, and feral sounds issue from him. Moments pass before I realize that the man is sobbing. He covers his face with his hands, shoulders heaving.

I feel nothing. There's no sympathy in me for this man who, I suppose, now cries out of guilt and shame. It's too late for that. I wait out his squall.

When his crying subsides, he looks at me and says, "I'm dying . . . I got maybe six months."

And this is meant to excuse him! With fury I realize he was crying for himself, not his victims. He's a pathetic, vile man. I don't bother to ask where he was on the night of Lake's or Peace's murder because I'm convinced this squalid shell of a person is not the murderer. I feel disgust and need to get out of here. I turn to leave.

"You don't understand," he yells after me.

"You're right," I say, looking back at him. "I don't understand how a man can abuse little girls, beat up women."

"I'm dying," he says.

He doesn't get it. "You know what?" I say.

"What?"

"I'm glad."

He's shocked.

"I hope it's soon," I add, and leave him sitting there.

In the hall I take out my notebook and cross off his name. Shaking, I realize I wanted to hurt him badly. I wanted to *see* him die. I don't like these feelings; I run down the stairs as fast as I can.

Outside, the street is thronged. It's noon. For once I've lost my appetite, and the smells from the restaurants turn my stomach. I push my way through the swarms of people; their chatter gives me a headache. I cross Canal Street and head west to Watts.

As I clip along, I realize what an extreme reaction I've had to this man. Besides my obvious, appropriate revulsion, I question my response.

And then, like a bear emerging from its winter lair, the thought surfaces: my father verbally abuses my mother and always has. He puts her down. Sometimes it's blatant, often subtle. He never takes what she says seriously, barely listens. My insides feel webbed with live wires. At first I think it's anger at him, or empathy for her, but this doesn't last long. I can't evade the truth another moment.

As a teen, I colluded with him. I joined in the ridicule of my mother — all in fun, of course — and she accepted it as her due. Shame suffuses me as I acknowledge my culpability.

I devour despair.

◆

Watts Street is changing, though it will never be gentrified because it's too near the Holland Tunnel. Once there was a small movie theater here, called the Film Forum, which showed offbeat films, but they tore it down to make way for a high rise.

The roaring trucks shake the sidewalk under my feet; their exhaust suffocates.

Number 34 Watts is on the uptown side of the street, a small tenement not unlike the one on Pell, except that there are no smells of Chinese cooking here. Instead there's a sour stench, like spoiled milk.

Only six names appear next to the bells. I'm disappointed when I don't see ELLROY. Still, KRUPINSKI, J. is there. I push the buzzer, but there's no response. After ringing a second time without success, I hit all the bells, and someone buzzes open the door.

Inside, I wait under the stairs, but no one asks who's there. Krupinski is on the second floor. As I climb the stairs I notice the peeling paint, water stains, and cracked steps.

At Krupinski's door I push a bell, but it doesn't seem to work, so I knock. I don't detect any movement, but from the other side of the door a woman's muted voice asks what I want. I realize she must've been there since I rang the downstairs bell.

I try my social-worker routine, but it doesn't fly.

"Go away," she says.

I try the truth. "I'm looking for Zach Ellroy."

There's a long silence.

"Ms. Krupinski?"

"He doesn't live here."

"But he did. I'd like to talk to you about him." I tell her who I am and that I'm investigating a homicide.

"Zach killed someone?"

"That's what I'm trying to find out. Won't you let me in, please, so we can talk?"

Silence.

"Ms. Krupinski?"

"I'm . . . the apartment's sort of a mess."

How many times have I heard this? "It's all right. I don't care."

After a few moments she unbolts the door, but leaves the chain on and looks at me through the six open inches with one eye, like a cyclops. I hold up my I.D. She closes the door, unhooks the chain, and opens it again, this time allowing me entrance.

She's tall, with skin like paper, and her hair, a seldom-seen shade of yellow, is long and disheveled. Separated strands stripe the right side of her face. She wears an old, food-stained blue satin robe.

"I'm not usually dressed this way at this hour," she says, fussing with the neck of her coral nightgown.

"It's all right," I assure her.

The one-room apartment is, as she warned, in total disarray. Krupinski leads me to a round table covered with papers, dirty plates, and glasses. After she clears a place for me, we sit down. She scrabbles around under some papers and comes up with a crumpled pack of Marlboros. I refuse her offer, and she lights up. It's then that the neck of her gown slips down and I see an angry smear around her throat. She catches my gaze and quickly pulls up the nightgown again. When she looks back at me, I detect shame in her eyes, as if whatever happened to her neck were her fault. Is she with a batterer? Is it Ellroy?

"Do you live alone, Ms. Krupinski?"

She nods hesitantly. But there's someone in her life. Someone who hurts her. I feel incensed again.

"When's the last time you saw Zach Ellroy?" I ask, trying to get on with it so I can leave.

"About a year ago, maybe more," she says sullenly, the way Kip has told me battered women speak.

"Do you know where he is now?"

"No."

"Do you know where he went when he left here?"

"No."

Krupinski reaches across the littered table for an ashtray, and I see part of a brilliant purple bruise on her arm. I have to check myself from asking about it.

"Is there anything you can tell me about him?"

"Like what?"

"Like where he might go?"

"Go? You mean, like, another state or something?"

"Yes."

A smile twists her mouth, like a garter snake. "Not with *her* still here. He'd never leave New York unless she did, and then he'd go wherever she went."

I'm confused, yet my detective's heart is doing a rumba because I suspect I'm on the verge of learning something big.

"Who?" I ask.

"His old lady. He never got over her. She kicked him out years ago, but he never got over her."

"You mean a wife?"

"Yeah. She divorced him, married someone else. But that didn't stop Zach. He never loved me, just used me for a punching bag."

So Ellroy is a batterer too.

"I think it was her he wanted to punch out," Krupinski says.

"Who? What's her name?"

"Helena."

"Ellroy and this Helena were married?"

"A long time ago. In the sixties."

I was lied to again.

Krupinski kills her cigarette in the overflowing ashtray as smoke seeps from her mouth. "He was always talking about her, saying he was going to get even."

"Even for what?"

"I guess divorcing him."

"Did he say *how* he was going to get even?"

"No."

I don't believe her. "Ms. Krupinski —"

"Could you call me JoAnn? I hate that *Ms.* shit."

Fitting. "JoAnn, why do you want to protect Ellroy?"

"I don't know what you mean," she says flatly, as if the words were coming off an assembly line.

"I mean that I think you *do* know how Ellroy was going to get even. You know, but either you're still afraid of him or . . . or you still love him." This last is hard for me to believe, but I see by her eyes that this *is* the reason.

"Is she dead? Is Helena dead?"

"No."

She sighs.

"Is that what he said? That he was going to kill her?"

"No. Really."

"Then what *did* he say?"

"Listen, I don't want to get Zach in trouble."

I can hardly believe my ears. But why am I surprised? I know of an abused woman who, after escaping her husband, leaving his house, went back every afternoon, made dinner for him, and left it in the fridge. She did this for a year.

Unable to stop myself, I say, "JoAnn, why don't you get help?"

"Help?"

"Counseling."

She recoils as though I'd suggested fire walking.

I barrel on. "It's clear to me that you're in another abusive situation. Please try not to be offended. I can't help noticing the bruise on your arm, the red mark around your throat, and —"

"I think you'd better go." She stands up, and moving slowly, like so many battered women, she goes toward the door.

I stay where I am. "JoAnn, it doesn't have to be like this. There're groups, there's help for women like you. You're not alone."

She stands silently at the door.

I realize that I'm not going to get anywhere this way. She doesn't want help, and I'm foolish to think that I could say something that would make a difference. Meg Lacey would never get sidetracked this way. I haven't come here to rehabilitate this woman, and it's arrogant of me to think I could. I try to be a P. I. again.

"Do you have a picture of him?"

She looks at me, her eyes glistening with unshed tears, and shakes her head no.

"Will you describe him to me?"

"If I do, will you go?"

"Yes," I lie. There's still one more question I have to have an answer to before I leave.

"He's skinny, or he was. Maybe he's not anymore. But he probably is because he's got that kind of energy. Like he's on speed, and no matter what he eats, he burns it off. And he's very tall."

I prompt her as I see her falter. "What color's his hair?"

"Black. Last time I saw him, he was starting to go gray."

"And his eyes?"

"Brown."

"Anything else? Anything that would distinguish him?"

She thinks, smiles sadly, as if she were touched by what she remembers. "He's got a big nose. I think he was always self-conscious about it."

"Anything else you can remember?"

"No."

"How did Ellroy say he was going to get even, JoAnn?"

"You said you'd leave if I told you what he looked like," she says with almost no indignation. The thoughts are there, intact, but not the emotions.

"I promise this is the last question. I have to know this."

"He might kill me if I tell you."

"He'll never know."

"You swear?"

"I swear."

"He said . . . he said he was going to make Helena suffer. He said . . . someday he'd kill her kid."

Chapter

Twenty-eight

I LIE on our bed, sick from my day. I've spent time with a dying batterer and a woman committed to being abused. And I've learned that Ursula and Helena have continued to lie to me, and that Zach Ellroy is almost certainly the murderer of Lake Huron and probably of Gordon Peace as well, though I haven't yet been able to figure out that connection.

But where is Zach Ellroy?

Why didn't Helena tell me she'd been married to him?

How did Ellroy know that Lake had been raped? I'm sure now that he chose to murder her when he did because he believed the rapist would be accused.

Lake's rape wasn't in the papers, so he must have been told about it. By whom? Helena? She said she didn't know about the rape before Lake's death. Is that true? I realize with a thud I've never checked it out. I sit up, switch on the light, punch in Ursula's number. When she answers, I go right into it without any preliminaries.

"Did Helena know Lake had been raped?"

"Of course."

Jesus. More lies. "Why didn't you tell me Helena is your half-sister and that Lake was your niece?"

There's a long silence, and then she says, "It's complicated."

I'm sick to death of this answer. "*Un*complicate it for me."

"I guess it doesn't matter now." She says this more to herself, I suspect, than to me. "Whitey and Helena did ask me to the commune, but they weren't together. Helena was with someone else."

"Zach Ellroy, her husband?"

"Yes." She sucks in her breath, but at least doesn't ask me how I know. "Whitey was in love with her. He always had been."

"So who was Lake's father?"

"Zach. But he didn't know."

"How could Zach not know he was the father when his wife had a baby?"

"Two reasons: he wasn't around when she was born, and because Lake was my child."

I'm stunned.

"Zach raped me many times. I guess I was too scared to say anything."

"What do you mean, you *guess?*"

"Remember when I said that parts of that summer were like blank pages to me? Well, I don't remember all the rapes. I don't even remember Zach, what he looked like, what he sounded like. I only know what I was told."

"And what were you told?"

"Helena finally caught him and kicked him out. By then I was three months pregnant, too afraid to have an abortion. So I had her — Lake. . . ." She's crying.

I wait.

"Helena and Whitey agreed to raise her as Helena's and say that Lake was my half-sister. When she was old enough, we were going to tell her that Zach had been the father of both of us, and that he'd been much older than Helena and had died. I thought Lake would feel closer to me than she would if we said I was her aunt. Of course, it never came to that.

"When Helena left, she didn't want Lake, so Whitey and I tried to make a home for her. But when Helena married Bradshaw, she suddenly asked for Lake. I didn't want to let her go. She *was* mine, after all. Whitey convinced me that Lake would have a better life with Helena and Bradshaw. There wasn't much I could do, anyway.

"I guess she did have a better life than I could have given her. But Helena never loved her. Lake felt that. She told me. You don't know how many times I wanted to tell her the truth."

"Why didn't you?"

"Harold Bradshaw threatened to cut Lake off if I told her. He had some crazy idea that she'd turn her back on them if she knew that Helena wasn't her real parent either."

"Did Mark know the truth?"

"No. That's what I told him when he asked me to marry him."

I recall her reference to "personal things" and Mark's going to the park to think things over. Since he loves Ursula, I can't imagine that he'd want to kill her daughter. And instinctively I know that Ursula wouldn't kill her own child. I'm ready to cross Ursula and Mark off my list of suspects.

She goes on. "After Harold died, I kept meaning to tell her, but something always stopped me. I guess I was afraid she'd hate me if she knew the truth. I thought one day, when I had more courage . . . I didn't know I'd never get the chance," she says sadly.

"Ursula, I think Ellroy killed Lake."

"Oh my God."

I tell her about my conversation with JoAnn Krupinski and Zach's threat. "Ellroy's a batterer and a rapist. I don't think he'd have any compunction about killing a child he didn't know — maybe even one he *did* know. It happens."

Ursula says, "What now? How do we find Zach?"

"Helena. She says she hasn't seen him since the commune, but I don't believe her. I think she's protecting Ellroy. She *was* in love with him at one time. Did he ever abuse her?"

"Yes. He raped her, too. Well, we didn't think of it as rape back then because he was her husband, but I heard them sometimes. . . ."

"You mean he forced her to have sex when she didn't want to?"

"Yes."

"Was Bradshaw abusive?"

"No. Basically he was a nice man, except when it came to Mark. It was wrong of him not to leave Mark some money, to have it go to him only after Helena's death. Mark didn't want to be a clone of his father, and Harold couldn't stand that. Do you know what I mean?"

"Yes." I think I know a lot about the cloning of American children, maybe children everywhere.

"It was Harold's one weak spot, this conceit that his son should follow in his footsteps. Other than that, he was a very lovely man. And that's another thing."

"What?"

"I don't think Helena ever loved Harold. This is terrible to say, Lauren, but I think he was too nice to her."

For a moment we're both silent, digesting the horrible truth of her statement.

Then I say, "Everything you've told me makes me more convinced that Helena has seen Ellroy, perhaps even started a relation-ship with him again."

"You don't think she had anything to do with Lake's death, do you?"

"Perhaps not knowingly. But I *do* think she told him about Lake's rape. Why else would she have lied to me, pretended she hadn't known? On some level, she was protecting Zach."

"You're probably right. She never got help, like I did. I've spent years in therapy and in an incest survivors' group. In a perverse way I think she avoided help *because* of me, as if her allegiance to sickness would somehow punish me."

"Punish you for what?" I ask.

"For Zach."

I understand. Helena felt forced to banish Zach when she discov-ered him with Ursula. If she hadn't done it, she would've been exactly like the mother she censured and despised. Still, some part of her blamed Ursula for ruining her marriage, for putting her into a position of having to give up a man she loved.

I tell Ursula that I'm going to shadow Helena in order to find Ellroy, and I thank her for her candor, say I'll keep her informed. We hang up.

I lie down on the bed again, overwhelmed by the amount of abuse in this case. It's like a diseased octopus. But why should I be surprised? This malady shows up everywhere: in the cavalier way men slap women around in movies and television; in the way they talk about them in comedy routines; in the easy portrayal of male-female violence in novels. Our consciousness has been raised by news stories, but what attitudes have changed?

The door opens, and Kip comes in.

"This is cheery," she says. "Why are you lying in the dark?"

I pat the bed next to me, and she lies down while I fill her in on the latest developments. When I finish, I say, "There's something else, something that's right there under the surface, but I can't get to it."

"Do you want me to hypnotize you?" she asks.

We've done this before when I've been stuck. "I don't know what it's about, what area I'm blocked in."

"That makes it tough."

I'm tired of thinking about the case. "What are we doing to-night?"

"We're spending it alone."

"Good."

"I'm cooking you a fabulous dinner."

I feel myself perking up. "What?"

"Skinless, boneless breast of chicken, steamed vegetables, arugula with lemon dressing, and raspberries for dessert."

"You can't be serious." My spirits slump.

She snaps on a light, leans on her elbow, looking down at me. "What's wrong with it? People would kill to have a dinner like that."

"What people? And don't tell me orphans and the homeless, I know that. I mean, what people leading average lives would kill for that meal?"

"Lauren, you're impossible."

"I thought you weren't going to police my food."

"I'm not. It's my turn to cook, and that's what I've decided to make."

"*I'm* impossible?" I say, laughing. "Okay, after the *fab-u-lous* meal, what are we going to do?"

"We have choices. We can rent a movie, read, listen to music, or . . ." She bends her head, kisses me.

"Let's do that first," I say.

"I thought you'd never ask."

◆

At eight A.M. I'm staked out across the street from Helena's apartment. The weather is wintry again, the air callous. A gray creamy color lights the sky. I huddle in a doorway, wearing an old green parka, jeans, and blue leg warmers. I've tucked my hair under a black velvet fedora, pulled down low to cover part of my face. I also wear a pair of shades. I wonder if Kat Colorado would ever dress like this. Thinking about last night with Kip helps keep me warm. This is an illusion, though I enjoy the recollection.

Various people leave Helena's building — on their way to work, I presume, where they'll spend the day in nice warm offices.

At eight-fifteen I feel frozen and wonder how the homeless manage. By eight-thirty I'm ready to call it a day. Of course, I can't. What I *can* do is reward myself with the coffee and chocolate doughnut I have in my backpack.

It's quarter to nine, and I'm incredulous that I only bought one doughnut. Was I crazy? As I deliberate over my sanity, the door across the street opens, and this time Helena comes out. I can't believe my luck.

She wears a brown fur coat (I hope it's fake but doubt it) and dark-brown boots, with matching gloves and purse and nothing on her head. What is it with people? Everyone knows you lose half your body heat if you don't wear a hat, and still they persist. I go through this all the time with Kip. She refuses to wear a hat. Why do I care? It's *her* head. I vow to never mention it again.

When Helena reaches the corner of Washington Place and Sixth Avenue, I start walking, staying on the opposite side of the street. She waits for the light to change, crosses the avenue, and continues west. Keeping well behind her, I try to tell myself that she'll lead me directly to Zach Ellroy. Chances of this are about a thousand to one.

She stops at the corner where Washington meets Grove, waits for the light, then crosses Waverly and waits on the corner of Seventh Avenue. My office is across the street, and for a moment I imagine that she's going there to see me. But this is ridiculous. I checked my messages earlier, and though there were the usual hang-ups, there was nothing from her.

When the light changes, she crosses the avenue, stands on the point of sidewalk outside the Riviera Café, crosses West Fourth, and goes directly into my building.

I'm bewildered. Why is she suddenly coming to see me? Has she finally decided to tell me the truth? I remove my shades and hat, stuff them into my backpack, and follow her into the building. When I come upon her in the vestibule, she's talking to Joe Carter.

"Helena," I say.

She jumps, startled.

"I'm sorry, I didn't mean to scare you."

"I . . . no . . . you . . ." She appears more flustered than the situation calls for.

Joe says, "She was just asking for you. I told her you'd be along any time now."

I nod my thanks to him and put my key in the front-door lock. "You've never been here before, have you?" I ask Helena.

"No."

In my office I tell her to take a seat as I hang up my parka. I sit behind my desk, look at her directly, and wait.

She says nothing. Her fatigued face reflects the toll this case has taken. Is it true, I wonder, that she didn't love Lake? I want to ask her, but it seems too cruel. We haven't spoken since I learned that

Ursula was Lake's real mother. But I think this is a delicate moment, and an important revelation could be forthcoming, so I wait.

And wait.

At last she says, "Mind if I smoke?"

I do, but I say no, reach into a drawer, and take out a brown tin ashtray. If they have to smoke in my office, I don't like to offer attractive accouterments. She looks at it with distaste.

I wait. Finally it's clear that she's not going to reveal the nature of this visit until I ask her, so I do. "Why've you come, Helena?"

She chews on her bottom lip, scraping lipstick onto her two front teeth. "I . . . I wanted to know why you're *really* continuing on this case, when they have the murderer."

"Why do you care? You're not paying me."

"It's just that . . . with you delving into it like this . . . there's no way we can put it behind us, get on with our lives."

"Who's 'we'?"

"The family."

I find this unconvincing and decide to be direct. "Why didn't you tell me you'd been married to Zach Ellroy?"

She takes a breath and says smoothly, "I asked myself the same question after you left. I don't know. It was silly not to." She flashes a wan smile. "I suppose Ursula told you."

"No. Zach's ex-girlfriend did."

She puffs her cigarette furiously, like a Bette Davis impressionist. "What else did she say?"

I notice she doesn't ask who the ex-girlfriend is, which tells me she knows. "Everything," I say cryptically.

" 'Everything,' " she repeats. "What's 'everything'?"

"Why don't *you* tell *me*?"

"Cute trick," she says, and rises.

"It seems to me that you're the one playing tricks. You've been seeing Zach Ellroy, haven't you, Helena? And you searched my office and knocked me out because you were afraid I might've found out what you suspected."

"And what's that?" She shakes with rage or fear.

"I think Ellroy killed Lake."

"Oh, no," she cries. "He wouldn't . . . he wouldn't. I can't believe that."

I tell her everything I know, outlining all the true relationships, then I feint to the left, so to speak. "Why'd you tell me you hadn't known about Lake's rape?"

She opens her mouth, closes it.

I ask again.

"I don't know."

"I think it was because you'd seen Ellroy and told him about the rape, and wondered yourself if he'd killed her. You're still protecting him, aren't you?"

"No. I — I don't know why I said I hadn't known about it. It was stupid."

"You have to have had a reason."

"I — I'm ashamed to tell you."

I wait.

Helena sits down again, hunched over like a woman twice her age. She shifts in her chair, taps one arm with long, crimson nails. "All right. I'm not proud of this. I wanted attention. I felt left out."

This makes no sense. I flash on the scene after the funeral. She was surrounded by mourners; I had to wait to talk to her. "You're lying," I say.

"I've had enough," she says indignantly, jumping up again.

I stand, too. "You've lied to me about every damn thing in this case."

We both move toward the door.

"Do you know where Ellroy is now?"

She doesn't answer.

"Did you tell him Lake was his daughter?"

She stops, whirls on me. "How could I have told him that if I haven't seen him?"

"You couldn't," I say reasonably. "But you have."

"I don't have to listen to this." She reaches for the doorknob.

"Just tell me one thing," I say.

"What?"

"Did you love Lake?"

She looks as though I've vilified her, then says, "She *was* my niece, you know," as if this were somehow an equation to love.

Before I can recover from this inexplicable reply, she's through the door, and it slams behind her. I consider going after her, but I know she won't say more. As for following her, I've blown my cover for now.

Why did Helena come to see me? I can't make sense of this. I don't believe it was to get me to drop the case. Perhaps she wanted to tell me something and then, at the last minute, found it impossible.

Or . . . had Helena meant to do me harm?

Chapter

Twenty-nine

IT'S QUARTER TO TWO in the morning. I can't sleep. I'm playing blackjack for time credits on the Funhouse BBS. I lose it all, and the screen message says: SORRY, LAUREN, YOU'VE EXCEEDED YOUR TIME. CALL BACK TOMORROW. Then come the usual code characters and NO CARRIER.

I call a multi chat line, log in, go to the teleconference. There's no one there but me. I log off. Pathetic. I could call a gay board, people are always talking on them, but they're usually men and, certainly at this hour, they don't want to talk to me.

This would be a good time to download some files — games, utilities, graphics — but when you're downloading, there's nothing to do. The modem does it by itself. I can call a board and read messages in different conferences. I decide to do this and am dialing Frenzy when I look up and see Kip.

"I thought this was over," she says.

"I couldn't sleep."

"You could read. You used to read, Lauren."

"I know."

"So even though you don't need to call these places anymore, you're still doing it?"

"Guilty as charged."

"Why?"

"It's fun."

"I forgot to tell you that yesterday Cobra called you from TDTM."

I say nothing because even though I don't know who Cobra is, I do know that TDTM stands for Talk Dirty To Me.

"I guess I'll never understand," Kip says.

"Maybe if you'd let me demonstrate it to you, you'd —"

"No. You think I want to get hooked like you?"

"I'm not hooked, Kip."

"Okay."

"It's relaxing for me." This is true.

"Okay. Fine."

"If you woke up and found me reading, it would be all right, wouldn't it?"

"But you're not reading. You're playing with your modem."

"So what?"

She looks at me for nearly three weeks. "You know, Lauren, you're absolutely right."

"I am?" A tingle of joy rushes through me.

"Yup. I'm being rigid because I don't understand it. Sorry."

She comes over to me, leans down, and kisses me lightly on the lips.

"Thanks." This is one of the reasons I love her. When she feels she's wrong, she admits it. I try to do the same, but I'm not always successful.

"Is it the case that's keeping you up?"

"Yes."

"Want to talk?"

"I don't even know what to talk about. Pieces don't add up, I can't make sense of them."

She sits down, folds her robe over her crossed legs. "Tell me about the pieces."

I do: about Ursula and Helena's being half-sisters and Lake's being Ursula's child. Then I go over Helena's unexplained appearance at my office, my curiosity about the whereabouts of Zach Ellroy, and, finally, the part that puzzles me most: Gordon Peace's murder.

"Have you looked into Peace's background?"

"Sure. He was who he said he was, and he had no connection to Lake or anyone else involved in the case."

"Except for one person," she says.

"Who?"

"You."

"*Me?*"

"I know it's farfetched, but you *are* the link, if there is a link — and there does seem to be one."

I want to tell her that this idea is crazy, but I can't. She's right. I hate it when that happens. Still, the connection is feeble, and I can't make the equation work.

"Okay, let's say I *am* the link — the link to what?"

"Information?"

"About the case?"

"Maybe."

"You mean somebody hired Peace to keep tabs on my progress?"

"Could be."

"Then why kill him?"

"I guess the same reason anyone in his position gets killed: he found out something."

Yes and no. It's hard for me to believe that Peace would hire out to be a snitch, but then would-be writers can always use money. The faulty premise is that he could have uncovered anything, let alone something worth killing him for. I say this to Kip.

"The office break-in," she says.

"He was dead by then," I remind her. I start to tell her that I think Helena was responsible for that, and then it hits me. Gordon Peace was dead, but Joe Carter wasn't!

"Joe Carter? What would he have to do with it? He was hired after Lake's murder — after Gordon's, too, for that matter," Kip says.

"Exactly."

"Exactly what?"

"Maybe it was Joe Carter who was supposed to keep an eye on my progress." I remember my mother's words: *Cherchez l'homme.* Lucky guess.

"And whoever killed Lake and Gordon got Carter the job?"

"Helena was talking to him," I exclaim. "I accepted what Carter said about her asking for me, but she was there to talk to *him*, because I'll bet she and Zach hired him. She certainly knew him; he was the bartender at the gathering after Lake's funeral."

"Sounds right."

"Oh, shit," I say.

"What?"

"I just remembered: when I returned to my office after the break-in, Carter said to me, 'I hear you were conked on the back of the head.' On the *back* of the head. How'd he know? I admit it could be an expression, a coincidence, but I remember being bothered by it at the time, only I couldn't put my finger on it. There was something about the certitude in his tone when he identified it as the *back* of my head. I have to find out *exactly* how Joe Carter got his job. Thanks, Kip."

"Anytime," she says, yawning. She starts for the door, stops, turns to look at me. "Well?"

"Well what?"

"Aren't you coming to bed?"

"I can't sleep now. I'll just fool around here for a while."

"Sick," she says, and leaves.

As I said, when she's wrong, she freely admits it.

◆

The Thompson & Churchill Company is in a new building on Washington Street. A siren in a parked car wails, alerting anyone who cares that a break-in has been attempted. No one cares. This area, too, is going through a facelift. The city feels like a horror movie: on the outside, things look good, but underneath everything is rotting, crumbling, bursting. A day doesn't go by but a water main or a gas pipe breaks; somebody falls through a subway grate; a building collapses.

The management company is on the fourth floor. I could've called, maybe gotten more information out of Ms. Mitz, but I don't want to push my luck, and this is too important.

The offices are unremarkable in their sterile design. Everything is gray, black, and chrome. Behind a front desk sits a woman in her twenties, hair the color of moribund marigolds, skin waxy white, with slabs of orange makeup.

"I'd like to see Mr. Thompson," I inform her.

"Appointment?"

The word from hell. We then go into the routine dialogue that not having an appointment entails. I tell her I'm investigating Peace's murder and show my license.

To my amazement, she appears impressed, picks up the phone, and hits a button. She tells Thompson why I'm here, and to my further astonishment, he agrees to see me.

I follow Marigold-Hair down a hall, left, right, straight, until we come to Thompson's door, which she knocks on, opens, introduces me, and leaves.

J. Thompson is not at all as I've pictured. He's a small, thin man, his chrome and black chair almost dwarfing him. His gray hair is like a pugnacious spiny-backed fish. Brown eyes peep out from below lazy lids and size me up. He wears a loud checked sport jacket. A defiant mop of salt-and-pepper chest hair fills the V of his open-necked tan shirt. Thompson indicates a chair with a long, narrow hand.

"So what's this about, sis?"

Oh, no. I take a breath and let it go, ask him about Joe Carter.

"What about him?"

"How did you happen to hire him?"

Thompson looks at me as though I were insane.

"He said he had his name on a list," I add.

"List? What list?"

"I don't know. How do you usually hire people for janitorial jobs in your buildings?"

"Look, sis, I don't dick around with stuff like that. I thought you wanted to talk about Gordon Peace."

"This *is* about Peace. It's important for me to know just how Carter got his job, and when."

He pushes a buzzer on a speaker. When it's answered, he growls a command. A moment later the door opens and a fiftyish woman joins us. She looks like an artichoke.

Thompson asks her about Carter. She blushes, turning into a persimmon.

"Yes, I hired him," she says.

Since Thompson hasn't seen fit to introduce us, I do. She turns out to be Margaret Mitz, and she remembers me from our conspiratorial conversation about men. It brings a hint of pleasure to her gloomy gray eyes. Still, I can tell she continues to feel embarrassment.

"Where did you get his name?" I ask.

"From him," she says guilelessly.

"When?"

"The day he came in for a job."

"And when was that?"

"Well, it was the funniest thing: he wandered in the very next day after Gordon didn't show up. I remember thinking how fortuitous it was, because when I'd looked earlier that day, the file with applicants in it was missing."

"What d'ya mean, 'missing'?" Thompson snaps.

She looks at him with trepidation. "I couldn't find it, Mr. T. The whole place helped me look, but it was gone. Then later this Mr. Carter wanders in asking for a job. Well, I told him we just might have something, and to check back the next day. As you know, Gordon never did show up — well, how could he?" Her color deepens, as though Peace's death were somehow shameful. "So when Mr. Carter got in touch again, I gave him Gordon's job."

◆

I sip a cappuccino at Vivaldi. I don't have to go to Scotland Yard to figure out that Carter stole the application file from Thompson & Churchill, and that he did it so he could get Peace's job. How did he know Peace wasn't coming back to work? There's only one possible explanation: he knew he was dead. How did he know that? There are two possibilities: either someone told him, or he killed Peace himself. Still, in both cases the question of *why* rears its annoying head.

Ms. Mitz showed me Carter's application form, and predictably, Carter had said he had no phone. The address he'd listed on West Eleventh Street was no good, either. So I can't find Carter unless he shows up at my building, but there's no reason he shouldn't since he doesn't have any idea I'm on to him. I've already had Cecchi run a make on him. Nothing came up — but then Joe Carter probably isn't his real name. I calculate and realize that if he keeps to his schedule, Carter is due at my place tomorrow morning. I'll have to try to get his prints, because everything tells me that Carter killed Peace, and if that's so, then he killed Lake, too. I look at my watch. I have seventeen hours to figure out why.

◆

Kip cooks a sumptuous meal for Rick, William, Jenny, Jill, and me. We talk about the case. And talk about the case.

Jenny says, "Okay, I admit it, I don't get it."

"Get what?" Rick asks.

"You won't believe this," Jill says, "but she's never read a mystery."

"I don't believe it," William says wryly.

"So what if she's never read a mystery?"

"Please stop talking about me like I'm not here," Jenny pleads.

"Is Jenny here?" William says.

"Very funny."

Kip says, "What is it you don't get, Jenny?"

"I don't get this whole thing. This whole mystery."

"God, I hate mysteries," William says.

"Me too," says Jenny. "I mean, do you understand who's who?"

"Who's who where?"

"Here."

"What?"

"When?"

"Hold it," I say. "Give me a for instance, Jenny, of what you don't understand."

"You have all night?"

"Probably."

"Okay. Who was Lake's mother?" she asks.

"Ursula. She was raped by Zach when she was twelve and got pregnant," I explain.

Rick says, "And Helena, who is Ursula's sister, was married to Zach. When she found out what Zach had done, she dumped him."

"Then Whitey Huron," Kip adds, "took Helena and Ursula on as his own little family. Ursula had Lake, but they all pretended that Lake was Helena's daughter instead of her niece."

"And then, Jenny," William tries to clarify, "because of Ursula's tender age, they decided to pretend that Ursula and Lake were half-sisters, that Helena was Lake's mother and Ursula had this other mother." He turns to me. "How were they going to pretend that Whitey was the father of both of them?"

"I don't think they thought that far ahead. But as it turned out, it didn't matter, because Lake never saw Whitey, and she just assumed he was old enough to be Ursula's father as well as hers."

Kip continues. "So when Lauren met Whitey and realized that that couldn't be true, she knew something was screwy. That's when she confronted Ursula, and Ursula lied again, insisting there wasn't a blood tie."

"Right," I say.

"See, Jen, Ursula wanted Lake to think they were half-sisters so they'd feel closer," Jill puts in.

"So then I met Ursula's mother, this homeless woman named Marion, tracked her background and learned that Helena was also her daughter, making Ursula and Helena sisters."

"And," William says, "Ursula finally had to admit that Lake was really her child, which actually made Lake Helena's niece."

Rick slaps first one cheek and then the other mockingly. "Jesus: my mother . . . my sister . . . my mother . . . my sister. This is worse than *Chinatown*."

"Bob Wise was Ursula's father, Helena's stepfather. Both of them were abused by him. Then Helena got involved with Zach Ellroy, and both she and Ursula were abused by *him*."

"The usual," Kip confirms.

"Do you get it now?" I ask Jenny.

"No."

We groan in unison.

"Hold everything," I say. "I know it seems complicated, but it's really not. This is all you have to know: Ursula and Helena are sisters; Helena raised Lake as her daughter but she was actually her aunt; Ursula was Lake's real mother. Get it, Jenny?"

"No."

Jill says, "Does she *have* to get it?"

A chorus of nos.

"So, where are we?"

We brainstorm some more (sans Jenny), but no one comes up with anything other than the assumption that some unknown person hired Joe Carter. We all agree that Gordon Peace was murdered so Carter could keep an eye on me. So it's Lake's murder that must be focused on.

With Lake dead, Helena's inherited the money. No one has tried to kill her, and that, along with other things, means that Ursula and Mark can be ruled out as suspects. Terrence Ford was a jilted lover, but I believe he's more in love with crack than he was with Lake. And he needed her alive to enable him.

"I think Ellroy got Helena back under his thumb, and this is a revenge murder, not to mention the money," I say.

"Would Helena have her niece — the child she brought up as a daughter — murdered?" William asks.

"It's not out of the question; we read about that kind of thing all the time. But I don't think she did. Quite the opposite. She let Ellroy believe Lake was his and hers. Helena doesn't — or at least didn't — understand the depth of Ellroy's pathology."

"Love is definitely blind," Rick says.

"So true, li'l honey," William agrees.

"Does Joe Carter have an alibi for the time of the murder?" Kip asks.

We all look at her. Then they all look at me. "It wasn't a consideration until today," I say lamely.

"So," Rick says, "that's the first thing you have to do: find out where Carter was when Lake was murdered."

"Easier said than done. I can't ask him; he'd know I was on to him. And frankly, I'm a little frightened of the guy."

Kip says, "And you should be. Lauren, you have to bring Cecchi into this."

"He's not on the case anymore."

"It gives me the creeps to think we had Carter build our cabinets," Rick says.

"*Somebody's* on the case," Jill suggests.

I know they're right, but being the stubborn person I am, I resist this. "My plan is to get Carter's prints tomorrow. I'll get him up to my office somehow, offer him a drink or something."

"*Somehow* and *or something* give me pause," Kip says.

"Not exactly what you'd call well-thought-out," Rick adds.

Jill solemnly asserts, "Sloppy, Lauren, very sloppy."

"Not to mention dangerous," Jenny says.

I say nothing.

Because I know they're right. It's a stupid plan. Hell, it's not even a plan.

Rick says, "I don't see why you can't get Cecchi to pull him in."

"For what?"

"Suspicion," William says.

"Of what?"

"How about stealing the application files at Churchill and Thompson?" Jill says.

"Everything is speculation. There's no hard evidence on this man."

"How about soft evidence?" Rick asks.

"There's no such thing," I say.

"Then why do they always say *hard* evidence, if that's the only kind there is?"

I say nothing, give him a "leave me alone" look.

"Never mind," he says. "Nothing's ever what it seems."

"What?"

"I said, nothing's ever what it seems."

"And neither is any*one*," I say, almost to myself. "Rick, you're a genius."

"No news to him," William says.

"You really think I am?" Rick asks, fishing.

"You are." And I lay out my new plan.

◆

I get to my office building at six-thirty in the morning and wait in the supply closet, coffee and doughnuts at my side. It's dark, of course, since I can't turn on the light, and the room smells like a cross between a stockyard and the locker room after the Super Bowl.

A decade has passed when I hear footsteps coming toward the room. Quietly, I stand up, take the safety off my gun, and assume the combat posture.

My detective's heart rattles and rolls as I listen to the key slip into the lock and turn. When the door opens, Joe Carter switches on the light.

"Hello, Zach," I say.

Chapter

Thirty

HE STARES at me as if I were an apparition — a ghost, perhaps.

"Hands over your head," I order.

"You have the wrong guy," he says, smiling.

"I don't think so." His nose looks enormous. Why haven't I taken this in before? "Up."

Reluctantly, he raises his arms. I move forward, forcing him back, so that I'm out of the broom closet. With my foot I close the door behind me, my gun pointed steadily at the middle of his chest, right at the R in WOLVERINE on his *MIDWESTERN* sweatshirt. I was right about his accent.

"Hey, you're making a big mistake. My name's —"

"Zach Ellroy," I supply.

"Never heard of him," he says smoothly, slowly inching his arms down.

"Why don't you just do that? I'd like a change," I say in my best Clint Eastwood manner, and wiggle my gun at him like the nose of a tiger sniffing prey.

His arms go up again. "This is stupid. You're making a stupid mistake." Fury flashes from his eyes.

I've seen this look before on more than one psychopath. They don't like to be thwarted. I'm on dangerous ground here because his low frustration tolerance could persuade him to make a dumb move. Whether it would turn out to be dumb for him or for me is the problem. I have the gun, but he has incredible strength. Whatever happens, I can't — not even for a fraction of a second — take my eyes off him.

"What do you think you're doing?" he asks.

That question again. Crazy responses tumble through my mind, but I've no time for them. "Why don't you tell me why you killed Lake?"

"I don't know what you're talking about. Put that fucking gun down." He starts to lower his arms again.

"Don't," I command.

He doesn't. I wonder when the first person will come into the building. "I want you to sit on the stairs," I tell him.

"Fuck you."

"Listen, Zach, I'm not afraid to use this gun. I've used it before." This is a lie. I've never used *this* gun, and I *am* afraid. The last person I shot was Lois.

"You wouldn't shoot me, you fucking dyke."

Oh dear. That. I decide this isn't the time to deal with his homophobia. "Sit down," I say.

"What if I don't?"

"Then I'll have to shoot you," I answer without missing a beat.

He stares.

I wait.

He glowers.

I wait.

He believes me and sits down.

I hide my relief.

"The cops have your fingerprints," I tell him, because I know they'll match.

Smiling slightly, he says, "That's a lie. I don't have a record anywhere."

"I mean they have the prints they took from Lake's and Gordon Peace's apartments."

I watch him calculating: unless they have *him*, they can't match the prints. True. What if he rushes me? Can I really pull the trigger? I remind myself that this man's a rapist and a murderer. It helps. "Helena told me everything," I lie.

The bright blaze of betrayal sails over his eyes and is gone.

"And so did Ursula and Whitey."

It's Whitey's name that seizes him, his eyes communicating rage. And it's then that I realize that Whitey's story about the three of them actually happened differently. It was *Zach*, not Whitey, who walked in on the scene with Helena, *Zach* who joined the other two.

"Mine," he mutters.

"Who?"

He catches himself, doesn't answer.

"Suppose I tell you how it went?" I say.

"What?"

I don't give him a proper answer but decide to tell his story the way I imagine it. "You and Helena were married, and she had an affair with Whitey. You caught them together." No need to mention the ménage à trois. "You raped Ursula to get even with Helena. Maybe you hoped that would frighten Helena into fidelity, but that's not how it went. Instead, Helena kicked you out and —"

"She didn't kick me out, I left."

I check my smile. Thank God for the male ego! "You left?"

He realizes that this admission means he's Ellroy, but he doesn't care now. "I left the fucking whore. Left her with that wimp. I knew I'd get even one day." He laughs. "When I found her again, I pretended I forgave her, but I didn't. I never would. She was mine. Everything was mine."

"Like Lake?"

"Yeah."

"And what you wanted to do with Lake was kill her?"

"I wanted to teach Helena a lesson."

"Helena told you Lake had been raped, and you thought the murder would be blamed on the rapist. Does Helena know you killed her?"

"No. Later. I was going to get her to marry me again, get the money, then tell her. That money is as much mine as hers."

I don't understand the rationale for this, but believe that Zach does. Whatever he wants is his.

"And you killed Gordon Peace to get this job, right?"

"I wanted to keep an eye on you."

"Why didn't you just kill me?" I ask.

"Tried to," he says, grinning. "You're a damn good driver."

My trip to Hurley. The blue Honda.

"Anyway, that bitch Ursula would've hired somebody else," he continues. "Maybe a guy."

So I was allowed to live because I was a woman. It's nice when my gender pays off; that doesn't often happen.

"Didn't you care that Lake was your child?" No need to tell him that Ursula was her mother, not Helena.

"Sure I cared."

"I don't understand, then."

"All the more reason I could do what I wanted with her."

Of course. Why would this sociopath care that he'd murdered his own child? And then we both hear it: a key in the lock. The door swings open. I keep my eyes on Ellroy as I say to the person, "Go call the cops. Right away. This man is dangerous."

"Hey, I don't want to get involved in —"

It's a man. "Do it. Now," I say in my most commanding tone.

He withdraws; the door slams shut. As soon as it does, Zach leaps up and flings himself on me. We fall to the floor, his huge hand around mine, the gun wobbling.

We struggle. His strength is overwhelming, as I thought it would be. But I hold on to the gun even though I feel he's going to break my wrist. This is a matter of life and death. I throw every ounce of strength I have into fighting him, and just as he brings back one hand and clenches it into a fist, ready to punch me in the face, I see my opening and knee him in the groin with everything I've got. The gun goes off.

◆

As I'm reading the messages Kip has left for me on the refrigerator door, she comes into the kitchen.

"There's another one," she says. "I didn't get to put it up there."

I look at her expectantly.

"Mastergru called from Death's Head," she says, as if this were a normal report.

"And?" I ask, playing along.

"He was validating you. Why didn't you tell me you needed validation, Lauren? I would've given it to you."

"What did he say?" I don't laugh, and ignore her question.

"He said you have full access to the system and to tell you that he was putting up a lot of new GIFs. GIFs?"

"G for *graphic*, I for *interchange*, and F for *format*."

"Crystal-clear," she says.

"They're computer pictures. And they're usually . . . well, raunchy."

"You serious?"

"Perfectly."

"Do you have any?"

"A few — a few very select ones," I say suggestively. "Anything else?"

"He asked me your birth date. That was how he validated you."

"What'd you say?"

"I told him."

"Oh, shit. And what did he say?"

"He asked me if I was sure. . . . I said I wasn't."

"Thank God."

"You lied about your age, didn't you?"

"Don't you want to hear how I solved the case?"

"Is it a good story?"

"Of course it's a good story."

"Is it as good as seeing GIFs?"

"Different."

She sits at the table. "Shoot."

"I already have."

I sit down across from her and tell the tale, ending with the gun's going off into Zach's kneecap.

"But how did you know Joe Carter was Zach Ellroy?"

"When I realized, with your help, that Carter was in on it, I remembered that I'd identified him as coming from Madison, Wisconsin, and that Helena had told me Zach was a Midwesterner. And when Rick said 'Nothing's what it seems,' it all fell into place. Joe Carter had to be Zach Ellroy."

"Did you ever think of becoming a detective?" she asks.

"No, but I'm thinking about becoming a magician."

"C'mere," she says sexily.

As I sit on her lap, the phone rings.

"I have the rest of the day off," she says. "Don't answer."

The machine picks up.

It's Susan.

"Oh, no," I say, and look at my watch.

"Hey, don't let it bother you, okay?" Susan says after the beep. "Don't worry that pretty little head of yours about standing me up for lunch seven times. I know you're trying to make the *Guinness Book of World Records*, and I'm here to help you, babe. So let's meet Monday at Woody's. How's one o'clock sound? Perfect? You bet. See you then." Click.

"We've got to take Susan and Stan out to dinner," I say.

"Be happy to, but I think she'd just like to have lunch with you alone."

"I know. I'll do that too. I mean, I want to."

"I know you do." She nuzzles me behind my ear, moves around to my neck.

"I don't know why I keep . . ."

Her lips trail across mine, and her hand slips inside my blouse.

It's not long before we're both excited, and we're barely able to contain ourselves as we climb the stairs to our bedroom. In record time we're naked and lying on the bed. I reach out to touch her and she grabs my hand, holding it by the wrist, as if it were in a vise.

"What?" I ask, confused.

"You want me, Lauren?"

"Yes."

"How much?"

This isn't like her, but I find it highly stimulating. "A lot."

She kisses me in a way that arouses me more.

"How much?" she asks again.

"More than I ever have," I whisper.

"Will you go crazy if you don't have me?"

"Yes."

"Will you scream and beg if you don't have me?"

"Yes."

"Really?"

"Really."

She whispers in my ear: "Then tell me your password, or I'm getting up!"

It's all romance!

I tell.